MIDLOTHIAN LIBRARIES

D1427411

'The king of the British hard-boiled thriller'
— *Times*

'Grips like a pair of regulation handcuffs'
— *Guardian*

'Reverberates like a gunshot'
— *Irish Times*

'Definitely one of the best'
— *Time Out*

'The mean streets of South London need their heroes tough.
Private eye Nick Sharman fits the bill'
— *Telegraph*

'Full of cars, girls, guns, strung out along the high sierras of Brixton
and Battersea, the Elephant and the North Peckham Estate, all
those jewels in the crown they call Sarf London'
— *Arena*

Other books by Mark Timlin

A Good Year for the Roses 1988
Romeo's Tune 1990
Gun Street Girl 1990
Take the A-Train 1991
The Turnaround 1991
Zip Gun Boogie 1992
Hearts of Stone 1992
Falls the Shadow 1993
Ashes by Now 1993
Pretend We're Dead 1994
Paint It Black 1995
Find My Way Home 1996
Sharman and Other Filth (short stories) 1996
A Street That Rhymed with 3 AM 1997
Dead Flowers 1998
Quick Before They Catch Us 1999
All the Empty Places 2000
Stay Another Day 2010

OTHERS
I Spied a Pale Horse 1999
Answers from the Grave 2004
as TONY WILLIAMS
Valin's Raiders 1994
Blue on Blue 1999
as JIM BALLANTYNE
The Torturer 1995
as MARTIN MILK
That Saturday 1996
as LEE MARTIN
Gangsters Wives 2007
The Lipstick Killers 2009

mark timlin

pretend we're dead

The Tenth Nick Sharman Thriller

NO EXIT PRESS

This edition published in 2015
by No Exit Press,
an imprint of Oldcastle Books
PO Box 394, Harpenden,
Herts, AL5 1XJ, UK

noexit.co.uk
@NoExitPress

Copyright © 1994 Mark Timlin

The right of Mark Timlin to be identified as the author of this work has been
asserted in accordance with the Copyright, Designs and Patents Act 1988.

All rights reserved. No part of this book may be reproduced, stored
in or introduced into a retrieval system, or transmitted, in any form
or by any means (electronic, mechanical, photocopying, recording or
otherwise) without the written permission of the publishers.

Any person who does any unauthorised act in relation to this publication
may be liable to criminal prosecution and civil claims for damages.

This is a work of fiction. Names, characters, places, and incidents either are
the product of the author's imagination or are used fictitiously,
and any resemblance to actual persons, living or dead, businesses,
companies, events or locales is entirely coincidental.

A CIP catalogue record for this book is available from the BritishLibrary.

ISBN
978-1-84344-628-6 (print)
978-1-84344-629-3 (epub)
978-1-84344-630-9 (kindle)
978-1-84344-631-6 (pdf)

Typeset by Avocet Typeset, Somerton, Somerset
in 11pt Garamond
Printed in Great Britain by 4edge Limited, Essex

For more information about Crime Fiction go to @CrimeTimeUK

For The Cookie Crew

One more radar lover is gone

1

The phone call came on the morning of my wedding day.

That's what I said. My wedding day. No, don't laugh.

Ten am sharp, Saturday morning, the 12th of May. Only I wasn't. Sharp that is. Anything but.

The original idea had been for me to have my stag night on the Thursday, thus allowing plenty of time for the hangover to consume Friday, then up early, bright-eyed and bushy-tailed, on Saturday morning to get ready for the ceremony that was going to take place at Brixton registry office at noon.

Only I wasn't bright-eyed and bushy-tailed either. Trouble was, the sort of people who'd come to a stag night of mine didn't know when Thursday ended and Friday started. Or stopped for that matter. In fact I hadn't got rid of the last one until about six o'clock on Saturday, just four hours earlier. Then I'd fallen into bed and set two alarm clocks for nine-thirty. Thank God I'd heard them. Dawn would never have forgiven me if I was late.

So there I was at ten o'clock in the morning, standing in the middle of the carpet in my tiny flat, shaking hard enough to register on the Richter scale, and wondering if it had been a good idea to agree to plight my troth for the second time in my life.

After three rings I picked the phone up. The sound of the bell was echoing around my head like a fire alarm. I held the receiver a few inches away from my ear, but said not a word. My mouth was dry and I had an overwhelming desire to throw up.

'May I speak with Nick Sharman?' said a cheery American male voice. A cheery American voice of either sex at that time on my wedding day I did not need. Especially when I just knew that a dead pig was probably in better shape than I was right then.

I grunted. It was a 'yes' kind of grunt. About all I could manage in my condition.

'Good morning. I believe it *is* morning in London.'

I looked at the curtains that were tightly drawn across my windows. Outside it could have been dark midnight for all the light they let in. In my flat it certainly was, except for a tiny forty-watt bulb in the lamp sitting on top of the dead TV set. Forty watts was all I could handle then. Probably all I could manage for the rest of my life, the way I felt. And it still seemed to be as bright as the Blackpool illuminations.

I grunted again. A sort of non-committal grunt that time.

I assume he took that one for a yes too, or totally ignored it. Either way, he introduced himself. 'My name is Lamar Quinn,' he said just as cheerily. 'I'm calling from Los Angeles, California. It's one am here, and it's been a beautiful day. I'm in the offices of Lifetime Records right now. I trust you've heard of us.'

I'd heard of them. Who hadn't? They were one of the biggest music conglomerates in the world. But I refused to be impressed. A third grunt. What the hell did this geezer *want*? A weather forecast from London?

'I work here in the royalty department. I'm first vice-president,' said Quinn.

From what I'd gathered about American business practices, there were probably five hundred first vice-presidents at the company. All driving identical BMWs, wearing identical Armani kit, and drinking identical mineral water with lunch.

'And we have a problem,' he continued.

Don't we all, I thought, as I sat on the bed and tried to put my head between my knees and listen to what he was saying at the same time.

'What?' I said. My first intelligible word of the day. Things were looking up.

'Do you remember Dog Soldier?' he asked.

'The band?'

'Yes.'

'Sure,' I said, and I did. People of my age do. What age? I hear you ask. The kind of age where you remember Elvis before he got fat, and you've seen every episode of *Star Trek* at least three times.

Dog Soldier. Jesus, I'd bought all their records when I was a spotty-faced kid. They had been one of the biggest American bands in the world in the late sixties and early seventies.

'And Jay Harrison?'

'Of course,' I said.

Christ! He *was* Dog Soldier. All hair and cheekbones and Greek God looks and skinny chest. There had been a famous poster of him at the time, wearing a crown of thorns and being crucified on a rough wooden cross. I read somewhere that in 1970 it sold three million copies. I mean, a poster. Shit! I had one myself, hanging on the wall of my bedroom over the record player.

'You know that he died in London in 1972?' said Quinn.

'I know,' I said.

In the bath of heart failure. But it was reckoned that the big H had finally taken its toll of his life. Long after it and the booze had taken their toll of his good looks and talent. He was buried in Highgate cemetery close to Marx's tomb.

'Well,' said Quinn. 'We had a letter from him a month ago. Posted in London W1.'

'Did you?' I said. 'What kind of letter?'

I heard an exhalation of breath down the line. It was so clear that he might have been in the hall outside my flat.

'When Harrison died – to be blunt, Mr Sharman, you couldn't get arrested with a Dog Soldier record. The sales figures were well down. Almost off the graph. But since then we've released a greatest-hits double, and all the earlier albums on CD, plus a lot of in-concert recordings. And then John Sloane made the movie a couple of years ago. Remember it? Just called *Dog Soldier*?'

I remembered it. I've got it out on video. For old times' sake, I suppose. It was crap.

'And frankly the sales are way up again. Higher than a lot of contemporary hit acts,' Quinn went on. 'All his share of the royalties are still being held by us. There's been some squabbling over it. Some! That's an understatement. All sorts of people have popped up claiming to have married Harrison, or to have had his children, or to have signed contracts at some time or other. We have a dozen law suits running currently. The money hasn't been touched, and there's a lot of it. Millions of dollars. The letter said that he was alive and wanted what was owing.'

'Wild,' I said.

'Precisely. And a big headache for us. We talked to Chris Kennedy-Sloane in London. He's done a lot of work for us over the past few years in the UK. We asked for his advice and he suggested that we, I, spoke to you.'

'What about?'

'About whether or not you'll try to find out who sent the letter. If it was Jay Harrison or an impostor. That's what you do, isn't it? You're a private eye.'

'That's what I do,' I agreed. 'But not today. I'm getting married in an hour or so.'

'*Married!* Congratulations. That's great to hear,' said Quinn as if he'd known me for years. But before his enthusiasm got too much for him he was all business again. 'Do you have a fax number?'

'No,' I replied.

'Oh,' he said. He sounded put out. As if everyone should have a fax number. Preferably from birth. Preferably tattooed somewhere prominently on their body.

'Anyway, I'm off for a couple of days. Honeymoon, you know,' I said.

'Sure. I had mine in Acapulco.'

'In my case it's in Hastings,' I said.

'Is that in England?'

'Just about.'

'Well I hope you have a good time and the weather keeps fine.'

There it was, the bloody weather again.

'So do I,' I said. 'And I'm sure it will. But do you think there's anything to this letter?'

'We don't know. But we have to check. This sort of thing happens all the time when a company has a deceased artist on its roster. Especially when it's a big name. Presley, Hendrix, Buddy Holly. But of course there's always been a certain mystery about Harrison's death. I'm sure you're familiar with the story...'

'Remind me,' I said.

'Well, he died over in London, thousands of miles away from home. There was no post-mortem. Like I said, at the time very few people cared. The only witness was his then girlfriend, Kim Major. She died less than a year later from a drugs overdose herself. The doctor who signed Jay Harrison's death certificate is also dead. It was a closed-casket funeral within a few days. No one from his family or any other friends attended. By that time he'd alienated the former, and there were very few of the latter. None at all in Europe. There have been rumours for years that Harrison is still alive.'

'Dig him up,' I said.

'Rumours, Mr Sharman. No evidence. Your British authorities take some convincing before they'll supply an exhumation certificate.'

I grunted again.

'So I'd like to fax over a copy of the letter and the envelope, plus some background information.'

'Doesn't Kennedy-Sloane have a fax number?' I said.

'Yes.'

Probably several, I thought.

'Then send the stuff through to him. I'll collect it when I get back next week.'

'You'll take the job then?'

'Sure,' I said. Why not? I was getting married. Becoming a responsible citizen. I needed the money. And I suppose I'll never forget that poster that used to hang in my room.

'Do you know my rates?' I asked.

'Chris tells us you charge a thousand pounds sterling per day, plus expenses. We'll arrange for you to pick up the money from him. And please. Remember that these enquiries are strictly confidential. Have a nice day, Mr Sharman, and enjoy your wedding. We'll speak again soon.' And he broke the connection.

I looked at the dead phone in my hand. A grand a day. Very good, Chris. A tasty little wedding present.

And then I remembered that I had to get dressed.

2

I'd bought a navy blue, single-breasted suit from Paul Smith for the occasion. And teamed it with a soft, white, Oxford cotton shirt with a button-down, roll collar, a dark blue knitted tie, a new pair of wool-mix socks from Marks and Sparks, and a favourite old pair of black loafers that I'd polished to a brilliant shine. I'd figured that a new pair of shoes would be a disaster. Who needed sore feet at their own wedding?

I showered, shaved and got dressed in my new suit, and when I looked into the mirror I didn't look half bad, if I do say so myself. Much better than I deserved after the caning I'd given to the twenty-year-old Scotch the night before.

Waiting by the door was my suitcase packed for the honeymoon. We were going to Hastings for a couple of days, like I'd told the American. I knew exactly why. Dawn had spent her childhood holidays there. She said the town was old and a bit past it, but with plenty of front. She also said it reminded her of me. I didn't quite know how to take that. I'd suggested Spain for a week, but Dawn hated flying. So I'd booked a couple of nights at the best hotel in Hastings, and we were due to drive down there after the reception.

I lit a cigarette, and looked at my watch. By then it was almost eleven, and I was getting a bit worried about my best man. I hadn't heard a word from him, and my last clear recollection of the night before had been that he would give me a call about ten-thirty to make sure that I was still alive. After that, everything was a blur.

My best man's name was Chas. He was a reporter for a tabloid Sunday paper now, but I'd met him when he wrote for the *South London Press*, and he'd become involved in a couple of cases of mine over the past year or so. So involved, in fact, that he'd nearly been killed by a rogue copper the previous autumn. He was OK now. Except that sometimes he went all quiet and introverted, like he was looking back down a long, dark tunnel where monsters lurked. It was at those times that I worried about him, but he said they were getting fewer and fewer and I had to believe him.

I'd thought that the call from America had been him checking in early. I looked at my watch again, and decided to call him up. I didn't want anything going wrong. The plan for the day was as follows. My wife-to-be, Dawn, was going to be collected from her flat in Wandsworth by one of a pair of brothers I knew who bought and sold American cars for a living. As a sideline they hired out the white Cadillac convertibles they owned for weddings.

Dawn and I had gone down to have a squint at the motors and choose which one she wanted for her big day, and she'd fallen in love with an oversized 1984 five-litre Chevrolet Caprice station wagon that they'd imported from California, and bought the damn thing. Just like that. Three and a half grand's worth. And that's not counting insurance. When I protested, she told me tartly that it was her own money, and that the boys had thrown in car tax and a T-shirt. Christ! I ask you. You buy a car and all you get is one lousy T-shirt. That morning, the Chevy Caprice was parked outside my front door, next to my E-Type, like a cart horse next to a thoroughbred racer. Chas was due to come round, dump his Ford Sierra, and we'd drive to Brixton in the Chevy. Then he was going to take it on to where the reception was being held. As it was a full nine-seater, there'd be plenty of room for anyone who turned up without a motor. Me? I'd be off with the blushing bride in the Caddy.

And talking of blushing, Dawn was getting married in scarlet. From the skin outwards. We'd choked over the thought of a white dress, and I'd told her that full black, which was her first choice, was a little too funeral for our nuptials, even if it was second time for both of us. So we'd settled for fire-engine red.

Dawn was, if plans had gone smoothly, getting dressed right now. She shared a flat with her friend Tracey, who was going to be matron of honour. My daughter Judith, who was going to be our one and only bridesmaid, had been fetched down from Scotland by my ex-wife, Laura, and was staying the night with them. Laura was safely ensconced at the Connaught, where she always stayed when she was down in London, now that she was married to a seriously rich dentist with a large private practice in Aberdeen.

With me so far?

Tracey had arranged a hen night for the Friday night, at the local boozer in Wandsworth that she and Dawn both used. I was supposed to believe that Judith was going to be cosily tucked up in bed by nine with a good book and a mug of Bovril. Fat chance. I knew that plans were afoot to sneak her into the pub. Plans that I wasn't supposed to know anything about. Of course I'd sussed that one out early, but was prepared to turn a blind eye. Judith was thirteen after all, and these days kids grow up fast. And it was a rare occasion. But I also knew that if her mother ever found out where she'd been, my life would be a misery henceforth. Laura was good at making people's lives a misery. I should know, I was married to her for long enough.

As I was about to pick up the telephone, it rang, and I jumped. My nerves were raw. I didn't let it ring twice.

'Hello,' I said.

'Nick?' The voice seemed to come from far away.

'Chas?'

'Yeah. What's happening?'

'I'm getting married this morning. You're the best man.'

'Oh God. For a moment I thought I'd dreamt the whole thing and I could go back to sleep.'

'Don't do this to me, Chas,' I said.

'Sorry. I'm almost ready.'

'You don't sound like you're almost out of bed, and I'm getting hitched in...' I looked at my watch, '... sixty-two minutes exactly.'

'Nick. Don't worry. I'll be there.'

'No, Chas. Be here.'

'That's what I mean.'

'How long?'

'Thirty minutes tops.'

Chas lived in Docklands. A cute little development by Tobacco Wharf. He was going to have to move his arse to do it.

'Do you want me to meet you at the registry office?' I said. 'It's closer.'

'No. Trust me. I'll be there.'

'Don't forget the ring,' I said. But he was gone.

I put the receiver down carefully and made the second big mistake of the day. I went over to my little collection of bottles and poured out a stiff Jack Daniel's.

Oh yeah – the first had been taking the Jay Harrison case, but I didn't know it yet.

3

I went over to the window, drew the curtains back and winced at the brightness outside. I stood for half an hour, thirty-five minutes, three-quarters of an hour, smoking cigarettes, sipping at my JD and chewing on my fingernails. Finally at ten to twelve I saw Chas's red Sierra tear up the road and screech to a halt in front of my house. I shook my head sadly and went downstairs to meet him.

He looked like a wreck inside a smart suit. His face was pale and his hair had obviously been plastered down with water. He stood by his car and shrugged apologetically. 'Come on,' I said. 'We're going to be late.'

I got into the Caprice and started it up. I leant over and opened the passenger door, and Chas joined me on the wide bench seat. 'Sorry, Nick,' he said. 'It took me longer than I thought to get here.'

'Forget it,' I replied. 'Got the ring?'

His face crumpled.

'Chas,' I said. 'If you've lost it...'

He started patting his pockets and I saw him relax as he reached into one and pulled out the twenty-four carat I'd bought for Dawn. 'No problem,' he said.

I stuck the column change into reverse and pulled smoothly out into the street, put the car into drive and headed for Brixton.

We arrived at the registry office at one minute to twelve. A Chevy Caprice is almost twenty feet long and not the easiest car to park, but luckily I found a space and manoeuvred it in and switched off the engine. There was no sign of the Cadillac, or Dawn, Tracey and Judith, although I saw a couple of people who'd been invited to the wedding, lurking about in the street smoking cigarettes and pretending they weren't there.

I said hello to them, and got the usual offers of fast cars and ferry tickets. My friends have never been noted for the originality of their wit.

Chas and I went inside the foyer, where the previous wedding group was standing around having their photographs taken, and looking self-conscious on a carpet of cheap confetti and a few rose petals.

Chas went off to see the registrar and I lit another cigarette, which contravened all the local bylaws, and stood and waited for something to happen.

The previous wedding party made for the door, and I smiled at the bride who smiled back and wished me luck. With my track record I was going to need all the luck I could get, and I wished her the same.

Chas returned to the foyer and gave me the thumbs up, which I took to mean that no one had expired or been arrested overnight. He came over and said, 'Any sign of Dawn yet?'

'Not so far,' I said, 'but with her and her pals, and unlimited booze, anything could have happened.'

'The registrar's getting a bit antsy,' he said. 'Saturday's their busy day. They've got another wedding booked for half past. I'll go and have a look outside.' And he did. I lit another cigarette and wished I was anywhere else but there.

A minute later Chas stuck his head back through the front door and said, 'They're here. Where did you get that bloody car?'

'Don't ask,' I said.

The guests started filtering in, straightening ties and adjusting hats as they came, and Chas pulled me into the registrar's office, where she was waiting, book in hand, looking at her watch.

Chas and I took our places at the front of the room, and the guests sat in the chairs provided, and I turned and looked at the door, as some cheesy organ music filtered through the cheap speakers on either side of the big window covered in a dusty Venetian blind.

At ten past the hour precisely, the door opened, and Dawn, Tracey and Judith came in. Dawn looked like a flame in her red dress, Tracey had gone the Nashville route in an outfit of denim and lace teamed with spike-heeled ankle boots, and Judith was a picture in an ivory dress and matching shoes. All three carried bouquets of white roses. I looked at Chas and raised my eyebrows, and he raised his eyebrows back, as the music on the tape changed to the Wedding March.

I won't bore you with details of the ceremony. But by twelve-thirty, Dawn and I were husband and wife and Judith had a new step-mum. So the world turns.

When we left the registrar's office, we stopped in the foyer to have our photographs taken.

Then my new bride and I, plus her matron of honour and bridesmaid, went out to the ridiculously bulbous Cadillac convertible, complete with spotlights and sirens that was blocking the Brixton Road outside, to be carried off to the bar where the reception was taking place. No one threw confetti. But then no one threw bricks either.

The bar was in West Norwood. I'd actually worked there once for a while when times had been hard. Not that they were ever much else. The geezer I'd worked for, JJ Jeffries, had sold up and moved to Hollywood. Hollywood in Ireland, that is. And the place had been bought by a bloke called Simon. He was all right, except for his penchant for red glasses. But then, changing times make fashion victims of us all.

Simon ran the place with his wife and kept a couple of small children barking in the flat above.

We'd hired the place for the whole day, twelve to twelve. I knew the kind of people who'd been invited, and I didn't want them let loose on the streets of south London until well past the end of licensing hours.

The driver of the Caddy dropped us off outside the bar, at just before one, and the four of us entered the premises to be greeted by the guv'nor and two barmaids.

The counter was covered with dishes containing a buffet lunch, and half a dozen bottles of champagne were standing in a big tub of ice. They were just for starters. Like I said, I knew the kind of people who'd been invited. Simon and the barmaids congratulated us, and cracked open the first bottle, as the vanguard of guests started arriving. I pulled Judith to one side.

'Did you have a good time last night?' I asked.

She went pink and nodded.

'Don't ever tell your mother,' I said. 'Or I'm dead meat.'

She shook her head.

'I hope you didn't get drunk.'

'I only had orange juice,' she protested, and I smiled.

'I believe you. Do you want some champagne?'

She nodded.

'With orange juice?' I said.

She nodded again, and I ordered a Buck's Fizz from one of the barmaids and a glass of champagne for myself. Not that I like the stuff, but it was that kind of day, and I needed something as an antidote for the JD I'd been swigging at home earlier.

When the drinks arrived Judith bobbed up and kissed me on the cheek. 'Congratulations, Daddy,' she said. 'I think Dawn is terrific.'

I almost cried.

'So do I, love,' I said, and we toasted each other and drank.

By then, the bar was starting to fill up, both with people who'd been to the ceremony and with those Dawn and I had asked just to the reception. As I looked through the big plate-glass window into the street, a bright red Porsche 911 with full racing trim pulled up outside, parked on the bus stop, and out from behind the wheel appeared the rotund form of my old pal Christopher Kennedy-Sloane, one of the last of the city whizz-kids who still had a seat to his pants. He ran round to the passenger door as fast as his little legs would carry him, opened it, and gave his hand to whoever was sitting inside. The world seemed to hold its breath as a dream in cream silk emerged, unfolded herself to her full six foot, and stood dwarfing Kennedy-Sloane as he closed the door behind her and set the locks and alarm with the little remote control he held in his hand.

I looked round and found Dawn's eye and she followed mine to the scene outside, and I saw her smile and shake her head as Kennedy-Sloane and his companion entered the bar.

I hadn't been the only one to witness the two of them arrive. I think every geezer in the bar stood pop-eyed as Kennedy-Sloane ushered her inside, and the conversation level dropped to the floor.

I pushed through the crowd to welcome them.

'Nick,' said Kennedy-Sloane. 'I was in two minds whether or

not to venture down into the badlands where you insist on living. I thought the whole thing would have ended in tears by now.'

'Thanks, Chris,' I said. 'Your confidence in my new marriage is duly noted.'

'I just didn't think you'd go through with it, old boy. You or your lady wife. More likely the latter, as she discovered what a reprobate you are. I take it the ceremony did take place.'

'We're street legal, son,' I said. Then looked at the woman he was with, who close up I saw was no more than a girl. At least twenty-five years his junior, whose doe eyes were fixed intently on mine. 'Aren't you going to introduce us?' I asked.

He looked up into her face. 'Of course,' he said. 'Do forgive me. Angela Shakespeare-Lane, allow me to introduce the blushing bridegroom. An old adversary of mine, Nick Sharman. Who is just about to make a comment about double-barrelled surnames.'

'No I'm not,' I said, and stuck out my hand in Angela's direction. 'How do you do,' I said. 'Welcome to the party.'

Angela took my hand in her gloved right. I could feel her bones through the fabric and the skin and flesh beneath it. 'Delighted,' she breathed.

'Angela is a clothes horse,' said Kennedy-Sloane. 'Eighteen years old and making a mint. Front cover of *Vogue* as we speak.'

'From which you take your percentage,' I said.

'Certainly. You don't mind, do you, Ange?'

She shrugged.

'Can I get you both a drink?' I asked. 'Champagne. And don't ask about the vintage, Chris.'

'Wouldn't dream of it,' he said. 'Not in this neck of the woods. You're likely to get a kick in the head if you do, I imagine.'

I turned and rescued two glasses of bubbly off the counter behind me, and passed one to Kennedy-Sloane and one to Angela, who had pulled a cigarette out of her handbag and stood with it between pursed lips while as many lighters as you see at the encore of a Barry Manilow concert were fired up and stuffed under her nose. She didn't flinch. Just took a light from one, inhaled and breathed the smoke out through her nose in two grey streams, and nodded regally at the lucky man who'd ignited her cigarette.

'I've got a little something for you in the car by way of a wedding present,' said Kennedy-Sloane. 'I was going to get you a pair of engraved, his and hers pump-action shotguns, but I imagine you've already got all you need of those.'

Funny man.

'So instead I settled for a couple of lead crystal tumblers. Super king size. Just right for a couple of gin and tonics when you come home after a hard day's sleuthing.'

You had to give it to the man. He was a prat of the first order. 'Thanks,' I said. 'And thanks for putting that American geezer on to me.'

'Lamar. He phoned you did he?'

'He sure did. First thing this morning. At least, first thing for me.'

'And?'

'And I took the job. I was always a big fan of Dog Soldier.'

'I suspected you might have had leanings towards the gothic in your youth.'

I just nodded, then said, 'He's sending a fax over with a copy of the letter and some other stuff to your office. He seemed positively offended that I didn't have a machine of my own.'

It was Kennedy-Sloane's turn to nod. 'Fine. I'll keep an eye out for it. And I've got authorisation to pay you a week's fee in advance. Plus something towards your expenses. Lamar wants me to oversee the job this end. So it looks as if I'll be your boss. At least temporarily.'

'That's terrific,' I said drily.

'At a grand a day, I should think almost anything would be terrific for a newly married man,' he said. 'Plus exes. When will you come in and pick up the cheque?'

'On Tuesday. I'm taking Dawn away for a few days' honeymoon.'

'Paris?'

'Hastings. We're driving down later.'

'You're an incurable romantic, Sharman.'

'She likes Hastings,' I said.

'I like Langan's Brasserie. But I wouldn't want to go there for my honeymoon.'

'You'd have to find somebody to marry you first,' I said.

'Bitchy,' said Kennedy-Sloane. 'Well, enjoy yourself, and try not to expire from the excitement of the place.'

'I'll try,' I said, then noticed over his shoulder someone who'd just come through the door and was scoping the place in a professional way. 'Excuse me a minute,' I said. 'There's someone just arrived who I must say hello to.'

'Carry on, dear boy,' said Kennedy-Sloane. 'It's your day, and I can see that you've spared no expense to get your friends together. It's a bit like *This Is Your Life* on angel dust in here.'

'I try to please,' I said, and with a nod to Angela went to greet an uninvited guest.

He was standing by the door, sort of half in, half out of the bar, when I reached him. 'Hello, Mr Robber,' I said. 'This is a surprise.' I didn't say if it was a pleasant or an unpleasant one. Only time would tell.

Detective Inspector Jack Robber was his usual grubby self, in an old trench coat unbuttoned over a shiny suit, greyish-looking white shirt, and food-stained tie.

'I think my invite must have got lost in the post,' he said. 'So I came anyway.'

I ignored the comment. 'How did you know?'

'I heard it through the grapevine,' he said. 'They've been taking bets up the station whether or not you'd go through with it.'

'I did,' I said. 'Have you met my wife?'

'I think I nicked her once for tomming. Her and her mate.'

'I don't think we have to go into all that today, do we?' I asked.

'No, son,' he said. 'Let bygones be bygones. I don't give a fuck anyway. I'll be retiring soon. I've had enough of this shithouse of a town. I'm off to the coast. I've got a sister down there. Her husband died last Christmas. Children gone. She wants to look after me. Make sure I eat regular.'

I'd never previously pictured Robber as having a family. 'That's good,' I said.

'Maybe. I'll probably have a heart attack within a year. It often happens you know.'

I nodded. It was a fact. It did. Take coppers away from the stress of the job, the late nights and bad food, too many cigarettes and too much booze, and they dropped like flies.

He shrugged. 'Whatever,' he said. 'Anyway, I came to wish you two the best of luck. Maybe she'll keep you in order, and you her.'

'We'll try,' I said, strangely touched by the ugly old detective's words. 'Want a drink?'

'Do rabbits fuck? A single malt. Large one.'

'I wouldn't dream of getting you anything else,' I said. 'Won't be a minute. Help yourself to food.' And I went over to the bar and caught Simon's eye. When he came over I said, 'Check out one of the local Old Bill. The geezer I was talking to, who looks like a flasher gone bad.'

I saw Simon's eyes move in Robber's direction.

'Get me a triple single malt for him,' I said. 'Stick it on the tab.'

Simon nodded, and got down the best in the house, poured out three measures, and gave me the glass. 'Cheers,' I said. 'See you in a minute.'

He nodded again, and I took the drink over to Robber, grabbing another glass of champagne on the way. Robber had moved to the bar and was piling up a plate with food. 'She won't have much trouble, will she?' I asked, as I put his glass down.

'Who? What?' he said.

'Your sister. Making sure you eat properly,' I explained, gesturing at his plate.

He almost smiled. Almost, but not quite. I don't think Inspector Robber smiled much. Then he nodded. 'But this is buckshee,' he said.

'Enjoy it. And the barman will get you what you want to drink. I'll see you in a minute. I think I'd better find my wife and mingle a bit.'

'Not in public, son,' he said. 'You can get arrested for that.'

It was the first time I'd ever heard Robber crack a joke. Blimey, I thought. Things are looking up.

I smiled, and nodded, and turned towards the back of the bar where Dawn, Tracey and Judith were holding court.

I battled through the crowd, accepting congratulations and greeting people I hadn't seen before, until I reached the restaurant at the rear, where my wife, her matron of honour and bridesmaid were sitting at a table covered in bottles and glasses.

'You haven't wasted much time,' I said.

'Hello, darlin',' said Dawn. I knew from the tone she used that she was getting pissed. And why not? It *was* her wedding day.

'I hope you're not corrupting my daughter,' I said to her.

'No more than she was before,' she replied.

Judith grinned. Tracey giggled. I could tell she was getting pissed too.

'It's a great party,' said Dawn. 'Come and sit down. Have you seen all the pressies we've got?'

Behind her, stacked against the wall, was a pile of gift-wrapped boxes.

'Twenty-four toasters,' I said.

'Don't be so cynical, Daddy,' said Judith. 'Mine's not a toaster.'

Cynical. Now my daughter was calling me cynical.

I sat down and found a half-empty bottle of Becks. I checked it for cigarette ends and took a sip. It was OK.

'I'm sure it's not,' I said. 'I was only joking.'

Dawn put her hand on my thigh. High up. Judith looked. I moved Dawn's hand away.

'Bashful?' she said.

Judith grinned again. Tracey giggled again, and put her hand over her mouth.

I felt as if the three women at the table were ganging up on me.

'You're married now, Daddy,' said Judith. 'You're allowed.'

'Not in public,' I said, repeating Robber's words. 'And don't wind me up. It's not a daughterly thing to do.'

All three women looked at each other, pulled faces and burst out laughing.

'You can be a pompous sod, Nick,' said Dawn.

Funnily enough, I can remember an old girlfriend of mine saying exactly the same.

'Sorry,' I said. 'You're right.' And I pulled her close and gave her a big kiss. Tracey and Judith both applauded. 'Is that better?' I asked.

Dawn nodded.

'What time are we off?' I asked.

'Not yet,' said Dawn. 'I haven't said hello to everybody. And there's more to come. And we've got to cut the cake. And I want some more pictures taken.'

In the face of that many excuses, what could I do? 'It's your honeymoon,' I said. 'And if we're not leaving yet, I'm going to get another drink.'

4

I suppose I should have insisted that we leave then. But I didn't. Like I said, it was her wedding day as well, after all. Bad mistake. Because from there on in, the reception seemed to take on a life of its own. A life with a death wish.

I went back to the bar and started on the JD again. I was surrounded by old friends and well-wishers, and I suppose all that went to my head. Just like the alcohol.

By three o'clock or so, the place was packed. Simon collared me and told me that the bar tab was getting close to a grand and a half, and that he was going to shut it down and start charging. That was a relief. With the food and all I was looking at a bill for two thousand quid or so. Mind you, that was only two days' work on my new case, which wasn't so bad. Thanks, Chris. I told Simon to carry on, and ordered another round.

Every time that I was aware what was happening, I seemed to be talking to someone new. I must have started thirty or forty conversations that went absolutely nowhere. And I must have copped for twenty or thirty drinks that went straight down my throat.

The next time I looked at a clock, it was five-thirty and where the afternoon had gone I knew not.

At six o'clock a cab came to collect Judith to take her back to her mother at the Connaught. She dragged me out into the street with her, and said, 'Daddy, you're drunk.'

I agreed.

'You're a very bad man.'

I agreed again.

'But I love you.'

'And I love you too,' I said.

'Mum sent you a wedding present too,' she said. 'I didn't mention it before.'

'Did she?' I asked.

Judith nodded.

'What? A razor blade or a hundred aspirin?' I asked.

'That's not nice, Daddy.'

And it wasn't.

'Sorry,' I said.

'She thinks about you more than you know.'

'And I think about her too,' I said, suddenly a lot more sober than I had been. 'But it's too late for all that now.'

Judith nodded once more, and I opened the cab door for her.

'Give me a ring next week,' I said. 'Will I be seeing you soon?'

'I've left a bag at Tracey's flat. With my other clothes in it. I'll have to come down and collect it sometime.'

'The sooner the better. We'll all go out for dinner. You can stay at the flat.'

'I'd like that, Daddy,' she said, and she stepped into the taxi, and for the first time I knew that I was father to a young woman and not a child.

She pulled down the window and leaned out and kissed me. 'Take care,' she said. 'Don't drive tonight.'

Some fat chance, I thought. State I'm in. Maybe we'd have to get a train to Hastings. The cab pulled away, and I stood waving like a berk, then went back into the bar and someone bought me another drink.

A few minutes later, the real trouble started. Or the real fun. It depends how you look at things like that.

Arsenal had been playing Crystal Palace at Highbury. One of those end-of-the-season matches that aren't supposed to matter. Except this one did. A London derby. North versus south. It mattered all right. And Crystal Palace beat Arsenal three nil. And the biggest Arsenal fan of all lived close to the bar. Well into Crystal Palace partisan territory. And he'd had to come home on public transport, all the way from north London, still wearing his Arsenal scarf, with all the Crystal Palace boys, and take all the digs on the way. So of course the first thing he wanted was a drink. And we were in his local. Which was shut for a function. But of course I knew him, and let him in. My third big mistake of the day so far.

He collared me in one corner and bought me a drink, and himself four. One after the other. 'Shit,' he said. 'Three fucking *nil*. I wouldn't let that cunt of a manager choose a Sunday morning side up Brockwell park. Three fucking nil. And at home. To fucking Crystal Palace of all people. We should have walked it. A doddle. But three nil. I wouldn't have minded if it was bleeding Chelsea. But fucking *Crystal Palace*. I ask you.'

I commiserated. Not that I know shit about football. Then I tried to move away, but he grabbed my shoulder and kept talking.

'And all those bastards on the train on the way home,' he said. 'Crystal Palace supporters. They're fucking animals. Do you know that?'

I nodded.

'Who do you support?' he asked me.

'No one,' I said.

'Best thing,' he said after a moment's thought. 'Fucking football sucks. Did you get married today?'

'Yeah.'

'Good luck.'

And then the worst possible thing happened. A geezer I knew slightly came over, and seeing the Arsenal scarf, said, 'Who won?'

'Crystal fucking Palace,' said the Arsenal supporter.

'What was the score?'

'Three nil.'

'Fucking great,' said the geezer, and started dancing about. Just our luck. We'd found a Crystal Palace supporter. Or he'd found us.

'Do what?' said the Arsenal fan.

'Fucking great,' said the geezer, and went off to tell his mates.

'*Bastard!*' said the Arsenal fan and ordered another drink.

'I'd leave it if I were you,' I said. 'There's half a dozen of them, and only one of you.'

'Sod 'em,' he said. 'Sorry. It is your party after all. I'll swallow it.

I've been swallowing it all afternoon.'

'Good idea,' I said. 'Have a good time,' and I left him to it.

Except they wouldn't let him swallow it. They were drunk, and at home as it were, and their team had just thrashed his.

Anyway, I went back to Dawn and Tracey, who were both by that time steaming drunk, and had decided to show off the garters they were wearing as part of their wedding outfits. Of course for a pair of ex-strippers it was just like old times. And I've got to say that they did have good legs. Better than good.

So there you have it. At one end of the place, a disgruntled football fan being baited by supporters of the team that's just beaten his, and at the other, two recently retired exotic dancers, dying to prove that they hadn't lost the knack. And in the middle, about a hundred and fifty drunks whose ears were being battered by a re-mix of a re-make of an old Stevie Wonder tune. A recipe for disaster I'd say, and it wasn't long in coming.

First of all the Crystal Palace supporters formed a conga line, and forced their way through the crowd singing 'Paul Merson is a wanker' to the tune of 'Don't worry 'bout a thing'. Then Tracey, not to be outdone, starts to get her kit off. At least Dawn, as the bride, had the decorum to keep her dress on. But not Tracey. Oh no. Before you can say knife, she's unzipped the back of it, and let it drop to the floor, so's we can all see that underneath she's wearing a black corset with suspenders attached. And also, I might say, that her figure is just as good as the last time I saw her in her underclothes. Of course Dawn's having hysterics at all this. She's nearly choking with laughter, and calling for more. What a pair! And don't forget I've just got married to one of them.

Meanwhile, the Arsenal supporter has had all he can stand of the Crystal Palace mob, and catches hold of the last one in the conga line as he passes him by for the second time, and clocks him a good 'un right round the ear. And that, as they say, is all she wrote.

Suddenly the place erupted like one of those saloon brawls in an old Western. The Arsenal fan is up on the bar with an empty beer bottle in each hand, wading through the remains of the buffet lunch, and fighting off his rivals in front and Simon and the bar staff behind. The tune on the stereo finishes, and the next one up is 'Waterloo' by Abba, which used to be part of Tracey's set down the clubs, so she starts undoing her stockings and rolling them down her legs. From where I'm standing, by the entrance to the ladies, all I can see is fists flying, best hats being pushed crooked, bodies jumping up on to the bar and being knocked back to the floor, bottles and glasses whizzing through the air, and Tracey coming close to committing a gross public nuisance. Then I catch sight of Inspector Robber, who's trapped behind an overturned table in one corner, and he's got out his personal radio. So I push my way through the mêlée, pick up Tracey's dress and put it round her shoulders, grab her in one hand and Dawn in the other, and make my way to the emergency exit at the back of the restaurant. Luckily Chas had given me back the keys to the Chevy, and told me it was parked in the service road next to the bar. So, dragging the two protesting women, who believe it or not wanted to stay, behind me, I made for the motor, opened it up, pushed them in, and, drunk as I was, got it started, and away towards Tulse Hill, just as I heard the first sirens heading down Knights Hill to break up the fight.

I think Dawn got Tracey dressed, and we went out for a Chinese. To tell you the truth I can't remember much until the next morning.

5

I was woken up by someone hammering on the street door of my house. I sat upright in bed and almost screamed out in pain. My head felt as if it had been put into a vice and squeezed so tightly that I was surprised my eyeballs weren't bleeding. My mouth was so dry and coated I almost had to put my fingers under my tongue and massage the saliva glands to get some moisture going. I sat there looking at the curtains in front of me, hoping I was having a bad dream. Then the hammering on the door started again, and was echoed by the hammering inside my cranium, and I knew I wasn't. This was reality, and I could have done with less of it. I knew it was reality, because I could feel every root of every hair on my head, and they all hurt. I looked at the figure lying next to me, and envied the way she could sleep through all the racket. I got out of bed, went over to the window, drew back the curtains, pulled up the sash and looked out. On the parking area that had once been the front garden of the house two coppers were just about to start knocking on the door again.

'All right,' I croaked, 'I'm here.'

They both stepped back from the porch and looked up. 'This your car?' said the taller of the two.

I looked behind him. The Chevy was parked with only its nose on the parking spot. The long body of the car blocked the pavement, and its rear end stuck out into the street.

'It's my wife's,' I said.

'Can you tell her to move it?' said the shorter copper. 'We've had complaints.'

'Sorry,' I said. 'I'll get the keys.'

I turned, and went back over to the bed and shook Dawn's shoulder. She groaned and pulled the pillow over her head. I persisted. She groaned some more and rolled over, pillow and all. I pulled it off her face and did a double take. I hadn't been in bed with Dawn. On my wedding night, instead of consummating our passion in the bridal suite of the Grand Hotel, Hastings, somehow I'd ended up in my own bed, in my own flat, shacked up with my bride's matron of honour.

So the next question had to be, where was Dawn?

I shook Tracey's shoulder again, and she groaned some more, but didn't wake up. I leaned over her, sat her up and shook her harder. As I did so, the sheet that was covering her slid down her body, and I saw that she was naked to the waist. Jesus! Whatever next?

And *still* she wouldn't wake up. So I pinched her nose between my finger and thumb and held it tight. She snorted, snored, coughed and opened her eyes.

'Whad der fuck are you doid?' she said.

'Where's Dawn?' I said. Still holding her nose.

'Whad?'

'Where's Dawn?' I repeated.

'I dode dow. Led go ob by nobe.'

I did. 'Where is she?' I asked again.

Tracey shrugged.

'And how come you're in bed with me on my wedding night?' I asked.

She shrugged again, then said, 'If you fucked me on your wedding night, does it mean that we're married?'

'I didn't,' I said. 'Did I?'

She fluttered her eyelashes at me.

'Did I?'

More fluttering. I almost felt the draught.

'Don't wind me up, Trace,' I said. 'Did I or didn't I?'

'You couldn't. Not for the want of trying, mind. You were too pissed.'

I felt a great sense of relief, but that didn't explain what had happened to Dawn, and why the motor was parked like that.

I struggled into a pair of jeans and a T-shirt and forced my bare feet into a pair of loafers. I ran to the tiny bathroom beyond the open-plan kitchen, and threw open the door. The room was empty. I went back and looked for the car keys. They were nowhere to be found.

'Have you seen the keys to the Chevy?' I asked.

Tracey shrugged again, and her bare breasts, with their pink nipples hard and erect, jiggled.

'Christ,' I said, 'cover yourself up. There's two coppers downstairs.'

She smiled. 'Are they handsome?' she asked.

'Sorry,' I said. 'I didn't have time to notice.' The car keys were still nowhere to be seen. 'Fuck it,' I said. 'I'd better go down.'

I opened the flat door and went downstairs and out of the house. The two coppers were looking inside the back window of the car. 'There's someone asleep in there,' said the taller of the two.

'Or dead,' said the shorter.

I went and joined them. The windows of the car were steamed up but inside, clearly to be seen, was the figure of a blonde woman in a red dress, with the skirt hiked up around her shapely thighs, stretched out on the back bench seat.

We tried all the doors, but they were locked.

'Do you know her?' asked the taller copper.

'It's my wife,' I said. 'We got married yesterday. We should be in Hastings.'

The looks on the coppers' faces said that they wished we were.

'But we got delayed,' I explained. 'You know how it is.'

It didn't appear that they did. I knocked on the window by Dawn's head, but she didn't move. For one horrible moment I thought that she might be dead, she was so still.

Then Tracey decided to get into the act.

'What's going on?' she said from the open window of my flat.

The three of us standing by the car looked up in unison to see her leaning out of the window, breasts still bare, and her nipples harder than ever in the chill morning air.

After a minute, the taller copper dragged his eyes away and said to me, 'You're sure the one you married is in the car?'

'Quite sure,' I said. 'She,' I gestured in Tracey's direction, 'she was matron of honour.'

'Looks like she took her job seriously,' said the shorter copper.

I didn't reply.

'Nick. What's the matter?' Tracey said.

The three of us looked up again.

'It's Dawn,' I replied. 'She's asleep in the car.' I leant down and peered through the window again. 'And the keys are in the ignition. Trace. Go in and put something on... Please,' I added.

She looked down at herself, pulled a face, and withdrew. The two coppers looked disappointed.

'Shall I break the window?' the shorter copper asked the taller, drawing his truncheon.

'No,' I said. 'They cost a fortune to replace. I'll wake her. Just give me a minute.'

I banged on the window closest to Dawn's head again. Hard. With my fist. And I banged the door too, and after a moment I was relieved to see her move her head. I banged harder, and she opened her eyes, and looked up into mine. I mimed rolling down the window, and after a few seconds she sat up, straightened her skirt and did it.

'Are you all right?' I asked.

'Hello, Nick,' she replied. 'Are we at the seaside yet?'

'No,' I said. 'Not quite.'

She looked up at the house, and I turned and saw that Tracey had put on Dawn's dressing gown and was back at the window.

'I might have known,' said Dawn. 'That girl will do anything for a bed.'

'Why did you sleep in here?' I asked.

Dawn shrugged. 'Dunno,' she said. 'It seemed like a good idea at the time.'

'But it was our wedding night.'

'If you were so worried, why did you leave me here?'

There was no answer to that. Except that I'd been too out of it to realise I had. So I just stood there without saying a word. Then I realised that the two coppers were listening intently to our conversation, and I knew they could get free teas in the canteen back at the station for weeks on the strength of it.

'I'll move the car,' I said to him. 'Sorry to have bothered you.'

They looked at each other, shrugged, sighed, then the taller said, 'I'm sure we could do you for something here.'

'I'm sure you could,' I agreed. 'But give us a break, mate. I'm in enough trouble as it is, can't you see?'

They both looked at me, Dawn, and then up at Tracey who was still leaning out of the window watching us, and I saw them both smile before the taller one said, 'All right. I'm a married man myself, and it looks as if you'll have your hands full for the rest of the day with these two. But we'll be watching out for this heap, and if you as much as park on a yellow line...'

'Not a chance, officer,' I assured him. 'From now on, you'll have no more trouble from me.'

'OK,' he said, and the two of them walked towards their patrol car parked opposite.

As they went, the shorter one turned and called out, 'Congratulations, by the way. Enjoy your honeymoon,' and I heard them both laughing as they got into their car.

I blew a sigh of relief, and reached in and unlocked the driver's door, opened it and slid behind the wheel. The Chevy started on the button, and I pulled it on to the front, well out of harm's way, then turned to Dawn and said, 'Who drove home last night?'

'Tracey.'

'Christ. She's never driven a car like this.'

'She did all right.'

'Up until the end at least. Come on, let's go inside and have some breakfast. We've got a room booked in Hastings, don't forget.'

'Did you fuck her?' said Dawn as we got out of the car.

'No. Course not.'

'Are you sure?'

'Course I am.'

We went upstairs in silence and when we got inside my flat, Tracey had the kettle on and was spooning instant coffee into three mugs.

'Hello, Dawn,' she said. 'Enjoy your honeymoon night, did you?'

'Did you?' asked Dawn back, as she sat at the stool by the counter I like to refer to as the breakfast bar.

'No. Lover boy couldn't get it up.'

'Just as well for lover boy,' said Dawn, giving me a slitty-eyed look.

'Oi,' I said. 'I am here you know.'

'Fancy,' said Dawn.

'Are we going to Hastings?' I asked, trying to change the subject.

'Are you sure you wouldn't rather take Tracey?' asked Dawn, and the two women collapsed into giggles.

'Sorry, darlin',' said Tracey, as she passed us each a mug of steaming coffee. 'I didn't mean to spoil your big night.'

'From the sound of it, it wouldn't have been all that much cop,' said Dawn. 'Now, are you sure you don't want to come to the seaside with us? I'm sure we could find you a bed.'

Oh Christ, I thought. What the bloody hell have I got into here? And my head started thumping again.

6

The two of us did eventually get away on our honeymoon, just before eleven. Without a third party, thankfully, although it was touch and go there for a while. I phoned ahead, and spoke to the hotel manager, and, although he was a little miffed that we hadn't arrived the previous evening, business wasn't so good that he'd let the honeymoon suite go. I promised to pay for the night we'd missed, and ordered a couple of bottles of champagne to be put on ice, and he was a lot less frosty when he put down the phone than he'd been when I first told him who I was. We dropped Tracey off at her flat and picked up Dawn's bag, and headed back down the south circular towards the A21. We arrived in Hastings at about four, after stopping for a sedate lunch and a couple of pints at a mossy old pub on the outskirts of Tunbridge Wells. By then Dawn had seen the joke and forgiven me. A very forgiving woman is Dawn. Just as well really, knowing me as I do. I'm the sort of person who needs forgiving often.

At the hotel we were greeted by a uniformed porter, who, on hearing that we were the tardy honeymooners, whisked our bags away to the lift and left us to check in.

The manager was at the desk to take our particulars personally. He was a tall character in a black suit, gleaming white shirt and conservatively striped tie.

'Mr and Mrs Sharman,' he said. 'At last. Your room is ready if you'll just sign the book. It has a view over the cliffs, and I hope you enjoy your stay. Until Tuesday morning, I believe?'

I nodded assent, and he banged the bell on the counter, and a juvenile in a similar uniform to the porter's arrived to show us the way to our room. The porter was waiting to show us around the suite when we arrived. There were flowers everywhere, a big bowl of fruit, *three* bottles of champagne in the fridge – my two, plus a complimentary from the management – next to half a dozen bottles of imported beer, and the usual miniature spirits and mixers. The bed was big and round and covered in a scarlet satin bedspread. The sitting room had a huge TV set in one corner, and a scarlet three-piece suite. Then the porter took us back into the bedroom and threw open the door to the bathroom. It was massive. The jacuzzi was big enough to hold a round-table meeting inside, and even the shower stall had plenty of room for two. I tipped the staff generously, and they left us in peace informing us as they left that dinner was served at seven.

'Not bad,' I said, when they were gone and I looked round.

'Tart's parlour,' said Dawn. 'But what am I but an old tart anyway?'

'*My* old tart,' I said. 'And don't you forget it. Want some champagne?'

She nodded, and I opened a bottle and poured two glasses.

'Want a joint?' she asked. 'Chill out.'

'OK,' I said, and she hunted about in her bag, and pulled out a crumpled ready-rolled, which I just knew would taste of her perfume. She lit it and took a long hit before passing it over.

I won't elaborate on our honeymoon. It's kind of personal. But we had a great time. I always have a great time with Dawn. She helps me forget. And I couldn't ask anything more from anyone than that.

Tuesday morning I paid the bill, thanked the manager, and we headed back to London. On the way I told Dawn about my new case. What with one thing and another, or *the* other, if you want me to be crude, there hadn't been time before.

'Jay Harrison,' she said as we joined a traffic jam on the outskirts of Sevenoaks, close to the M25. And that sodding road was built to *ease* congestion. 'He was in that band they made a film about, wasn't he?'

I agreed that he was.

'They were great. Bit before my time of course.'

'Of course,' I said.

'Can I help?' she asked.

'Do what?' I turned and looked at her, and almost rear-ended a Mini-Metro, which the Chevy could have eaten up and spat out without rippling a bumper.

'I've got nothing else to do. You wanted me to stop work.'

Work, in her and Tracey's case, being taking her clothes off in sleazy pubs and clubs and occasionally allowing punters to have their evil way. For cash.

'Well, I'm all for a woman having a career, but when it entails her coming home with her knickers all crusty, even I've got to draw the line,' I said.

'You know it never meant anything.'

'It started to mean something to me.'

She leant over the length of the bench seat and put her hand over mine on the steering wheel.

'That's one of the sweetest things I've ever heard,' she said.

I turned my hand and gripped her fingers.

'So *can* I?' she said.

'If you want. I don't know what's going to happen yet. It could be a hoax. Probably will be. It's not the first time this has happened apparently. A chancer going for a few quid. I mean, the geezer's supposed to have been dead for twenty years. So we just go through the motions. A couple of days' work and that's that. A nice little earner, and us back at the Grand Hotel for our second honeymoon.'

'Fair enough. If that's what it is, that's what it is. At least you'll have company.'

'All right, Dawn,' I said. 'You've got a deal.'

'And we're partners?'

'I wouldn't go as far as to say that. But you can carry the sandwiches.'

She punched me in the ribs. Hard. 'Chauvinist,' she said.

I nodded, and overtook a McDonald's truck that was big enough to carry a million burger patties.

'When do we start?' she asked.

'Today. I've got to phone Chris Kennedy-Sloane. He should have a copy of the letter by now. And he's paymaster on the deal. He's got a big fat cheque for me.'

'Us.'

'Us,' I agreed, as the suburbs got more citified, and we drove into London proper.

We were home by eleven, and Dawn stuck on the kettle, and I unpacked our bags and put our washing into the machine. Domestic bliss. When our undies were having a significant relationship under the Daz Ultra, and I'd copped for a cup of tea, I called Chris Kennedy-Sloane on his hot line.

'How are you, dear boy?' he asked, after I'd been sieved through a receptionist, two secretaries and a personal assistant. 'How was the honeymoon? A little less fraught than the reception, I hope.'

'You'd be amazed,' I replied. 'Did you get away in one piece?'

'The lovely Angela cut a swathe through the mob, brandishing one of her stilettos. We were just one step ahead of the cops, if you'll excuse the pun.'

'Much damage done?' I asked.

'Who'd know in a place like that? Rustic is the word that springs to mind.'

'I must go and see the guv'nor. What's new your end?'

'A sheaf of faxes for you, and a cheque.'

'Sounds good to me. When can I come in and pick them up?'

There was a pause. 'I have a window at three,' said Kennedy-Sloane.

'Don't give me all that window bollocks,' I said. 'If you mean you're available then, just say so.'

'Sorry, Nick. You know it impresses the clients.'

'But I'm not a client.'

'Precisely the opposite. An employee almost.'

'Very almost,' I said. 'And don't you forget it.'

'Wouldn't dream of it, old boy. I know how exact you always are.'

'How much is the cheque for?'

'Seven days at a thousand per. Plus, I thought another K for exes. Does that suit you?'

'Chris. I'll almost admit to being your employee for a cheque like that. You don't know how much this weekend has cost me so far.'

'Always ready to oblige a friend. So three o'clock it is. What are you driving these days?'

'A Chevrolet.'

'Dear God. Why don't you get something sensible?'

'Like a Porsche?'

'Touché. Anyway I'll tell Craig in the parking garage to expect some trans-Atlantic leviathan at three o'clock. Parking round here is a pain. Just drive round the back and head downwards. He'll put you right. Then the lift will bring you straight up here. You remember where I am?'

'How could I forget?' I asked. 'And I'm bringing Dawn.'

'My word, we are taking the marriage stakes seriously. This is not like you.'

'I've turned over a new leaf,' I said.

'Delighted to hear it. So until three,' he said, and hung up. I told Dawn what was happening.

'*Eight thousand quid* for a week's work?' she said. 'It's all right for some.'

'Yeah. But it might be the only week's work I do this year.'

'Even so.'

'I'm just the best,' I said. 'You didn't know who you were marrying.'

'And half the money's mine.'

'Not so fast,' I said. 'I think we'd better go up the bar, see Simon, and find out what the damage was for that do on Saturday. Chris and Ange had to beat a hasty retreat. I don't know what happened after they left.'

'Was there a lot of trouble?'

'Enough. We'd better go up and settle the bill. And don't forget, half's yours,' I added.

'Charming. I thought you were standing for it.'

'I was, until you decided you wanted to be my partner.'

'All right. Come on then,' she said, and we got ourselves together and went to see Simon. I took my cheque book with me.

The place was deserted when we walked in except for a barmaid behind the counter, polishing a glass and looking a little puzzled at the concept, and Lenny Kravitz, whose latest album was on the stereo.

'Hello, Ash,' I said. 'How's tricks?'

She pouted and shrugged.

'That good?' I said.

She nodded, and went back to the glass, then put it on the counter and said, 'Drink?'

'Rattlesnake,' I said.

'Mineral water,' said Dawn.

As Ash got the drinks, I said, 'Simon in?'

'Out back,' she replied. 'Getting the food ready.'

I went through the restaurant to the kitchen, tapped on the door and opened it. Simon was mixing a big bowl of tuna, onion and mayonnaise for sandwich fillings.

He looked up as I went in. 'Hello, Nick,' he said. 'Where've you been?'

'Hastings. I came in to settle up for Saturday… And apologise?' I queried.

'No apology needed. There weren't a lot of breakages, and what there was I've put on your bill.'

'I thought you would. What's the damage? Break it to me gently.'

He pulled a face and smiled. The sort of smile bar owners wear when there's a great deal of readies about to enter their sphere of influence. 'I've got the bill in the office. Let me finish this and I'll get it.'

'OK. No rush,' I said, and went back to join Dawn.

I sipped my beer and saw Simon come out of the kitchen and go out the back way and up the stairs at the back of the place. He came back carrying a till roll which he gave to me.

'What's this?' I asked.

'The bill. Almost a complete roll. I changed it that morning. You can check it if you want.'

I shrugged. 'And this is the total?' I pointed at the end where, neatly printed in light purple ink, was £2465.91.

'That's the baby.'

'Jesus. You'll have to take a cheque. I don't carry that much petty cash these days.'

'Sure,' said Simon.

Dawn took a squint over my shoulder, and raised her eyebrows, but said nothing. There was nothing to say.

'I'm getting some dough this after,' I said. 'Can I post-date the cheque 'til Friday?'

'I suppose so,' said Simon.

'It's good,' I said. 'I just want to get the cheque I'm being given cleared.'

'All right,' said Simon. 'I trust you.' And I took out my cheque book and wrote him a kite.

'What happened to that geezer?' I asked.

'Which one?'

'Whassisname. The Arsenal fan.'

'Oh, the Crystal Palace lot tried to hang him from a lamp post with his scarf.'

'I bet they had a job,' said Dawn. 'He's a big lad.'

'Big enough to put three of them in hospital. Then he escaped across the cemetery,' said Simon.

'Did he get captured?' I asked.

'No,' said Simon, folding the cheque and putting it into the breast pocket of his shirt. 'Got away clean as a whistle. They've got wings on their feet, Arsenal fans, when they're running away.' But he supported Tottenham, so he would say that. 'By the way, I've got a whole load of parcels that belong to you in the back. Your wedding presents I think they are.'

I'd forgotten about them in all the excitement. 'Cheers,' I said.

'Want another drink while I get them?' he asked. 'On the house of course,' he added. And I should think so too, as I'd just about paid for his eldest daughter to go to private school for two terms with that cheque I'd given him.

I nodded, and he fetched me another Rattlesnake, and Dawn was tempted into having a gin.

7

We got to Chris Kennedy-Sloane's office just before three. It was up by Tower Bridge. I followed his directions, drove round the back, found a sign pointing to the garage, and took the ramp down. There was a young guy sitting in a booth at the bottom of the ramp. He came over when I drew up and I told him who I was. He directed me to park the Chevy in a shadowy bay at the far end of the garage, and Dawn and I walked back to the lift and took it to the top floor. The receptionist in the front office of Kennedy-Sloane & Partners was as cute as nevermind, and did she know it. Her breasts were perfectly lifted and separated under a white blouse that was just translucent enough to show the lace of her bra beneath. Her lips were pink and bowed, her false eyelashes hovered over her baby blues just enough to drive you crazy, and her helmet of blonde hair could have been sculpted from gold. I don't think Dawn liked her much.

With one perfectly manicured fingernail she pressed a button on the intercom and breathily told someone that Mr Sharman was in reception. She didn't mention Dawn. Somehow I think the dislike was mutual.

Another blonde dream opened the door that led inwards and beckoned to us to follow her. She led us through to Chris's office. I had to fight to keep my eyes from following the roll of her buttocks under a very tight, very short grey skirt. I knew Dawn was watching me out of the corners of hers. I turned and smiled at her and nearly collided with a palm in a pot. She shook her head. Marriage. A wonderful institution. But, as the old joke goes, who wants to live in an institution?

Kennedy-Sloane was waiting in his office with the killer view of the city stretching away to Essex. He jumped up when we entered and showed us to a pair of chairs in front of his desk. At least he paid attention to my wife which raised the temperature a little.

'Drinks?' he asked. 'Tea, coffee or something stronger?'

I asked for a beer. Dawn took an Evian water. Chris poured himself a vodka on the rocks.

In the centre of his otherwise bare desk was a plain folder. When we were all sitting comfortably he opened it.

'These are the faxes that arrived yesterday,' he said, and fanned them out in front of us.

I looked at the top one. It was a copy of a handwritten note. The handwriting was large and whorly, and it read:

To whom it may concern,
Royalties Section,
Lifetime Records/Music,
555 La Branca,
Los Angeles,
California,
USA.

I understand that you are holding a large sum of money that belongs to me. It being the royalties accrued since my death was wrongly reported on 7 April 1972.

I will write again with details of where I wish the money to be paid.

Yours sincerely
Jay Harrison.

'Short, sharp and to the point,' I said.

The next fax was a copy of the envelope in which the letter had arrived. It was in the same handwriting and the address was as on the top of the letter. It was postmarked 'London W1', and dated 14 April. The next sheet was a copy of the last page of a recording contract dated June 1967 between Lifetime Records and Dog Soldier. It was signed by all four members of the band, and as far as I could tell, the signature that was scrawled under the neatly typed 'Jay Harrison' on the contract was the same as that on the letter. Pretty damn close anyway, considering twenty-six years had passed. The third fax was a copy of a death certificate made out on 7 April 1972, stating that Jay Harrison had expired from a heart attack. The attending physician's name was Dr Malcolm Priest. The final three faxes were contemporary reports of his death. The one from the London *Daily Mirror* was pretty typical.

POP STAR DIES OF HEART ATTACK

read the headline. Then the story followed:

Jay Harrison, lead singer of the American pop group Dog Soldier was yesterday found dead in the flat he rented in Hyde Park Mansions, London.

Twenty-nine-year-old Harrison had been living in England for the past eight months preparing new material for the band's forthcoming LP. The singer was found in the bath by his girlfriend Kim Major (26) when she awoke to find herself alone at 3am. Earlier, the pair had attended a party given by Track, The Who's record company, at the Café de Paris. She immediately called Harrison's doctor, who declared him dead at 3.45 am.

Dog Soldier, part of the acid revolution of the so-called 'Summer Of Love' hippy explosion of 1966/7, had long been the centre of controversy, coming to a head when Harrison was arrested for using profanity in public and indecent exposure during a concert in Houston, Texas last year. He was still awaiting trial at the time of his death.

Dog Soldier had many top ten hits in Great Britain including the number one, 'Just Do It', plus five best-selling long-playing records. At the time of going to press, Miss Major was not available for comment, and believed to be staying with friends in the country.

Details of the funeral are to be announced later.

Beneath the story was printed a photograph of Harrison before he went to seed.

The newspaper was dated 9 April 1972.

I passed the faxes one by one to Dawn as I read them. 'Did you know him?' I asked Kennedy-Sloane.

'No. A bit before my time, Nick. I knew *of* him of course. Who didn't? But when he died I'd just started working for a brokerage in the city. In those days it wasn't the done thing to admire acid-rock bands. Engelbert Humperdinck was more our style.'

'Still is, isn't it, Chris?' I said.

He pulled a face.

'I'll need some more information,' I went on.

'Such as?'

'The exact address of the flat where he died. It's a long shot, but I'll go take a look. Someone there might remember what happened that night. There's a distinct lack of witnesses to all this. The girl and the doctor both being dead. And where was the body taken? Do you know?'

Kennedy-Sloane shrugged.

'Try to find out, will you, Chris? Someone alive's got to have seen this dude dead.'

'You have such a way with words,' he said.

'Cheers. Now, about that cheque.'

Kennedy-Sloane took a large envelope from his inside breast pocket and handed it to me. I opened it. I pulled out a company cheque for eight thousand quid. It was drawn on Coutts. The royal bank. I don't think I'd ever seen a Coutts cheque before. It felt like cash.

'Good bank,' I said.

'Not as good as it used to be. All the statements used to be handwritten in fountain pen. But times change.'

'Don't they just,' I agreed. 'So what do you reckon to all this, Chris?'

'God knows. What about you? You're the detective.'

'The signature on the letter looks like the business to me. If it's not the real thing, whoever wrote it has seen Harrison's handwriting somewhere.'

'An autograph book,' said Kennedy-Sloane. 'Or the back of a record sleeve. A menu, an airline ticket. Anywhere. Harrison must have signed his name a hundred thousand times for fans over the years.'

'True enough,' I said. 'And assuming the letter is a fake, which we have to, anyone interested enough would have had a long time to get the handwriting off pat.'

Kennedy-Sloane nodded.

'How much dough do you reckon is involved here, anyway?' I asked him.

'Millions,' he replied. 'Ten million, twenty. Who knows? Dog Soldier have sold an awful lot of records since Harrison died. Even splitting the take four ways, there's a bundle waiting in LA for someone. And the music isn't all. He's had half a dozen books of poetry published posthumously. And of course there was the movie. The band all got money from that. It's a lot, Nick, and the pot is getting bigger every day.'

'And the cash is all tied up.'

'That's right. No one's touched his share since April seventy-two.'

'And this sort of thing happens all the time? People making claims on the estate?'

Another nod.

'And do they always hire private detectives to investigate?'

'I don't know. But as far as I *do* know, there's never been a claim from this side of the pond before.'

The pond. I ask you.

'And Lifetime have heard nothing since this letter arrived?' I said.

'Not a peep.'

'It's been a month since it was sent. And it says he's going to send instructions about where to pay the money.'

'He's optimistic,' said Kennedy-Sloane tartly.

'I agree,' I said. 'I know how difficult it is to separate record companies from their money. But still, I wonder why there's been no further communication.'

Kennedy-Sloane shrugged again.

'Well, we'll press on,' I said. 'If you can find out that address for me, and anything else relevant, I'll get on the case straight away.'

'*We'll* get on the case straight away,' interrupted Dawn.

'We'll get on the case straight away,' I agreed. 'Come on then. Let's leave this man to make a load more money. We've got work to do.' And we left Chris Kennedy-Sloane in his ivory tower overlooking the river, and went back to the car, and home.

8

Kennedy-Sloane was in touch the next morning before I'd washed up the breakfast things and while Dawn was still in the shower. He gave me the exact address in Hyde Park Mansions where Jay Harrison had shuffled off his mortal coil, and, as a bonus, the name of the managing agents who looked after the place.

'I don't know if the flat is still rented, or if it's been sold off since,' he said. 'But it's somewhere to start.'

'Cheers, Chris,' I said. 'That's a great help.'

'I thought that was your job. Finding out things. I don't know why I'm paying you and doing all the hard work myself.'

'It must be my beautiful eyes,' I said. 'And you're not paying me,' I reminded him. 'Lifetime is.'

'Whatever. But from now on, you can earn that excessive fee that I negotiated for you without my help.'

'We're on the same side, remember?' I said. 'If you're the man with the information I'll be knocking at your door. Just like I would anybody else.'

'I've got other things to do,' he said.

'Course you have. Although if I asked, I bet you'll be hard pressed to tell me what they are.'

'Talk to me soon, Nick,' he said and hung up.

I looked at the clock. Quarter to ten. And any self-respecting managing agent should be right on the job at that time. So I gave them a call.

As I was dialling, Dawn came out of the bathroom, towelling her hair. She gave me a grin, took off her robe, and stood naked in front of me.

'Calling up your girlfriend, when I'm out of the room,' she said.

'Business,' I replied. 'Get dressed. You're distracting me.'

'That was the idea, my love,' she said, and ground her hips at me.

'Get dressed,' I said again, trying to ignore what she was laying out on display.

She wrinkled her nose, took a clean pair of panties off the bed, and stepped into them.

The phone was answered on the fourth ring. I asked the telephonist to put me through to whoever dealt with Hyde Park Mansions. There was a click, a single ringing tone and a woman answered.

'Marion Hartley,' she said. 'How can I help you?'

'Do you deal with Hyde Park Mansions?' I asked.

'I do.'

'I wonder if you can help me. Is the whole place rented?'

'It's a mixture of rented properties and privately owned.'

'I wonder if you can tell me about number twenty-two.'

'In what connection?' she said.

I told her that I was a journalist. A music journalist. Freelance. And that I was doing a story on Jay Harrison. She said that she'd heard of him. I told her that he'd died at number twenty-two Hyde Park Mansions, and that I was trying to trace whoever had rented or bought it after Harrison had died. She sounded vaguely interested. But not fascinated. I suppose it filled in the time between getting to work and her coffee break. After I'd finished she went and got the file, warning me that she only had details on the rented properties in the block. I was lucky. Number twenty-two was still rented. In the name of Simmons. Simmons, C. That was it. No more details. Marion Hartley told me that the company she worked for had only managed the place for about six months. She also told me, but not in so many words, that managing a place like that was a pain in the arse. It probably was. Trying to collect rents off tenants, and being deluged for requests to fix the central heating, while the owners lived it up in the sun somewhere. I could almost feel sorry for her. But not quite. I asked her who had managed the place previously. She told me, and gave me a phone number and the name of the person who had taken care of the building. I thanked her and hung up.

'Music journalist,' said Dawn. Who by then was looking most appealing in very tight, very faded blue jeans, a white blouse and black suede ankle boots. 'I really must get you a new pair of Ray-Bans.'

'It's all part of my chameleon-like character,' I said.

'You're just a bloody liar, you mean,' she said back, and I winked at her.

'Is there anything you want me to do?' she asked.

'Not yet. But stick around, and I'll find you something to do.'

She dropped into the armchair opposite me, and lit a cigarette.

Before I rang the number that Marion Hartley had given me, I checked the phone book. There was no listing for a C. Simmons at the mansions. Directory couldn't help either. Probably ex-directory. If the worst came to the worst, I could pretend to be a policeman and try to bluff the supervisor to check. I still knew the patter. But not yet. There was plenty of time for that later.

I tapped out the number of the previous managing agents, and asked for the name that I'd been given. Once again I told my story, and the bloke I was talking to told me that his company had only managed the place for two years. He asked if I'd hang on while he found out who had done the job previous to *them*. I did, and he was back within a couple of minutes with the name of the company, but no phone number.

I went back to the phone book. By the time I'd told my story to the fifth estate agent, my mouth was dry and I was still only back to 1981. Then, on the sixth try, the company I was looking for had vanished into thin air. Gone out of business. End of story.

I went to the fridge and got a cold beer for myself and one for Dawn.

Next I got out the A to Z and located the corner where Hyde Park Mansions stood, and searched around for the nearest hospital. There were several in the vicinity, but the closest with an accident and emergency department was St Mary's in Paddington. The closest one *now*. Twenty years ago there were more hospitals and more casualty wings. I wanted to know if an ambulance had been called on the night Jay Harrison died. And if so, when, and what had happened when it arrived. I rang the switchboard and crossed my fingers. The telephonist confirmed that Hyde Park Mansions was in their catchment area. When I asked if that was true in 1972, she put me through to records. It was a miracle. It had been. I asked if by any chance their A&E files went back that far. Whoever I was speaking to, a young woman with a faint Irish accent, confirmed that they did. The last five years on micro-film. The previous five in filing cabinets and anything before that in bales somewhere deep in the heart of the hospital's storage system. From the way she said it, I got the impression she thought that dragons lurked there. I asked if I could see the records. She asked why. I gave her the freelance music journalist story again. She told me that she loved music, and that I should come by any time. Ask for Mary in records. Mary at St Mary's. Easy. I said my secretary would be along soonest. With a donation to the hospital fund. Mary sounded genuinely sorry when I said I couldn't make it in person. I had to interview Michael Bolton at his hotel I told her. She sounded impressed at that. I wouldn't have been.

We parted the best of friends. Mary and I.

When I put down the phone, Dawn said, 'Another conquest?'

I was beginning to think that my wife understood me too well. 'Just part of the job. I keep telling you that,' I said. 'Now about that something I said I'd find for you to do...' And I explained to Dawn exactly what I wanted.

'Do I get all the dirty jobs?' she asked.

'That's right. If you want to be a detective, you've got to pay your dues.'

She pursed her lips.

'Of course, if you don't want to do it...' I let the sentence hang in the air.

'I do,' she said quickly, slashed some lipstick on her mouth, picked up the keys to the Chevy and went to the door.

'Give Mary a hundred quid for the hospital charity,' I said. 'Out of expenses.'

'And your love?'

'Just the money. I'm saving all my loving for you,' I said, and Dawn cracked a smile, blew me a kiss, and left.

I went back to the fridge for another beer.

While Dawn was gone, I read through the file of faxes that Chris had given me the previous day. As I read the press cuttings about

Harrison's death, I made a few notes. Not many. There weren't that many to make. I wrote down 'Undertakers', and underlined it heavily. If anyone knew who was in that coffin it would be them. And I wondered who the hell had buried him, and how I could find out after all this time. Twenty years. It was a bloody lifetime. Talk about a cold trail. This one was deep frozen.

I made myself a solitary lunch of Sainsbury's sliced turkey breast, coleslaw, red onion, tomato and lettuce on white bread and wandered the floor thinking, and played Otis Redding CDs while watching afternoon soaps on TV with the sound turned down.

Busy. Busy. Busy.

Dawn came back about four. Her jeans and blouse were filthy. She gave me a look almost as dirty as the clothes she was wearing, peeled them and her underwear off, and went and took another shower. I said nothing. Just made a jug of martini cocktails. Gin. Six to one, with olives. And waited for her to finish.

She wasn't long. She came out of the bathroom, towelling her hair for the second time that day, sat in the armchair, lit a cigarette and accepted the chilly glass I gave her.

'Hard day at the office, dearest?' I enquired.

'Fuck right off.'

'That's what I like to hear. Someone who's happy in their work.'

She downed half the martini in one swallow, catching the olive between her teeth, as I sipped at mine.

'Well?' I said. 'Don't keep me in suspense. What did you find?'

'Your girlfriend Mary is very pretty. But a little short for you, and her thighs are too heavy.'

'Bitchy,' I said, and helped myself to a cigarette.

'But she was very helpful.'

'And?'

'And I found the file you wanted.'

'Good for you.'

She got up, went over to her jeans, reached into the back pocket and took out a piece of folded paper. 'I took a copy,' she said, and handed it to me.

The paper was lined and the contents were the logs of the emergency ambulance calls for the 7th of April 1972. Halfway down the sheet an entry was marked. It read:

7/4/72... Origin 999... 3.05am... 22 Hyde Pk. Mans... 723–
   0821
See Miss Major... Patient Harrison... Suspected heart attack
Delta six despatched... Arrived 3.12am... Patient DOA
   Attending MD. Dr Priest, present... No action taken

Simple as that.

'So, at least we know he never made the hospital,' I said. 'Well
done, love. I wonder if the ambulance attendants saw the body? I
suppose the crew's names weren't on the files?'

'No. But there was this though.' She went back to her jeans and got
out another sheet of copy paper. 'I went through the previous pages,'
she said. 'And I saw this. It may not mean anything. But...' She pointed
at an entry at the bottom of the page. It must have been the one directly
before the one with the details of the shout for Harrison. It read:

7/4/72... Origin 999... 1.14am... Hyde Pk. Mans...
No flat number given/No tel. no./No contact. Caller male.
Suspected drug OD. No patient name.
Romeo four despatched... Arrived 1.28am
Nothing known. No action taken.

'Like I say, it may have no connection...' Dawn said.

'And it might,' I said. 'You're brilliant. We'll make a private
detective out of you yet.'

'Thank you, kind sir, for your patronising remarks,' she said,
curtsying in her towelling robe. 'Why don't you stick them where
the sun don't shine?'

I grabbed at her, and caught her dressing gown, and dragged her
protesting on to my lap. 'Sorry, Babes,' I said, licking at her face,
which still tasted slightly of soap. 'Won't you forgive me?' And I
stuck my hand up the skirt of her robe, and started tickling her
thighs, which I know just drives her crazy. She was laughing so much
she was crying, and beating at me to let her go. But I had a good grip,
and eventually she screamed that she forgave me, and I kissed her on
the mouth and held her tight.

She went back to her chair, and filled her glass from the jug. When
she'd taken a sip and regained her composure, she said, 'So what do
we do next?'

'Next, we go to Hyde Park Mansions,' I replied. 'And have a nose about. We'll go in the morning. See if there's anyone still there who was there at the time, and also try to find out who buried our American friend. I mean, there must be someone alive who actually saw the body. And at some point, we're going to take a look-see at where his mortal remains are buried. Highgate cemetery. I've heard it's beautiful up there. Perhaps we'll take a picture. But first I think you should get dressed, and then we'll go and have a drink, and I'll treat you to the best Indian dinner we can find.'

9

Dawn did as I suggested, and we spent the evening in the fleshpots of Tulse Hill, culminating in a pleasant hour or so at the Taj Mahal restaurant and take-away for a chicken pasanda, two onion bhajis, two vegetable samosas, fried rice, chickpeas in hot sauce, a few Kingfisher lagers and several Irish coffees. When we got home, we went straight to bed. Dawn rolled a grass joint without tobacco, and after that I'm afraid I'm a little hazy as to the details. But as far as I remember, a good time was had by all.

The next morning we were up early, and Dawn made a huge fry-up and a pot of freshly ground coffee. Something told me I'd done something right the night before.

'So what's the plan?' she asked, when our plates were empty, and we were on our second cups of coffee.

'No plan. We vamp it. This place is going to be pretty exclusive, I reckon, and we've got to look the part.'

I showered, shaved closely and put on a dark blue Hugo Boss suit, pale blue button-down shirt, a tie of muted hues in blue again, and polished my black leather Bass Weejuns to a shine that would shame a new mirror. Dawn wore grey. A grey two-piece double-breasted suit that made her look like an assistant bank manager, a pale grey silk blouse, matching tights, and black mid-heeled court shoes. Her make-up was understated, and she carried the tan Burberry I'd bought her for Christmas. All in all, we looked the right business.

Hyde Park Mansions *was* as exclusive as I'd guessed it would be. Concierge. The whole works. But even the most perfect organism sometimes breaks down. When Dawn and I arrived, the concierge must have gone for his tea. The front door was locked and the seat behind the desk in the foyer was empty. There was a huge entryphone system mounted on one side of the door, and I buzzed number twenty-two. There was no answer, and I buzzed again. Luckily, as we were waiting, the lift doors opened and an elderly couple walked across the foyer and opened the front door from the inside. They gave us a quizzical look, and I said, 'We're here to see Miss Simmons in number twenty-two,' and quoted the name of the managing agents.

It did the trick, and the male half of the duo held the door open for Dawn and me to enter the building. She gave the bloke a dazzling smile, and his wife hustled him out and down the front steps.

'You scored there,' I teased her.

'When have you ever known me to fail?' she asked.

We walked over to the lift, and I checked the flat register on the metal plate by the side of it, found that number twenty-two was on the fourth floor, and we took the lift up. Like I said, Hyde Park Mansions was as exclusive as I'd guessed it would be. Posh even. Smart. Well up-market. But number twenty-two was the exception. The paint around the door frame was old and peeling. The door itself looked a bit out of true, and the brass furniture was green with age and lack of attention. There was no bell-push, just an old knocker in the shape of a fish. I looked at Dawn, and she looked at me. 'Go on then,' she said. 'Knock.'

So I did. Not that I expected to get a result. The buzzer at the front door had gone unanswered, and even if anyone *was* at home, it had been twenty years since Jay Harrison had dropped off his perch behind that door. And twenty years is a very long time.

There was no answer at first, and after about two minutes I rapped hard on the door again. Somewhere way back in the flat I heard a noise and Dawn heard it too. She pulled a face at me, and I pulled one back. Then there was the sound of locks and bolts being turned and pulled, and the door opened six inches on a brass chain, and a little, old, wizened female face, topped with snow-white hair, appeared, and a pair of black eyes behind thick, rimless spectacles peered out at us.

'Hello,' said Dawn. 'Mrs Simmons?'

'Miss,' said the old lady who had answered the door. 'What do you want?'

'We're making certain enquiries,' I said.

'Enquiries. What kind of enquiries?' the old lady demanded.

'We wondered how long you've been living here,' said Dawn.

'Why?'

'There's a few questions we'd like to ask you.' Dawn again.

'Are you more of those fans? How did you get in? I thought the porter was keeping you out.'

'We're not fans,' I said, and pulled out one of my cards before she slammed the door in our faces, and held it in front of her. 'I'm a private detective. This is my wife. Someone going out let us in. The porter wasn't on duty.'

'Lazy devil. He's always disappearing when he's needed.' Her little black eyes sparkled. 'Are you both detectives?'

'Yes,' said Dawn. I didn't argue. I could feel the conversation going our way.

'Like *The Thin Man*,' said the old lady. 'Nick and Nora Charles. They're on television sometimes in the morning. I like television in the morning, don't you? What a coincidence you having the same Christian name,' she said to me, clocking my card closely. 'Have you got a dog?'

'No,' said Dawn, not the least fazed by the question.

'You should get one. Nick and Nora have got a beautiful dog. A terrier. Asta's his name. He's ever so clever. Knows loads of tricks. He's always rescuing them from trouble.'

'I know,' said Dawn. 'I watch those films too.'

I might've guessed.

'What kind of case are you on?' asked the old lady, suddenly well into crime-busting.

'That's why we're here,' explained Dawn. 'It's about someone who used to live in this flat.'

'Who?'

'Jay Harrison.'

'That pop singer. I knew it. People used to get in here all the time. But lately I haven't seen so many.'

'How long *have* you lived here?' I asked.

'Since it happened.'

'Since 1972?'

'Yes. I took the lease over when his friend left.'

'Kim Major?'

'Was that her name? I forget. My memory's not what it used to be.'

'That's all right,' said Dawn reassuringly. 'Don't worry. It's just that we'd be grateful if you could spare us a few minutes to answer some questions. May we come in?'

'I'm sorry. Where are my manners? Of course.' And the door shut in our faces, and I heard the chain rattle, and then the little old lady opened it all the way.

She *was* tiny. No more than five foot tall, and sort of bent in the middle, and wearing a shawl over a brown woollen dress that touched the tips of her round-toed shoes.

'Come through,' she said. 'Would you like some tea?'

'Yes please,' said Dawn, and I nodded.

The flat was dark and smelt of damp and old cooking. But it was huge, and the ceilings were so high that they all but vanished into the gloom. The old lady led us down the hall into a large living room where the curtains were drawn across the windows and a dim bulb shone in the ceiling fixture.

'Sit down,' she said.

'Thank you, Miss Simmons,' said Dawn, as she sat in a lumpy-looking old armchair. 'This place is massive. Do you live here all alone?'

'I'm afraid so,' said Miss Simmons sadly. 'I never married. There was someone once. But he died.'

'I'm sorry,' said Dawn.

'So am I,' said the old lady. 'I still think of him every day, even though it was over fifty years ago that it happened. In the war. You know.'

Dawn nodded, and I chose an upright chair next to a table covered in a dingy white lace cloth.

'Milk and sugar?' asked Miss Simmons.

'Yes please,' Dawn and I said in chorus, and the old lady left the room.

'Poor soul,' said Dawn. 'I think it's very sad.'

I nodded agreement. I did as it happened. It's shit to have someone you love snatched away by untimely death. Both of us knew that.

Dawn and I sat in the silence of the flat, silence broken only by the tinkle of metal on china from the kitchen.

It took Miss Simmons only a few minutes to make the tea, and she came back into the room carrying a huge silver tray covered in crockery.

'Here, let me,' I said, and took the tray from her and placed it on the table next to where I'd been sitting.

'Thank you,' she said. 'You're very kind.'

She fiddled around pouring out three cups of tea and offered us some digestive biscuits, which Dawn refused and I accepted, then sat down in the armchair opposite the one in which Dawn was sitting.

'This is lovely,' she said. 'I get so few visitors these days, and now here you are, a pair of real live detectives. So how can I help you? Why are you interested after all this time?'

I thought that honesty would be the best policy. She seemed like a nice old party, and frankly there was no reason to lie.

'Some evidence has turned up that he might not be dead at all,' I explained. 'And we've been hired to look into the matter.'

I clocked Dawn's stare at the 'we've'.

'Fancy,' said Miss Simmons. 'What sort of evidence?'

'A letter.'

'How exciting. I hope I can help.'

'So do I,' I said. But I didn't give it much hope. 'You say you moved in here straight after Kim Major left,' I said. 'How long after Jay Harrison died was that?'

'About three months, I think. I'm sorry I don't really follow popular music. The last record I can remember was by Al Bowlly, before he died in the Blitz. I didn't even know who the boy was who died, but there was a lot of gossip from the neighbours at the time. I'm sorry,' she said again. 'I'm not being much help, am I?'

I smiled reassuringly. 'That's all right, Miss Simmons,' I said. 'We're lucky to find anyone who remembers anything after all this time. What sort of gossip?'

'The usual. Parties. Noise 'til all hours. You know.'

I did.

'How come you got the place?' I asked. 'Didn't you mind that someone had died here?'

'I got the place because I was on the waiting list. And no I didn't mind that someone had died here. After what I saw during the war,

I know that the dead can't hurt you. Only the living. The place isn't haunted, if that's what you mean.'

She might have been old and stooped, but Miss Simmons definitely retained all her marbles.

'Has it changed much?' I asked, looking round. It definitely didn't look like a pop star's gaff. But then, like I said, twenty years is a long time.

'No. I'm afraid I'm a bit of a fly in the ointment for the owners. Since I moved in, this block has been sold about fifteen times. Property developers, you know. They've improved most of the flats and sold a lot of them, and I'm on a very long lease, with a fixed rent. A very low fixed rent. They've tried to buy me out dozens of times. But I'm used to living here, and where would I go? So they think that if they don't do anything for me, I'll just disappear... They're wrong,' she added.

'Good for you,' said Dawn.

'In fact it hasn't changed much. These are all the same decorations as when I moved in. And they were here when they moved in too, from what I can remember from talking to the girl at the time. I don't think they had much money when they came over here. I can remember she was forced to leave. She couldn't afford the rent, low as it was. She told me that she was penniless after he died.'

'You actually knew her?' I said.

'Yes. We met twice. Once the day I took over the place, and once later. But I never knew what happened to her. She never came back for the last of her stuff.'

'What stuff?' I asked.

'The stuff she left here.'

'Kim Major left stuff here?'

'Yes. When I moved in there was a lot. A whole room full. She came over one night and picked most of it up. But there wasn't room for everything in the taxi, so she asked me if I'd mind looking after it for her. Of course I agreed. She was in a terrible state. I made her tea, and we chatted for ages. I liked her. But I never saw her again. Do you know where she is?'

Dawn looked at me. 'I'm afraid she's dead too, Miss Simmons,' she said.

'*Dead?* But she was so young. And pretty.'

'It was drugs,' said Dawn. 'The same as killed Jay Harrison.'

'So sad,' said Miss Simmons.

'What did she leave?' I asked.

'A mattress, some pots and pans, a chair, some clothes and a suitcase.'

'And it's all still here?'

She seemed almost offended at my question. 'Of course. She asked me to keep it for her, and I did.'

'And no one's ever asked for it?'

Miss Simmons shook her head. 'The people who came here, the fans, and sometimes newspaper writers, were only interested in him. Not her. And besides I didn't want to tell them about it. It was none of their business.'

'But you've told us,' said Dawn.

Miss Simmons's eyes twinkled again. 'You're different,' she said. 'I can tell. The others who came didn't care about the girl. I could see it in their eyes. But you two did, and you're in love. I can tell that in your eyes too. And that makes me trust you.'

I swear I blushed, and I know Dawn did.

'I'm sorry,' said Miss Simmons. 'I didn't mean to embarrass you. Forgive an old woman.'

I mumbled something, but Dawn laughed out loud. 'Of course we do. I'm very flattered, and glad that you could see. We just got married recently.'

'I thought so,' replied Miss Simmons. 'And I hope you have a lot of years together. Not like me and my young man. Or that girl and her friend.'

'Thank you,' said Dawn. 'I hope so too.'

'Did she have anyone?' asked Miss Simmons. 'The girl. A family or anything?'

'Not here,' I said. 'In America.'

'Would you be able to trace them?'

'Yes. The people I'm working for are American. They'd know,' I said.

'Would you see that they get what she left?'

'I could try. Can I see it?'

'Of course. The furniture and clothes are still in the box room. But I put the case up in the loft with the water tank. You'll have to get it down. I haven't been able to get up there for years.'

She got up and I followed. Dawn stayed where she was. Miss Simmons took me further back into the flat, and opened the door to a tiny room full of junk. At the back was a single mattress leaning against the wall, a big, heavy wooden chair with dusty arms, piled high with hippie-looking dresses, and a stack of saucepans standing next to it. It wasn't a very interesting find. I glanced at the stuff, then Miss Simmons pointed up at the ceiling to a recessed trapdoor with a handle attached. 'Pull it down,' she said.

I had to stand on the chair to reach, the ceiling was so high. But I managed, and caught the handle, and with a squeak the door opened, and the end of a folding ladder appeared. I tugged it down, got off the chair and climbed up the ladder. I stuck my head into the dark space inside the door and saw the end of a leather suitcase in front of me. I reached in and pulled it to the edge of the opening, then slid it, and what must have been twenty years of muck, down to the ground. The case was heavy and awkward, and I got a faceful of dust. I coughed and rubbed my eyes, and Miss Simmons took a duster from the pocket of her dress and wiped the top of the case. It was worn and scratched, about two and half feet long, by two wide, by nine inches deep. There were a bunch of worn-out airline stickers on the top next to the inscription 'Dog Soldier', stencilled on in white paint that had faded to grey. I tried to open it, but it was locked.

I pushed the ladder back up, got on the chair again, and slammed the trapdoor shut. 'I'll take this now, if I may,' I said, picking up the case. 'I'll let you know about the rest of the stuff. I don't know if anyone will be interested. But I'm sure they'll be grateful that you kept it.'

'It was the least I could do,' said Miss Simmons. 'For that poor, sad girl.'

I took the case back into the living room and placed it on the floor next to my seat. Miss Simmons offered us more tea, but both Dawn and I refused. When we'd finished what we had, we both rose to leave.

'Just one other thing,' I said. 'And there's no reason why you should. But I don't suppose you know the name of the firm who buried Jay Harrison. Or the names of local undertakers who were in business at the time.'

Miss Simmons clapped her hands with glee. 'But I do,' she

said. 'Of course I do. It was Cousins and Co.'

'How can you be so sure?' I asked.

'Two reasons. I used to live just around the corner before I moved here, and Jasper Cousins did nearly all the funerals in the area. And then when I did move in here, they sent a letter to this address. Major, of course. I remember now. Miss K. Major. That was the name on the envelope. It must have been the bill. I can see it as plain as if it were yesterday. You couldn't miss old Jasper's bills. Big white envelopes they came in, with Cousins and Co...' she shook her hands about, lost for words, 'you know. Punched into the paper, so that it stood out.'

'Embossed,' I said.

'That's the word. Embossed. They had their name and address embossed on the top left-hand corner.'

'What did you do with the letter?' I asked.

'I sent it back of course. Wrote "MOVED AWAY" in big black letters across the back.'

'Whereabouts are Cousins and Co?' I asked.

'Oh, they've gone now. Jasper retired, oh, ten years or more ago. More like fifteen. Time flies. I heard he moved to Stamford Hill. Somewhere like that. He'd be eighty now if he's a day. He left the business to his son, who used to work for him, but it was never the same after Jasper left. I heard that the son got an offer for the premises that he couldn't refuse, and he sold out. They pulled the old shop down and built a supermarket.'

'Do you remember the son's name?' I asked.

Miss Simmons looked into the distance for a moment, then shook her head. 'Do you know, I can't,' she said. 'I'm sorry. It's my memory again. I didn't really know the son at all, you see. Not that I knew Jasper. But he was such a local character, that I felt that I did.'

Another dead end, I thought. But maybe old Jasper was still alive and kicking. Fighting the day when he'd be in need of a wooden overcoat himself, instead of screwing other people into them.

'Miss Simmons,' I said. 'You've been marvellous. A great help. Thanks.'

'It was a pleasure.'

Dawn took her hand and thanked her too.

'There is one thing,' the old lady said.

'What?' asked Dawn.

'Will you let me know what happens?' asked Miss Simmons, as she saw us out of the flat. 'As I said, life is rather dull these days. I'd be intrigued to know what you find out.'

'I will,' said Dawn. 'Perhaps I could call round for tea again some time.'

'Any time at all,' said Miss Simmons. 'I usually pop out every other morning to the shops. But apart from that I'm always here. I'm not on the phone, I'm afraid. And the buzzer to the front door is broken, and the landlords won't fix it. But just tell him on the desk that I said you're welcome any time. And don't take any nonsense from him.'

'I won't,' said Dawn. 'And as soon as we find out anything, I promise that I'll come round and tell you all about it.' And I knew that she would, and I loved her all the more for saying it.

10

When we got down to the foyer, the concierge was back on duty. He ignored us as we left the lift, but Dawn marched up to him and said, 'The door buzzer to flat twenty-two is broken, isn't it?'

The concierge was a big bloke with a lot of five o'clock shadow and an ill-fitting braided green suit and matching cap.

He shrugged at Dawn's question. 'Is it?' he asked.

Not the correct answer.

'Yes, it is,' said Dawn. 'And you should be ashamed of yourself. Miss Simmons hasn't got a telephone, and she's all alone up there. I know what your boss's game is. Now I want that buzzer fixed. And quickly. Do I make myself clear?'

'Who are you then?' he asked, and looked at me. But I stayed quiet. I put down the suitcase I was carrying and lit a cigarette. This could be a long conversation.

'What does that matter? Are you going to get it fixed or not?' said Dawn.

The concierge shrugged again.

Dawn took out her purse, and took a twenty-pound note from it. 'What's your name?' she asked.

He looked at the note and licked his lips. 'What do you want to know that for?'

'Because if I give you this to get the buzzer fixed, and it's not when I come back next week, I want to be able to find you.'

'I'm always here,' he said. 'My name's Bruno.' And he reached out for the note.

'You're *not* always here,' Dawn contradicted him. 'You weren't here earlier when we arrived.'

He mumbled something about a call of nature.

'Well, Bruno,' said Dawn, 'against all my better instincts, I'm going to trust you. But I promise, when I do come back, and it'll be soon, that if the buzzer isn't fixed, I'll find some way to make your life even more miserable than it is now. Understand?'

Bruno nodded, and Dawn put the twenty down, and it vanished inside his uniform.

'Just remember what I said,' she warned, and came over to me and took my arm.

'She means it,' I said over my shoulder as we left the building. 'I should know. I'm married to her.'

I could almost see pity in Bruno's dull eyes before I turned away.

When we got outside, I said, 'd'you think he'll do it?'

'He'd better,' Dawn replied. 'Or I'll have his legs.'

'You're amazing, babe,' I said. 'I don't think I'd've got through her door.'

'I told you I'd make a good partner.'

'And you do.'

'And I will go back and see her. And make sure that her buzzer's fixed.'

'I know,' I said again.

Dawn looked at the case I was holding. 'So what's in there?' she asked.

'Dunno. It's locked. Let's get it home. Have something to eat and a drink, and I'll open it. Of course it may be nothing. Just a bunch of rubbish. She did leave it behind, after all.'

'Will you send what's inside back to Kim's family?'

'Course I will, if it's anything decent. But I want a squint first. Who knows what's in here.'

'Used works probably. Knowing them. Or dirty knickers.'

'Maybe. But it might not.'

We got back into the car and I drove home. When we got in, Dawn made us each a drink, found the makings of a Spanish omelette in the fridge, and got busy at the stove while I tried a couple of old keys in the lock of the suitcase. I didn't want to bust it open if I didn't have to. I was lucky. The third key I tried slipped the lock, and I opened the lid of the suitcase.

On top was a tapestry shawl or tablecloth, fringed at the edges. I opened it out. Its colours were still bright after all the years it had been locked away, and I laid it over the sofa where I was sitting. It took me back to being a teenager, and seeing the hippy revolution break out all over London. Underneath the shawl was a pile of record albums. A complete set of Dog Soldier releases up until Harrison had died. I looked at the laminated sleeves, and that took me back too. I'd had most of them myself, then lost or sold them as I got older.

I put the records on the floor, and went back to the case. All that was left were three books and a large brown envelope. The books were *The Tibetan Book of the Dead, On the Road* by Jack Kerouac and *John Lennon in His Own Write*. Pretty much par for the course for anyone into the alternative society at that time, I guessed. I put the books next to the records and opened the envelope. It bulged with eight-by-ten photographs. They were all of Harrison. Harrison and Kim together, or the pair of them with other people. Mostly at receptions or functions at clubs or restaurants. The group photos had been taken in London from what I could see. Posters and price lists in the background told me that. And in one photo, taken outside a restaurant, the back of a black cab. Everyone in the pictures looked like they were drunk or stoned, or both. The pair of them might not have had much money when they came over to England, but from the state of them in the photos, life looked like it had been one long party.

I looked closely at the groups. I didn't recognize anyone straight off. Why should I? I certainly hadn't been part of the swinging set as the sixties turned to the seventies. I was too busy taking my A levels.

Dawn started to serve up the food. 'Anything interesting?' she asked.

'A complete set of Dog Soldier LPs. A little light reading. A new tablecloth, and a bunch of pictures of our happy couple with a load of people I've never seen before, which look like they were taken when Harrison and Kim were living over here.'

'Let me look,' she said, and I took the pictures over to the table and gave them to her, before I sat down in front of my omelette.

She leafed through the photographs. 'What are you going to do with these?' she asked.

'I'm going to find someone who knows who all those people are,' I replied. 'There must be some old hippies still around with enough brain cells to remember. And I'm going to find one.'

'The best of luck,' said Dawn.

Next morning I took my problem to Chris Kennedy-Sloane. He was the only person I could think of who might know the kind of people I wanted. I called him early and told him about the photos that I'd found.

'Old hippies,' he said. 'I hope you don't mean me.'

'No,' I said. 'Anyone who was around at the time. This mob looks like the Chelsea set, circa nineteen seventy. They were all hippies then, weren't they? Flower power and all that shit. LSD. Joints. Smack. All of them look like they were half dead when the pictures were taken. Most of them probably are by now. But the ones that aren't are the types that you have as clients. Old money. Eton, Oxford, then straight down to Notting Hill Gate to get high. Rich fucking kids who've come into the family fortune since. Come on, Chris, you must know someone who could help me.'

'Let me think about it. I haven't had my coffee yet.'

As a matter of fact, neither had I. 'Call me back,' I said.

'What now?' said Dawn, who was lying next to me in bed looking superb in a black lace nightie that had slipped down to expose one round, white breast with its dark red nipple enlarged in the air. She saw me looking and smiled, and I felt her hand brush my thigh.

'Not what you think,' I said. 'Up and at 'em.'

'No nookie?'

'Not this morning, honey. We've got to earn our bread and butter.'

'Honey and butter. Sounds good. As a matter of fact, I'm feeling pretty greasy myself. You know, slippery and wet.'

'Dry yourself on the sheet, sweetheart,' I said. 'We haven't got time.' And I kissed her, and the kiss might have turned into something more interesting if I hadn't reluctantly dragged myself out of bed and into the kitchen to put on the kettle.

'Spoilsport,' she said, and pulled a face at me as I went. I pulled one back, and went into the bathroom and by the time I was finished she was up and making coffee. 'What do you want to eat?' I asked.

'A bacon sandwich,' she replied. So I got a fresh packet out of the fridge and put eight slices under the grill while she buttered some bread.

'Come on then,' she said as the bacon sizzled, 'if we're not going to have a fuck, what are we going to do this morning?'

'Me,' I replied. 'I'm going to phone Chas at the paper and see if I can go in and look through the cuttings on Jay Harrison. There must be loads. I'll try to come up with some names. Any names from the time he was living over here.'

'And me?' asked Dawn.

'Jasper Cousins from Cousins and Co., the undertakers. I want you to go through the phone book. Start with the Js Miss Simmons said he'd moved to Stamford Hill or somewhere like that. Try to locate him. See if the old boy's still alive. And if you have no luck, keep trying. There was the son who worked with him. The one who sold the business. He might have been around at the time. Maybe he knows something about Harrison's funeral. Perhaps he saw the body, and can tell us for sure who it was that they buried. If you have no luck with the Js, go back to the As and keep trying.'

'Yes, Boss.'

'That's what I like,' I said, as I scooped the bacon onto the bread. 'A staff who know their place.'

As soon as we'd eaten and I was dressed, I called Chas at his office in Wapping. He was at his desk.

'Morning,' I said when he answered. 'What's cooking?'

'I hate it when you ask that,' Chas replied. 'It usually means you want something. And every time you do, someone ends up in hospital.'

'Well, I do, as a matter of fact,' I said. 'I want to go through your morgue, look up some old stories.'

'I wish you wouldn't use that word,' he said. 'It makes me go cold.'

'That's what you hard-bitten hacks call it, isn't it?' I asked.

'Yeah. But when you say it it has connotations. Bad connotations. I take it you're on a new case.'

'Correct.'

'I thought as much,' he said mournfully.

'Relax, Chas,' I said. 'This one's harmless.'

'That's what you always say.'

'This time it's true.'

He was silent for a second. 'OK,' he said eventually. 'But I want to know what's going on.'

'That's the trouble with you, son,' I said. 'You're too nosey. *That's* what gets you into trouble. Not me. But if you insist, I'll tell you. Can I buy you lunch?'

'OK. Be here at twelve-thirty. It's a quiet day today. We'll have a bite, you can tell me all, then I'll introduce you to Amy, the keeper of the microfilm.'

'Sounds good to me,' I said.

'Right, I'll see you then. How's Dawn by the way?'

'Fine.'

'And married life?'

'It's only been a few days.'

'And they said it would never last. Give her my best, and I'll see you at half twelve.'

'Half twelve it is,' I said, and hung up.

I passed on Chas's best wishes and checked the time. It was just after ten.

I got hold of the A to K telephone book. 'Cousins' filled just over a column, maybe a hundred and fifty entries. Maybe slightly less. But there were only about twenty with the initial J. Plenty to keep Dawn busy and our phone bill well up.

'I'll leave you to it,' I said. 'I'll take the Chevy. I'll see you later.'

'I didn't think you were seeing Chas until twelve-thirty,' she said. She doesn't miss much, does my wife.

'I'm not. But I've got a couple of things to do first.'

She didn't ask what. Just nodded and said, 'Enjoy your lunch.'

I kissed her on the cheek, took the car keys and left. I drove up to the river and sat outside a bar I know on one of the wharves until it opened and I could get a beer. The truth was I needed some time on my own to think about the case. Or maybe some time on my own, period. I wasn't used to being with someone all the time, living and working together, and I needed a little space. I felt a twinge of guilt, as if I was being disloyal to Dawn, but it couldn't be helped. Some habits are hard to change, and the one of solitude is possibly the hardest.

Fortress Wapping was just as I remembered it from my only previous visit. High, barbed-wire-covered fences with metal gates manned by heavy-looking security guards surrounded the grim-looking office buildings. It was like a scene from one of those American prison movies from the thirties.

Chas had left my name at the main entrance and I parked the

Chevy and went to find him. He was sitting at his work station, hunched over his PC, when I arrived. He punched in a number, closed down the screen and gave me a grin when he saw me.

'Hello, Nick,' he said. 'How you doing?'

'Can't complain,' I replied. 'I see that this place is as cheerful as ever.'

'The boss man's paranoid,' he said. 'But it's a living. Where are you taking me for lunch?'

'It's your manor, pal,' I replied. 'You tell me.'

'Are you holding?'

'As much as we need.'

'Luigi's then. Just down the street. Best food in the area. And the best prices. I can only afford to go there on someone else's tab.'

'Lead me to it,' I said.

So he did.

When we were the right side of a couple of martini cocktails, Chas asked me what was happening, and I told him the whole story. There was no point in being coy.

'This is all off the record right now,' I said later, after we'd eaten, 'but if anything occurs you get the green light first on it.'

'It's a great story,' he said. 'But I've heard it all before. You'd be amazed how many times people see Elvis these days. Even round here.'

I shrugged. 'It's the story I've been hired to investigate. That's why I want to go through the cuttings here. I want to try to dig out some names. Someone who can confirm or deny that Harrison is dead.'

'Don't you think someone would have done it by now?' Chas asked. 'If he is alive there's a few bob to be made out of it.'

'God knows. I'm clutching at straws, Chas. But I'm being well paid for the gig, and I intend to go down every alley I can find. Whether they're blind ones or not.'

'Well, let's have some coffee and a brandy each,' he said, 'and I'll take you to the morgue.' He grimaced as he said the word.

'Don't worry, Chas,' I said. 'You're probably right. It's just some lunatic with a bee in his bonnet. A wind-up. A hoax. Nothing's going to happen.'

'I remember the last time I got involved in one of your cases,' he said. 'Something certainly happened then.'

'That was different. Anyway you're not getting involved. Just doing an old friend a favour.'

'You've convinced me,' he said, as I signed the credit-card slip for our meal. 'Come on back to the factory and I'll introduce you to Amy.'

Amy was Amy Brough, a chubby brunette of about thirty, with bitten-down fingernails, who looked like she'd kill for a cigarette. She was the dayshift on the microfilm files at Wapping. Queen of all she surveyed from nine to five.

Chas introduced us and I shook her podgy little warm hand.

'Nick's a freelance doing research on an article about Jay Harrison for the Sunday mag,' he lied.

'Jay Harrison from Dog Soldier?' she asked.

I nodded. Surprised that she knew. But then, why shouldn't she?

'I've got a CD of theirs at home,' she volunteered. 'They're great.'

She went over to the computer that sat on top of her desk and punched 'Harrison, Jay' into the keyboard. The screen burst into life in a snowstorm of white letters and numbers on a black background. I looked over her shoulder as it scrolled off the entries for him. There were literally hundreds, starting in 1967 and going right up to the present day.

'Christ,' I said.

Amy said, 'Popular bloke. Do you want to see the entries for the band too?'

'Not now,' I replied. 'Just him.'

She scrolled back to the first entry. It was dated 20 February 1967. 'That must have been when his band got started,' she said. 'I was four.' She let the screen roll. The entries increased year by year until 1972, when there was a blizzard of them around April time. 'And that was when he died,' she said. She knew her stuff, did our Amy. I bet she owned a copy of *Simon and Garfunkel's Greatest Hits* too. 'But of course you'd know that, writing about him,' she said, turning round and looking up at me.

I nodded, and she turned back and let the scroll continue.

As the seventies went up the entries got fewer, then increased around the mid-eighties until eighteen months or so ago when there were entries for almost every day. 'That was when the film came out,' she explained. '*Dog Soldier*. I saw it. Did you?'

I nodded.

'Like it?'

I shook my head. 'Not particularly,' I said.

'I did. I got it out on video. I thought the actor who played Jay Harrison was dishy.'

I smiled at her, and she blushed slightly. 'So what period are you particularly interested in? For the article?' she asked.

'The early years,' I said. 'Up until his death.'

'I think I'll leave you two to it,' Chas interrupted. 'Come and see me before you go, Nick.'

I nodded and said, 'I will. Thanks for your help.' And he left the room.

'Right,' said Amy. 'There's a machine over there. Pick any one,' and she pointed to the bank of green-screened boxes lined up on a table by the wall. 'I'll sort out the films for you.'

It took me hours to go through the entries I wanted. The first was a small item about a new rock band from Los Angeles who were getting a lot of interest from the psychedelic community there. The lead singer being a beautiful, charismatic, young, ex-film student called Jay Harrison. Then Dog Soldier signed to Lifetime Records that summer after a bidding battle between them, Elektra and Warner Brothers. Their first single was rush released within a few weeks of the signing, and the band went into the studio to record their debut album, to be simply called *Dog Soldier*. The first single dented the US top forty, and was immediately followed by their first big hit, 'Just Do It', which broke into the top three in the autumn of that year. The album came out in November, and was number one by Christmas. Meanwhile 'Just Do It' was a worldwide success, and in November reached the top spot in Britain, where the album was also a massive hit.

The band toured Europe, stopping off in England to play the Roundhouse in Chalk Farm. I remembered the night well. I'd wanted to go, but my old man had put the block on it. Dog Soldier made a rockumentary for Granada TV, played a free concert in Glasgow, then split the country leaving a welter of unpaid hotel bills and assault and battery charges. No wonder I'd liked them so much at the time.

Then the cuttings got more interesting. Harrison wandering the streets of Los Angeles late at night stark naked. A rumour about Harrison marrying a white witch in Las Vegas, and consummating the union in the open air at the Joshua Tree, which was later proved false. Harrison almost crashing the band's private jet after insisting that he could fly after taking a massive dose of acid. Tales of drunkenness, cruelty and drug excess on tours of America. And as the success of the band grew, the stories of Harrison's overindulgences got worse. He was arrested for violence against women, for drunk driving, for assaulting the police, for possession of drugs, and finally the famous arrest on stage in Houston in 1971 for using profanity in public and for indecent exposure.

It was a great story. Harrison had got drunk and stoned prior to the gig, copped hold of a young girl backstage, got hassled by a policeman who was picking up some extra cash moonlighting as security for the promoter, had a fight with the guy, who'd then gone off to get a load of his pals to wait at the front and side of the stage and give Harrison a smack when he came off after the set. Harrison had sussed out what was going on and enlisted the aid of the thirty-thousand-strong crowd of stoned hippies by cursing the pigs over the PA, whipping out his wedding tackle and pissing all over the cops out front, and screaming that he'd been beaten by the local law prior to the concert. The crowd had promptly trashed the place, doing half a million dollars' worth of damage in the process, while Harrison and the young girl got away in the excitement to a local motel where they'd been arrested later that night for trying to burn the place down. Rock and roll, or what? Maybe I'd missed my vocation.

But looking at the photos that accompanied the stories, I wasn't so sure. During the five-year period, sixty-seven to seventy-two, Harrison aged twenty years. His once-beautiful face bloated out, and he grew a full beard to hide it. And his skinny body grew fat and unhealthy. The newspaper stories told of vast ingestions of booze and soft drugs, and hinted at worse. Coke and smack seemed to be the favourites, and from the pictorial evidence, I believed them.

After the arrest in Houston, things seemed to quieten down for a while, and there were several short reports that he was living in London with his latest girlfriend, preparing material for the new Dog Soldier album. Then a load of rumours about the band splitting as Harrison made no effort to return to America. And finally, in 1972, he died. And that was where I came in, as we used to say.

Not that all this information was set out as neatly and chronologically as that. I had to scrounge a pad off Amy and she lent me the pencil that poked out of the bouffant hairstyle that seemed in danger of slipping off one side of her head. I think she thought it was weird that the journalist I was supposed to be had no paper or pen with him, but she didn't mention it.

By the time I'd finished it was past five, my eyes were sore and I had a sharp pain in my right temple.

What I didn't have were any names from the period Harrison had spent in London.

I tore out the pages I'd written on in the notebook, gave Amy back her pencil, closed down the microfilm machine and thanked her for her assistance. Then I went off and found Chas.

'Any luck?' he asked.

I shook my aching head. 'Not really. I've filled in a lot of background, but nothing specific about the time he spent here.'

'Sorry.'

'Not your fault. And without your help I would have wasted days, instead of a couple of hours.'

'Fancy a quick one?' he asked.

'No thanks,' I replied. 'I'm knackered, mate. I'm going to head off home. We'll make it another time, yeah?'

'What married life will do to a man,' he said teasingly. 'But then I don't blame you. If I had someone like Dawn waiting, I'd be straight home after work myself.'

'I'll catch you later, Chas,' I said. 'Give us a call and come over one night.'

'Will do.'

And we made our farewells and I left.

Of course I got caught up in the rush hour, and it took me more than an hour to crawl back to Tulse Hill. When I went into the flat, Dawn was sitting with a drink in her hand watching the news on TV, and I could smell something good in the oven.

'Hiya, babe,' I said as I collapsed on to the sofa beside her. 'I missed you.'

'Had a nice day at the office, dear?' she asked, ignoring my comment. Dawn never forgets.

'Funny,' I said. 'Very funny. And in a word, no. A waste of time. What are you drinking?'

'G and T. Want one?'

'Not many. Make it a large one.'

She got up and went into the kitchen where I heard the rattle of ice cubes followed by the clink of a bottle on a glass, and she came back carrying a cool-looking glass of clear liquid with a slice of lemon nestling next to the ice. I took the glass from her gratefully and sunk half its contents in one.

'So how was *your* day?' I said.

She grinned. 'I thought you'd never ask,' she said. 'I found him.'

I looked at her in amazement. 'Who, Jasper?' I said.

'No.'

'His son?'

'No.'

'Who then?'

'His grandson. Jasper died a few years back, and his son, Jake, a year later. But after about thirty calls I turned up Clive Cousins.'

'Did he work for the firm?'

She nodded. 'When he was at school he worked for them on Saturdays and in the holidays.'

'Was he there in seventy-two?'

She nodded again.

'Did he see the body?'

This time she shook her head. 'No. He wasn't allowed to. He wanted to see the dead pop star, but the casket was brought in sealed. Jasper and Jake did the business at the flat.'

'Shit. And they're both dead. I don't believe this. Everybody involved in Harrison's death is brown bread. What else did… what was his name? Clive?' – she nodded – 'say?'

'He said he'd see us tomorrow at his house. He's intrigued by the whole thing. He was a fan of the band at the time, and he badgered his father and grandfather to let him see the body, but they wouldn't.'

'He sounds like a right morbid sod.'

She shrugged. 'Who knows? I've made an appointment to see him tomorrow at ten.'

'Where?'

'Highgate.'

'He lives there?'

She nodded for a fourth time.

'Coincidence,' I said. 'Harrison is buried at Highgate cemetery. After we've seen Clive I think we'll take a look at the grave. From what I can gather it's become quite a shrine. Maybe we'll learn something there.'

'Like what?'

'God knows. Maybe he was beamed up by aliens to a starship. Maybe they're still around.'

'Maybe they are.'

'Whatever,' I said. 'There's nothing more we can do tonight. What are you cooking? I'm starving.'

'Chicken casserole.'

'Sounds good to me.'

'I'd better take a look at it.' She got up and went into the kitchen and I watched her hips roll as she walked. I got up and joined her to get a refill of my glass. We stood close together and I could smell her perfume. She was wearing a black dress that stretched tightly across her bottom as she bent down to open the oven. 'Dinner will be in half an hour,' she said as she closed the oven door and straightened up.

I moved closer to her and put my hands on her waist.

'Did you really miss me today?' she asked.

'Yes.'

'Why?'

I shrugged. 'I'm getting used to having you around, I suppose.'

'Like the furniture?'

'No.'

She smiled.

'I'm sorry about this morning,' I said.

'What about it?'

'Having to get up early.'

'So you're sorry *now*, are you?'

'That's right. I don't suppose you're still feeling greasy, are you?'

'Could be. There's only one way to find out.'

I slid my hand down and tugged at her skirt until it rode up her thighs, and I pulled it up higher until it slid over her hips. She wasn't wearing anything underneath.

'Well?' she said breathlessly as I gently explored between her legs.

'I'd say yes,' I said.

'And I'd say you were right.'

And she put out her hand and turned the oven down to its lowest setting.

11

Clive Cousins's house was about halfway up Highgate Hill not far from the famous suicide bridge at the Archway. It was big and old and set well back from the road in overgrown grounds. The pointing was in need of renewing and the slate roof was sway-backed and delicate-looking. I parked the Chevy on the empty drive in front of the closed doors of the double garage, and Dawn and I got out of the car and walked up to the front porch.

It was one of those funny old days you get in London from time to time. Well warm and muggy, as if a thunderstorm was hiding somewhere, just waiting to pop up and drench all the unsuspecting souls who'd gone out into the morning heat without a coat.

I rang the bell beside the front door at exactly ten o'clock. It was very quiet where we stood. The trees in the front garden soaked up the traffic noise, and left us in a well of silence that could have been a hundred miles away from civilization.

'House of Usher,' I said, and I saw Dawn shiver and I pulled her close. She looked up at me and smiled, and I smiled back.

I saw a shape behind the cloudy glass panels of the door and with a jerk it opened to reveal a tall, youngish geezer with a shock of long, dark hair, dressed in a T-shirt and old jeans.

'Clive Cousins?' I said.

'That's me,' he replied. 'You must be the detectives.'

'That's us,' I said. 'Thanks for seeing us.'

'It's a real pleasure, believe me. I've never met any private detectives before. Come on in.'

He stood back, and we went inside the hall, which was dark and dusty, and he led us through to the back of the house, and into a comfortable-looking room with French windows opening on to a garden that stretched away to a line of tall trees.

'Sit down,' he said. 'Excuse the mess. I don't get many visitors these days. Coffee? Tea?'

'Coffee,' said Dawn, and I nodded assent. He went out of the room and we heard his footsteps recede down the uncarpeted hall.

'Some place,' said Dawn.

I agreed with her, and as she sat on the sofa in front of the dead fireplace I took a wander round. There was a big table next to the windows which held a state-of-the-art word processor and printer, a load of pens and notebooks, and a brimming ashtray. One wall was taken up with bookcases that held a thousand or more luridly covered paperback crime novels. I took out one. It was called *The Turnaround*. I'd never heard of the author.

As I replaced the book, Clive Cousins came back into the room carrying a large wooden tray with a coffee pot, cups, saucers, milk, sugar and a plate of assorted biscuits on it.

He put it on the table, asked our preferences, and poured out the drinks.

When we were all sitting down, he said, 'So what's all this about Jay Harrison?'

I told him some of the story. Not all of it. I put it to him that someone was trying a con on Lifetime Records.

'Really,' he said. 'That's amazing. It would make a great plot.'

I looked at him quizzically.

'That's what I do,' he explained. 'Write detective novels. Hence all those,' and he waved at the shelves full of books.

'Sometimes I need a plot and I rip one off from some old potboiler from the fifties, dress it up, and Bob's your uncle. Petty larceny. But I'm sure the people who wrote those wouldn't object. Most of them weren't past a bit of petty larceny themselves.' And he smiled to himself at the thought. 'Hence the fact that I was intrigued to meet you two. I use private eyes a lot in my books, and, like I said, I've never met one in real life. I'm afraid research isn't my strong suit.'

'Are you published?' I asked.

'Under various names. Paperback originals. You know. I don't make much money at it, but since Dad died and left me a few bob and this place, I don't need to. Anything so I don't have to get a steady job.'

I knew the feeling and warmed to the guy immediately.

'You live here alone?' I asked.

'Yes. Criminal, isn't it? All this space. I was one of the lucky few who did well out of the poll tax. The rates on this property were crippling.'

'You're not married?' asked Dawn.

He shook his head. 'Used to be. She left because I wasn't making anything of myself. I used to drive a laundry van. But when the old man kicked off, I could do what I wanted. And what I wanted to do was write.'

He saw the look on our faces.

'No. We never got on, my father and I. He was another who thought I wasn't making enough of myself. But he had nobody else to leave the place to. The funny thing is, he'd've been proud to have a published writer as a son, but he never saw it.' Clive Cousins looked towards the ceiling. 'But maybe he's up there somewhere looking down. A big believer in the afterlife was my old man... And talking of that, let me tell you what I know about Jay Harrison's brief afterlife at Grandfather's place.'

'Go ahead,' I said.

'Thinking back, which I did last night, after your call, it was weird, you know. I was still at school. About fourteen when it happened. I'd been a big Dog Soldier fan. They had that gothic thing about them. Death and destruction. I was well into that in those days, what with working with dead bodies and all. Still am, I suppose, considering what I write about. Grandad wanted me to come into the firm, but it was all the other things about the job I couldn't stand. Dressing in black, pretending to be sorry. Walking around with a long face all the time. That wasn't for me. But anyway. I can remember hearing Dad say that they were preparing this rock star to be buried, and when he told me who it was I couldn't wait to get round to Grandad's to take a look. The funeral was all done in a rush. I remember that. His girlfriend handled it. Harrison's that is. No one much went. He was well past his prime by then. But I sneaked in on the evening before the funeral to see him...' He paused.

'And?' I said.

'And the coffin lid was bolted down tight. They used Allen screws. You need a special tool to open them. Normally, even on a closed-casket ceremony, the coffin's only secured by finger-tight nuts. I mean, who would want to peep...'

'A curious fourteen-year-old boy,' interrupted Dawn, and Cousins gave her a big smile.

'Touché,' he said.

'Maybe they were worried that fans might get in, or newspapermen,' she said.

'Maybe. But I don't think so. Like I said, Harrison was a forgotten man by then. His records weren't selling. I can remember it as clear as day. I'd moved on to The Mothers and Velvet Underground by then myself.'

I nodded in agreement. So had I.

'So why do you think the coffin was so tightly sealed?' I asked.

He shrugged. 'I honestly haven't got a clue. And with Dad and Grandad both gone, I doubt we'll ever know. Unless of course you can dig the body up.'

'There is that, of course,' I said.

'But if there was something odd, I wonder why he wasn't cremated,' said Cousins.

'That's been bothering me too,' I replied.

'Have you seen where he's buried?' he asked.

'Not yet,' I said. 'As a matter of fact, we're going to have a look now.'

'It's weird round there,' he said. 'Spooky.'

'You've been yourself?' I asked.

He nodded. 'Sure. Lots of times. I like to go out walking when I'm stuck on a story, or just bored with writing. And the cemetery is a peaceful place. Except where Harrison is buried. It gives me the creeps.'

I put down my cup and stood up. 'Thanks for talking to us, Mr Cousins,' I said. 'We'll be off now, we don't want to waste any more of your time.'

'Not at all,' he said. 'It's been a pleasure. I'm sorry I couldn't be of more help.'

'You have been, believe me,' I said, and Dawn stood up too, and he showed us out of the house.

'Nice car,' he said as we walked to the Caprice. 'A bit heavy on petrol, isn't it?'

'With a car like that, petrol is the least of your problems,' I said. 'If you worry about things like that you should buy a Mini-Metro.'

He smiled again. 'Well I hope you get to the bottom of all this,' he said, and Dawn and I got into the car, switched on the engine, put the column change into 'drive', and pulled out into the street in the direction of the cemetery.

'He was dishy,' said Dawn as we went.

'Down, girl,' I said.

'A man of independent means with a beautiful big house like that... A writer too. Intelligent. Witty. Unattached. And so obviously in need of a woman's touch around the place. It needed taking in hand. And so did he.'

'And I suppose you'd be just the woman to do the job. Are you trying to make me jealous?' I asked.

I saw her nod. 'Am I succeeding?'

'You would be if I didn't know how crazy you are about me.'

'Says who?'

'Says you last night on the kitchen floor with your dress up round your neck.'

At least she had the grace to blush.

'Well, apart from meeting the handsome, witty, intelligent and unattached Clive, what did you think?' I asked.

'Apart from all that, I think it was a waste of time,' she said back.

'Not at all,' I said.

'Why?'

'Because for the first time we've got a handle that there *was* something strange about Harrison's death. All that locking the coffin top down. This is the first definite evidence that there was something going on that shouldn't have been.'

'It's not much help though,' she said. 'Not after all this time. And if there was, why didn't they cremate the body like Clive said, and not leave the evidence buried for all these years?'

'I don't know,' I said, and glanced over at her. 'But it does beg one question.'

'What's that?'

'If it wasn't his body in the casket, what did Jasper and Jake bury all those years ago?... Or who?' I added.

12

An attendant was on duty at the front gates of the cemetery as we drove up, and I asked him for directions to Jay Harrison's tomb. He looked up at me from under the brim of his dark blue cap, and his eyes registered nothing as he pointed me down one of the narrow tracks that ran between the gravestones.

The mausoleum was in one corner of the graveyard, behind an old brick building that could have been a crematorium, a stable, or a storehouse for Christ knows what in the old days. But now it was half derelict, with ivy clinging to the weathered brick, and a lot of slates missing from the roof, exposing the rotten timbers to the weather.

The storm I'd predicted seemed to loom even closer as the Caprice bounced over the rutted road towards Jay Harrison's last resting place. The sky was an uncomfortable shade of yellow that reminded me of stale piss, and somewhere over the other side of London heat lightning flared, and I heard a dull rumble of thunder drifting over the still, heavy air as Dawn and I left the car.

'I see what Clive Cousins meant about creepy,' said Dawn. 'I don't think I like this place much.'

'Me neither,' I replied. 'We won't stay long. Just take a shufti, then leave. It's going to rain soon. Looks like a bad storm coming.'

Dawn looked at the sky and nodded in agreement. 'What do you think we're going to find here?'

'Nothing, probably. That's what half this lark is about. Going places you don't want to go, and coming back none the wiser. Still, who knows what we might find? At least it'll be something to tell our grandchildren.'

I saw the sorrow well up into Dawn's eyes immediately, and I could have kicked myself. Why couldn't I learn to shut up? I put my hand on to her shoulder and said, 'Sorry, babe. Just me and my big mouth again.'

She smiled crookedly up at me. 'Don't be. It's just that places like this remind me…'

'I know,' I said. 'A quick in and out, and away. I promise.'

I locked the front doors of the car and we walked towards the tomb. It was surrounded on the three sides facing the building by a black iron railing, broken at one point by an iron gate which stood open. More ivy and creepers with sickly-looking white flowers snaked over the railing. For all the royalties that had accrued for Harrison in Los Angeles, no one was taking much care of the place where he lay on this side of the Atlantic.

Inside the railing were flat paving stones, from which the tomb rose like a giant concrete coffin. At one end was a bust of what I imagined must have been Harrison's head. But it was unrecognizable. It had been chipped at and broken until it resembled nothing more than a large, grey, pock-marked turnip. At the other end of the tomb were two stone urns containing dead flowers. Every inch of the monument itself, the wall behind and the flagstones was covered in graffiti and messages from fans, in thick, multi-coloured spray paint, or spidery felt tip, or scratched into the stone. Not that you could see much of what was beneath our feet because it was inches deep in litter. Cigarette ends, fag packets, roaches, used condoms, sweet papers, McDonald's cartons, and beer and softdrink cans that the strengthening breeze tossed with a faint rustle like the breath of a dying man. Each of the spikes of the railing had a can of its own forced down over the metal. It was right depressing. A panic-in-needle-park job, and it made me shiver.

Standing against the wall was a rough wooden bench, also covered with messages, plus three still figures. Two girls and a young bloke. None of them looked more than fifteen or sixteen. They were possibly even more depressing than the place itself. They sat and stared at Dawn and me as if we'd arrived from Mars. The girls were proto-punks, with dyed black hair in Mohawks with shaved sides, and long dreadlocks at the back. They were identically dressed in black leather jackets, black micro skirts, black fishnet stockings and high-heeled black boots fastened with silver buckles. They book-ended a whacked-out-looking skinhead who was holding a plastic bag full of glue in his tattooed and nail-bitten right hand.

Welcome to the pleasure dome. Kubla Khan, you've got a lot to answer for.

I looked at the trio, and two of them looked back at me with dark, dead eyes. 'What do you want?' said the girl on the right.

'Just looking,' I replied.

'Well fuck off. This is our place.'

'I thought anyone could come here,' I replied.

'It'll cost ya,' said the other girl.

'What?'

'Got any fags?'

I nodded.

'Give us then.'

I took a half-empty packet of Silk Cut from the pocket of my jacket, opened it, offered the packet to Dawn, who shook her head, took out one cigarette and stuck it in my mouth, and tossed the carton to the girl on the left. She caught it one-handed, looked inside, shrugged and said, 'Got any cash?'

I lit my cigarette. 'Yes thanks,' I replied.

'Give us some.'

I found a handful of change, about three quid's worth, and walked over and put it into the dirty palm of her hand.

I stepped back and she counted it, pulled another face, and was about to say something else when I interrupted.

'That's all for now,' I said.

She didn't argue. Just stuck the money into one of the zippered pockets of her jacket, took out two of the cigarettes, passed one to the other girl, and lit them both from a book of matches. I was worried in case she set fire to the fumes from the glue that the skin was holding, but she didn't.

'You a fan?' the girl on the right asked through a mouthful of smoke.

'I used to be,' I replied truthfully. 'You?'

She shrugged. 'He was all right,' she said. 'I prefer Marc Bolan meself.'

'Bollocks to that,' said the other girl. 'He was great. A right rebel.'

'Do you come here a lot?' I asked.

'Every day, nearly,' said the girl on the right.

'Why?'

'It's somewhere to go,' she replied.

'What's your name?' I asked.

'Bird,' she replied. 'That's Chrissie.' She poked a thumb at the other girl. 'And this is my bloke Malcolm.'

Malcolm just sat through the introductions and stared into another dimension.

'I'm Nick,' I said. 'This is Dawn.'

I saw two pairs of eyes move in my wife's direction, then back to me. 'You Old Bill?' asked Chrissie.

I shook my head.

''E could be, Bird, couldn't 'e?' she remarked.

Bird nodded wisely. And as she did so I realised where she'd got her nickname. She did look like a bird. A black-plumed bird of paradise washed up on to a rubbish heap.

'No,' I said. 'Just a punter.'

'Punting for what?' asked Bird. 'Anything we can do for you?' And she smiled lasciviously, looking much older than her age all of a sudden.

I looked at Dawn, wondering what she'd make of me being blatantly propositioned in front of her, but she didn't turn a hair. Where she'd been for so many years I guessed that she'd heard worse, from women who could eat Chrissie and Bird for breakfast. Mohawks and all. And scarf up Malcolm for afters.

'Maybe,' I said. 'But not what you're thinking. I'm looking for information.'

'What?' said Chrissie.

'Information,' I repeated.

'What kind of information?'

'About this place. And him.' I gestured with my cigarette at Harrison's tomb, then dropped it among the other rubbish and stubbed it out. 'You're here a lot. Are there any other regular visitors? Older people?'

'Like you?' she said.

I grinned. I was asking for the rise to be taken. 'Older,' I said.

'People that would be Jay Harrison's age now if he'd lived.'

'You sure you ain't Old Bill?' asked Bird.

'I'm a private detective,' I explained, and fished out one of my cards and passed it to her. She looked at it then gave it to Chrissie who did the same, then put it in another of her many pockets. She'd probably use it for a roach later.

'Loads,' she said. 'Wankers. Fuckin' old freaks with nothing better to do. Why'd you wanna know?'

'Just interested,' I said.

'You're the fuckin' same as them if you ask me,' said Bird. 'Why don't you get lost?'

'Don't be so hostile,' said Dawn suddenly, and the two girls and I looked at her again. 'You could mess up a good thing.'

'What kind of good thing?' asked Chrissie.

Dawn smiled. 'A nice little result. A few quid for you and your friend. And a little something for Malcolm too. He looks like he could use a little something.'

Chrissie's eyes narrowed. Dawn was obviously talking her language. Like I said. She'd been there.

'How much?'

'That depends,' said Dawn. 'On what you know.'

Chrissie looked at Bird and then back at Dawn. She seemed to have forgotten all about me. 'Know about what?'

'What he asked you. About the people who come here regularly.'

'There's loads,' said Bird. "Specially in the summertime. They come and hang out. Then they go away again.'

'How about the ones that don't go away,' asked Dawn.

Bird and Chrissie both shrugged. 'Dunno,' said Bird. 'But we know a man who might know.'

'Who?' I asked. I was beginning to feel left out.

'Dandy.' Bird again.

'Who's he?' I asked.

'He lives here,' said Chrissie.

'What, here?' I asked, looking round the dismal place that Dawn and I had found ourselves in.

The two girls nodded as one.

'Where does he sleep?' I asked.

'In there,' said Bird, using her thumb again to indicate the building behind her. 'He keeps this place tidy.'

I looked round once more at the mess that was Harrison's tomb. 'Not doing a very good job, is he?' I said.

'It's all right,' said Chrissie. 'Homely.'

If this was homely, I hated to think what her front room was like. 'Is he about?' I asked.

'Gone to get his breakfast, and some Cokes for us. He'll be back soon,' replied Bird.

'You'll have to pay him too,' said Chrissie.

'Depends what he knows,' I said. 'And no porkies.'

'He'll know if anyone does,' said Chrissie. 'And we don't tell lies.'

She sounded deeply affronted at the suggestion, and all of a sudden I saw through the disguise she was wearing to how she must have been as a little girl, and the kind of matron she'd probably become when she stopped being a punk. If the glue and other drugs didn't get her first.

'I believe you,' I said.

Just then I heard movement behind me, and a very tall, thin boy of about sixteen wearing a multi-coloured shirt and leather trousers, with long, floppy hair and a fringe that covered his eyes, appeared through the undergrowth. He was carrying a greasy package in one hand, and four cans of Coke, held together by loops of plastic, in the other. He stopped when he saw me.

'Here he is now,' said Chrissie.

I thought the boy was going to turn and run at the sight of Dawn and me, but Chrissie said, 'Don't worry, Dandy, they're not here to take you back.'

I wondered where 'back' was, but didn't ask.

Dandy stood and looked at us all. I could see that he was still poised to flee, and I said, 'Relax. I'm not going to hurt you.'

'Who're you?' he asked.

Chrissie answered for me. 'He's a private detective. She's his tart. They want to talk.'

Dandy went white. 'Are you from the council? Or me mum and dad?' he said.

'No,' said Dawn quickly. 'Look, Dandy. Don't worry. We're not interested in anything you've done. We want some help.'

He seemed to relax a fraction. 'What kind of help?' he asked.

Once again Chrissie jumped in. I felt like a ventriloquist's dummy. 'About this place.'

'What about it?' said Dandy.

'You live here?' I asked.

'What if I do?'

'You're here every day?'

'Don't tell him until he pays,' said Chrissie, who now appeared to be Dandy's business manager. 'And pass over those cokes. We're thirsty.'

Dandy came through the gate into the tomb, peeled off three of the cans and tossed them to Chrissie, who caught them one-handed. Good catchers, these girls.

'Eat your breakfast,' I said to him. 'Don't want it getting cold.'

He nodded, put the last Coke on top of the tomb and unwrapped the parcel. Inside were two soggy-looking sandwiches. Sausage, mustard and ketchup I guessed from the look and smell. A faint puff of steam leaked out from between the slices of bread. Chrissie and Bird popped their cans, and Dandy did the same with his. Malcolm's was put on the bench for his future enjoyment. Then Bird remembered her manners.

'Want a drink?' she asked us. 'Malc's well out of it. He don't want his.'

I shook my head, but Dawn nodded and took the proffered can and opened the top with a hiss.

Dandy picked up one half of one sandwich. The bread flopped damply, and he caught the crust in his mouth. 'How much?' he asked through his breakfast.

'Depends on what you know.'

'What about?'

'This place.'

He looked at me bemusedly. 'What about it?'

'Who comes here regularly. Anyone funny. Strange. You know.'

He shook his head. 'Most people who come here are strange,' he said. 'It's not normal to hang out in a place like this.'

'You do,' I said.

'Whoever said I was normal?' he replied, and bit into his sandwich again.

I wanted another cigarette, but I'd given all mine away, so I ignored the craving. I figured I was wasting my time but decided to have just one more try. 'OK. I give in,' I said. 'But try to think. I'm looking for someone who seems more than usually interested in him.' I switched my eyes to the tomb on which Dandy's Coke can was sitting. 'Not just a fan or a nutter. Someone who can't seem to stay away.'

'That fat fucker,' said a male voice. For a second I couldn't place it. Then I realised that Malcolm had spoken. I looked over at him and his eyes were gazing up into mine. 'Friar Fucking Tuck.'

I caught Malcolm's eyes with mine and said, 'Who's Friar Tuck?'

'Oh, Malcolm,' said Bird. 'Not that again. You were stoned.'

He turned in her direction and said, 'What the fuck do you know?'

'You're always stoned,' she replied.

Before it turned into a domestic, I said, 'Slow down a minute. Let him finish.'

Bird shrugged huffily, and I said to Malcolm, 'Come on then, son. Who's Friar Tuck?'

'Got any dough?' he said.

'Sure.' I reached into my back pocket and slid a note off the pile that was folded there. It was a twenty. I held it up between two fingers.

'Give us,' said Malcolm, reaching out his right hand. It was then that I noticed he had the letters LOVE tattooed on the backs of his fingers. I looked at his left hand. HATE. Obviously an original thinker, our Malcolm.

I shook my head. 'Not until you tell me what I want to know.'

'It's worth more than a score,' he said.

'I'll be the judge of what it's worth,' I said.

He spat on to the pile of garbage between his feet. What was another little piece of garbage among so much? I thought.

'Give us a drink?' he said to Bird.

She passed him her can of Coke and he took a long swallow, then stuck his snout back into the polythene bag with its layer of glue, grey like snot, in the bottom, and inhaled deeply, then dropped that too between his feet.

'Give us a fag,' he said to the girls.

Malcolm was beginning to get on my nerves.

Chrissie took my packet of Silk Cut out of her jacket and passed them round. All six of us present took one. Even Dandy, who stuck his under his hair behind his ear while he finished his second sandwich. I lit Dawn's and mine with my lighter. Chrissie lit hers, Malcolm's and Bird's with another match from her book. I wondered if she'd ever heard the superstition about the third light from a match. Probably not. She was too young. Or maybe she just couldn't care less.

Malcolm looked up at me again and slowly let out a mouthful of smoke, which the breeze, strengthening by the minute as it rushed the yellow clouds towards us, took and dispersed around his head.

'This geezer,' he said. 'Big cunt, fat. Bald on top. Never talks. 'E comes 'ere a lot.'

'Not lately,' interrupted Bird.

'Shut the fuck up,' said Malcolm. 'I'm talking.'

Charming, I thought. The mating habits of the young. And for a second I considered my own daughter Judith living up in Aberdeen, and wondered how her first boyfriend would treat her. If she didn't already have one. Not the way that Malcolm treated Bird, I hoped. Or he'd have me to answer to. Whoever he was.

'He used to come here all the time,' Malcolm went on. 'Never spoke to no one. Just hung about. You remember him, Dandy.'

I looked over at the tall boy, who nodded, swallowed the last mouthful of his breakfast, wiped his fingers daintily along the thighs of his leather strides, took the cigarette from behind his ear and lit it with a disposable lighter he kept in the top pocket of his shirt.

'Then I come up here one night late,' Malcolm continued. 'I was trippin'. 'Eavy fuckin' acid. Some cunt brought it back from Amsterdam. It was loaded with bleedin' speed and I couldn't sleep. Didn't want to neither. It was great.' He smiled at the memory. 'I wanted to come into the graveyard. See some spooks. I bunked in over the wall and he was here.'

'Friar Tuck?' I interjected.

'That's right. And he was wearing robes. Long black robes. Normally he wore jeans and a jacket. And he was kneelin' there.' He pointed to where the battered bust of Harrison stood. 'Prayin'.'

'Bollocks,' said Bird. 'You was dreamin'.'

'No I fuckin' wasn't,' Malcolm insisted. 'He was here, and so was I. I watched him from over there.' He gestured towards the gate. 'I keep tellin' you it 'appened. Do you think I saw it on fuckin' video?'

'Probably,' said Bird.

Malcolm backhanded her across the face. 'Don't tell me what I was doin',' he said. 'No one tells me that. Or what *to* do,' he added.

I guessed he said that a lot. People like him do, and I hated to disillusion him, but I did. 'Don't do *that* again, Malcolm,' I said.

'What?'

'Hit her.'

'She's my bird. I can do what I like with her.' He paused for a second, then grinned nastily. 'Bird. Geddit?'

I goddit.

'But don't hit her.'

'Don't you give her a whack?' he asked, looking at Dawn.

'I try to resist the temptation,' I replied. 'Mostly I succeed.'

'And if you don't?'

'It hasn't happened yet,' I said.

'Birds deserve a good 'idin',' said Malcolm. 'Keeps them in line.'

Bird touched her face where the imprint of his hand burned redly against the paleness of her skin.

'So do some blokes,' I said.

He looked up at me, and smiled nastily again. He got my message. 'And who's gonna give it me?' he asked. 'I'm fuckin' mad, me, when I get goin',' and his hand disappeared into the shiny green nylon bomber jacket with the orange lining that he was wearing, and came out holding a Stanley knife with the blade extended.

It was really no contest. One of the first things you learn as a probationary constable is how to take a knife away from someone. Two ways. The nice way and the nasty way. I did it the nice way but with just enough hint of nastiness that Malcolm might be able to form a fist with his right hand some time that evening. If I'd done it like our instructor had shown us one late night in a gym in Hendon, he'd've needed microsurgery.

Malcolm knelt in the garbage sobbing, and I tossed the Stanley knife into the undergrowth outside the iron fence.

Bird looked at me with a new softness in her eyes that was almost embarrassing. Dawn noticed and shook her head slightly and smiled.

'Does anyone else know anything about this Friar Tuck bloke?' I asked.

'Just what Malcolm told me,' said Dandy, who was also looking at me differently.

'Did anyone else ever see him here at night? Dressed like that? Or any other time, when he behaved differently from normal?'

Dandy, Bird and Chrissie all shook their heads.

'And he hasn't been here lately?'

Once again, three negatives.

'Well, thanks,' I said, and placed the twenty-pound note in Bird's hand. 'Don't spend it all at once.' And then for Malcolm's benefit, if he could hear me from the world of pain he now inhabited, 'I'll be back from time to time. See how you're all getting on. I'll bring some more cigarettes.' And I took Dawn's hand and led her through the gate and back in the direction of the car. By the time we reached it, the threatened rain was just starting and raindrops as big as ten-pence pieces were starting to kick up the dust from the roadway. We got in and I started the engine.

'I'm glad you hurt that little shit,' said Dawn. 'If you hadn't I was going to scratch his eyes out.'

'Now that I would like to see,' I said.

We sat there side by side with the big five-litre motor of the Chevy idling under the long bonnet, holding hands and watching the water stream down the windscreen.

'What made you ask that?' Dawn said.

'What?'

'About someone of Harrison's age acting strangely in here.'

'Because if he *isn't* dead, and that *isn't* him buried under that bloody great mausoleum, I reckon he might just pop by occasionally to see that everything's copacetic. Mellow-D. That the place is being looked after and no one's dug up whatever or whoever *is* buried there. And if anyone would know, it'd be those kids. They're there all the time.'

'But to come back at night, dressed in robes and pray there.'

'If we can believe Malcolm. He didn't strike me as one of life's more reliable witnesses. And he admitted himself that he was tripping. He probably dreamt the whole thing just like Bird said he did.'

'I don't like this job,' said Dawn. 'It's too weird, and we're meeting some nasty people.'

'It'll probably get worse before it gets better. Most cases I do are like this. But sometimes you meet other kinds of people. Decent ones. Miss Simmons for instance.'

'Yes. She was decent, wasn't she?'

As we were talking, the rain beat down even harder, drumming on the bodywork of the Chevy, and I switched on the wipers, double speed. The glass inside the car was misted up and I turned on the air conditioning.

'Do you think they're all right?' asked Dawn.

'Who?'

'The two girls and Dandy. It's pouring.'

I noticed she hadn't included Malcolm. 'Damp, I expect,' I said.

'Poor things.'

'I expect they're used to it.'

'That doesn't make it better.'

'For a hard woman, you're as soft as shit,' I said.

'Chris Kennedy-Sloane was right,' she said. 'You have such a charming way with words.'

I smiled. 'I know. It was what first attracted you to me, wasn't it?'

She smiled back. 'No,' she said. 'You were pissed and had far too much money for your own good, and Tracey and I decided that you could donate a little of it to us.'

'What was that about a way with words?' I said.

She smiled sadly.

'Do you want to go back and check how they are?' I asked. 'We could give them a lift somewhere.'

She shook her head. 'No,' she said. 'You're right. I expect they are used to being out in all weathers. Dandy must have a shelter somewhere. He'll look after them. They probably wouldn't thank us anyway.'

'Probably not,' I said, and switched the four big halogen headlights on full beam, put the car into 'drive' and pulled away.

'So what now?' she asked.

'How about lunch?' I said. 'I'm starving.'

13

We lunched at Camden Lock. By the time we got there the rain had stopped, the breeze had wiped the sky clean of clouds, and the sun was raising steam off the streets. We ate al fresco at an Italian restaurant with a terrace on the first floor, so that I could keep an eye on the motor.

The food was excellent, and when the coffee and brandies had been served, I said, 'OK, 'Olmes. You're the great detective. Lay it out for me.'

'What do you mean?'

'Tell me about the case. Frankly I'm confused. I want to hear what you make of it so far.'

'Starting when?'

'At the beginning.'

'Right back?'

'Right back. And if you miss anything I think is relevant, I'll interrupt. Maybe between us we can make some sense of this lot.'

Dawn lit a Silk Cut from the new packet we'd bought at an extortionate price from the restaurant and sat back in her seat. 'OK,' she said. 'Some time at the end of 1971, Jay Harrison and his girlfriend Kim Major come over to London from America. Things were getting too hot for them over there. He was awaiting trial for obscenity, and everything he touched went wrong. He was getting fat and ugly, and his band was on the skids. The pair of them took a flat in Hyde Park Mansions and proceed to party down. Cool, so far?'

I nodded. 'They were drinking up a storm, I imagine,' I said. 'That seemed to be par for the course for them at the time. And taking a lot of drugs from the state of the photos we've seen.'

'What kind of drugs?'

'Does it matter?' I asked.

'You wanted it all laid out.'

'Fair enough. Well, according to what I can make out, this pair were the original Furry Freak Brothers. They'd take anything. Anything and everything. Dope. Uppers. Downers. Coke. Acid. Prescribed drugs and smack. Especially smack. That's what a lot of reports reckoned finished him in the end. The dark drug. The killer.'

'I've never tried horse,' Dawn said. 'When I was on the game, that's what did for a lot of the girls. Before they moved on to crack. But heroin always scared me. Have you done it?'

'Once,' I replied. 'To keep a friend company.'

'What was it like?'

'Brilliant. That's why I only took it once. I knew if I tried it again I'd be hooked.'

'What was it like?'

'You really want to know?'

'Sure.'

I thought about it.

'It was strange,' I said. 'I snorted it. I can't stand needles. Never have been able to. First of all I puked. Then I was in heaven. No pain, see. We're all in pain all the time. Even if we don't know it. It's part of the human condition. A warning sign. But take some H, and you're in paradise. No pain. No worries. An excellent feeling.'

'Sounds dangerous.'

'That's half the attraction. But I reckon it's a coward's drug. A little pain's good for the soul. Makes you strong. Anyway, that's not the point at issue. Harrison is. Go on with the story.'

'Right,' said Dawn. 'Jay Harrison and his girlfriend are having fun in London town. Then one night they go to a party, then back home, where Harrison gets into the bath and croaks. Kim calls the doc who declares him dead... Why no post-mortem by the way?'

'According to the stories I read, he had been under the doctor's supervision for heart problems for months. On a daily basis. Hence the supply of prescribed drugs and the lack of a PM. His own doctor was in attendance and signed the death certificate. Everything legal and above board. In those days there were a lot of Harley Street quacks more than pleased to make up scripts in exchange for hard cash. Make up symptoms too. Or else get into the slimming-pill business. Very lucrative. Tenner a prescription. Thirty Black Bombers to get the weight down. Thirty Mandies to get you to sleep at night. So off the punter goes to the chemist, and in exchange for another fiver, he or she gets street-legal drugs worth sixty nicker. And that was when sixty nicker was a fair whack. Not a bad deal, Doll. And the doctor could do a hundred scripts a day and never bother to examine a single patient. Of course that was before the authorities tightened up on prescription abuse. Not that it still doesn't go on. It does. But not like it used to.'

'How come you know so much?'

'Used to be in the drug squad, didn't I? I did a lot of research on that sort of thing.' And a lot of drugs, I thought. Happy days. 'And with the doctor dead, we'll never know if the heart-symptoms story was a front or for real.'

'If it was true, then Harrison probably did die of a heart attack, just like it says on the death certificate,' said Dawn. 'I'm just surprised there wasn't more of a fuss made at the time. Christ, he wasn't even thirty when he died.'

'You know that no one was much interested in Harrison then,' I said. 'They were different days, the early seventies. The national press hadn't realised how fascinated the public are in pop stars' little foibles. Burnt out or not. In fact, especially burnt-out ones. It gives their readers a little warm spot inside when they see someone who used to be famous fall on hard times. Of course the papers have made up for it since. There have been loads of stories that Harrison isn't dead. 'Specially since they decided to make a film about him. He's been spotted running a gas station in New Mexico, shopping in Paris, begging on the streets in Berlin, and serving in Pizza-land in Oxford Street. But then again, John Lennon has been reported as being on a life-support machine at a special hospital in New England with inoperable brain damage. And of course Elvis gets seen *everywhere*. It's permanent conspiracy-theory time when it comes to famous people dying. Both Brian Jones and Jimi Hendrix were supposed to have been murdered. Hitler's in a home for old Nazis in

Argentina, and JFK is living on an island off Hawaii with a harem of beautiful girls. No one wants to believe that these characters can really die. It's weird.'

'You seem to have become an expert on dead celebrities,' said Dawn.

'I picked up all that when I went through the newspaper library,' I said. 'Frightening, isn't it? Anyway. Carry on.'

'Right. Now the story gets interesting. Jasper and Jake Cousins get called in to prepare Harrison's body for burial. They seal the coffin up tight and no one, but no one gets a peek.'

'And of course the four people that we know saw the corpse are all dead themselves,' I interrupted. 'A bit strange, wouldn't you say?'

'Hold on,' said Dawn, lighting another cigarette and signalling for refills of our brandy glasses. 'Don't you get carried away with conspiracies. It *was* twenty years ago. How old was the doctor at the time?'

'No idea.'

'Some detective you are.'

I accepted the rebuke. 'Middle-aged, I imagine,' I said. 'I could find out I suppose.'

'It doesn't really matter. Nobody lives forever, Nick. And Jasper Cousins was old. Then there was Kim Major. She was a fatality just waiting to happen by all accounts. So her death was no shock. The only one of the other three who died prematurely was Jake Cousins, and even he couldn't have been any spring chicken. These things happen.'

Shit happens, I thought. Course it does.

'Sure,' I said. 'But it would be good if at least one of them was still around for us to talk to.'

Dawn shrugged, and the waiter brought the brandy bottle again.

'To continue,' she went on. 'Harrison is buried under that lump of cement at Highgate Cemetery, and Kim Major moves out of the flat in Hyde Park, and we lose touch with her until she turns up dead too.'

'I wonder how come she was so broke?' I said.

'What do you mean?'

'Both Harrison and Kim Major were rich kids. His old man was a big wheel in the US Air Force and her dad owned a string of department stores in the midwest of America. And of course

Harrison made a fortune with the band. Relatively at least. Even with their lifestyle I'm surprised he could blow it so quick. So how come she couldn't afford to pay the rent on the flat?'

'Maybe his money was all tied up so that Kim couldn't touch it. And perhaps she'd been cut off without a penny by Daddy. It happens when a good girl goes to the bad.'

'You'd know,' I said, and immediately regretted it. 'Sorry, babe,' I said. 'Just my big mouth again.'

She shrugged. 'I would as it happens. I've seen it plenty of times.'

'I wonder who paid for that tomb then,' I said.

'His family?'

'I'll check it out,' I said. 'Speak to Chris.'

'It's a hell of a pile,' said Dawn. 'Whoever is under that will take a lot of getting out.'

'With what we've got so far, no chance. It takes a lot more than we've discovered in this country to get an order to exhume a body. In fact, what we've got so far would just about fit under one of your fingernails.'

She smiled. 'And after all that, nothing much happens, except, as you say, all the people who saw Harrison's body died and he got famous again. A cult figure. So famous in fact that kids are prepared to camp out at his graveside. And odd men dressed as monks come and pray there. And then, almost exactly twenty years after he's reported dead, a letter turns up, purporting to be from him, with a reasonable facsimile of his signature at the bottom, denying the fact, and demanding all the back royalties he's owed, and his record company freaks.'

'That's another interesting thing,' I observed. 'Like I said, there have been dozens of reports since seventy-two that Harrison is still alive. I wonder why this particular letter has caused such an upset.'

Dawn shrugged again, then said, 'So?'

'So what?'

'So, what do you think?'

'About the letter?'

'No. About the whole thing.'

I thought about it for a moment, then said, 'Babe, I think it stinks like shit. My intuition tells me that Harrison's still alive and running round London, and I think that with a bit of luck we're going to find him.'

14

After we'd finished lunch, and I'd paid with my badly dented credit card, I drove us back to Tulse Hill. The phone was ringing as I opened the flat door and I picked up the receiver. It was Chris Kennedy-Sloane.

'I was just going to call you,' I said.

'I must be a mind-reader. What did you want?'

'That can wait. What do *you* want?'

'You remember you asked me about finding someone to identify those people in the photographs you found?'

'Sure.'

'Well, I think I've come up with someone.'

'Who?' I asked.

'Tony and Pam Taffler,' he said. 'They've been around for years.'

'What do they do?'

'They're brokers.'

'What kind of brokers?'

'Time brokers.'

'What do you mean?'

'They buy and sell books, records, magazines, clothes, furniture. All sorts. Artefacts of the sixties and seventies. You name it, they can get it.'

'Who do they sell it to?'

'Anybody. Film and TV companies. Ad agencies. Private collectors.

But most importantly, they also sell information.'

'What kind?'

'Well, let's imagine you want to know what people were doing on any particular date. What was on the news. What they were wearing. You know the sort of thing. You call up the Tafflers and they'll tell you. Their whole flat is full of all kinds of junk, and they've got a lot of stuff in storage.'

'If you say so,' I said. 'But who buys it?'

'You'd be amazed who wants to know things like that. They even got called in as consultants for an exhibition at the V&A last year.'

'If it's good enough for them…' I said.

'It's good enough for you,' he finished. 'I've given them a bell. They're expecting a call from you. They're looking forward to seeing the photos.'

'Fine,' I said. 'Give me their number.'

He reeled off the ten digits and I copied them down on a pad.

'I'll call them right up,' I said. 'And I'll let you know if they're any help.'

'Fine. So what did you want from me?'

'I've just been up to Highgate to look at Harrison's grave. Very strange. I want to know who paid for it in the first place and who pays for the upkeep, what there is of it, now.'

'Shouldn't be too hard to find out,' said Sloane. 'I'll get back to you. And don't forget to let me know if the Tafflers were of any use.'

'I'll do that little thing,' I said, and hung up.

I told Dawn what was happening, and dialled the Tafflers number right off. A woman answered. 'Is that Pam Taffler?' I asked.

'That's right,' she said. 'Who's this?'

'My name's Nick Sharman. I believe Chris Kennedy-Sloane's talked to you about some photos I've got.'

'Of Jay Harrison?'

'That's right.'

'Yes. Sure he did. Tony and I can't wait to see them. We met him a couple of times before he died.'

'Then maybe you can help identify some of the other people in the pictures.'

'We'll do our best. Can you come over?'

'Sure. Where and when?'

She gave me an address in a block just off Shepherd's Bush Green, then said, 'How about tomorrow night? Say seven-thirty.'

'Fine,' I said. 'Do you mind if I bring my wife?'

'Course not. The more the merrier.'

'We'll bring a bottle of wine,' I said.

'What a lovely idea. We'll make an evening of it.'

'Suits me,' I said. 'See you then.'

Meanwhile I nipped down the doctor's. No, I wasn't ill. Just needed some information. This one had done me some good a while back when I'd had a run in with some nasty faces who meant me a great deal of harm. Permanent harm if they could've had their way, and they almost did. Then the good doctor came along and put Humpty together again.

I tracked him down in the social club at King's College. Social. From what I've seen and heard, if it was any more social there, it'd be illegal.

I asked him if he wanted a drink. He told me that he was operating later, so I'd better make it a large one, and I reconsidered BUPA.

'So what's the problem?' he asked. 'Prostate playing you up. Men of your age and your habits.'

'Bollocks. I ain't that old.'

'Prostate troubles are starting younger and younger. It's the modern age.'

'I wish you'd shut up about my fucking prostate. For the last time, I'm all right.'

'So what is it then?'

'Inquests. Post-mortems.'

'They're always interesting. You should've seen this bloke's body that they brought into the mortuary last week. He'd been lying dead in a flat in Catford for three months. His whole body was welded to the mattress. They had to bring him in still in bed. When we peeled him off, the maggots had eaten all his back away and there was a cockroach nest inside. I mean right inside his head.'

'Christ almighty,' I protested. 'I'm supposed to be eating out later. Give it a bloody rest, willya?'

'Sorry, Nick, I forgot how squeamish you are for a supposedly hard man.'

'Listen, Doc,' I persevered. 'How do you go about getting an inquest when someone dies?'

'Accident. Suspicious circumstances. No doctor seen for a period of time. Anything like that.'

'But if a doctor has been treating a patient on a regular basis, and everything seems kosher, it's straight down the boneyard?'

'That's right.'

'And if the doctor's at it?'

'Then Bob's your uncle. Do you know how many doctors are mentioned in old people's wills? Old people that they see all the time?'

'You're beginning to undermine my faith in the medical fraternity.'

'I'm sure we'll survive. The oldest profession, don't you know?'

'I thought that was something else.'

He grinned. 'But we're all brothers and sisters under the skin.'

Cynical bastard, I thought.

'Anyway, why are you asking?' he said.

'A case I'm working on. Young bloke. American. History of heart problems. Regular doctor from Harley Street. Used to visit him all the time, and make with the bedside manner. Dodgy quack, I reckon. But legit on the face of it.'

'I'll get him checked out by the BMA if you want. Always glad to help the mighty fall.'

'Too late I'm afraid. Brown bread years ago.'

'So why the interest?'

'The body of the young bloke in question was buried with almost indecent haste. No one saw him dead but his girlfriend, the doctor who signed the death certificate, and the undertakers.'

'Sounds iffy to me. When was this?'

'Early seventies.'

'Jeez. That was a long time ago. Prehistoric.'

The doctor was about twenty-five.

'Anything could happen in those days,' he went on.

'What? Like the Black Death?'

'Could be.'

'But you'd've asked for an inquest?'

'Definitely. Anyone under fifty dies of heart trouble. Call in the coroner. Safer all round. But why didn't the girlfriend? Or a member of the family?'

'That's just what I'm asking. Trouble is, the girlfriend's dead too.'

'High mortality rate around this bloke, isn't there?'

I nodded. 'But it's not impossible for no one to give a damn if someone dies? Just sling 'em in a grave to rot. So long as the paperwork's in order?'

'Obviously not. Come on, Nick, you used to be a copper. Stranger things have happened as you must be well aware.'

'Course I am,' I said. 'I was just thinking aloud, that's all.'

'Anyway, it must've. You just said it did.'

'You're right,' I replied, and left.

15

Dawn drove me up to Shepherd's Bush in the Caprice the next evening, and we parked in a side street next to the flats where the Tafflers lived. It was a better than average inner-city block. There were security doors at the front, and an entryphone. I buzzed through to the flat and I recognized Pam Taffler's voice. 'Nick Sharman,' I said into the mike.

'Come on up. Fifteenth floor,' she replied, and when the buzzer went, I pushed the door open, and Dawn and I went into the foyer. It was clean and looked recently swept, and the lift was waiting and working.

When we got out of the lift, the door opposite was open, and a good-looking brunette in her late thirties, wearing a long dress and thick-lensed bins, was standing waiting. 'Pam?' I said.

'Nick?' she replied.

I nodded, and introduced Dawn, and Pam let us into the flat. It was a fair size but felt smaller because everywhere you looked there were piles of books and magazines, and even about a hundred brightly coloured mail-order catalogues. The flash on the front of the top one said: Summer '67. Flower power fashions for teens and twenties.

Pam led us through the flat to the living room, which was illuminated by the sun starting to set over west London. A tall, olive-skinned bloke of roughly the same age as his wife, with medium-length wavy hair, just beginning to be streaked with grey, was sitting at a table by one of the windows leafing through an old copy of *Rolling Stone*. He got up when we entered. He had a friendly face and he looked enquiringly from Dawn to me and back again.

'Tony, this is Nick and Dawn Sharman,' said his wife.

He came over and shook hands, and smiled and asked us to sit. I gave Pam the bottle of wine, and Dawn put her bag with the photos inside next to an armchair which she sat in. As soon as she was seated, a big, grey tabby cat appeared from somewhere, sniffed at her shoes and jumped into her lap. Tony Taffler said, 'Shoo it off if it's being a nuisance.'

'It's all right,' said Dawn, and stroked the cat's head, who immediately started to purr like a steam engine. 'What's its name?'

'Hector,' said Tony.

'Hello, Hector,' said Dawn. 'Who's a good boy?'

'He's a she actually,' said Tony. 'A slight mistake when she was a kitten. By the time we found out, she was used to the name.'

Dawn laughed and apologised to the cat, who twisted round on her knees and went to sleep.

'Who wants some of this?' asked Pam, holding up our bottle.

We all made affirmative noises, and she went off into the kitchen to open the bottle and get some glasses.

Tony Taffler sat back at the table and said, 'So what exactly is the story with the photos?'

I told him the bare outlines. I said I needed to identify the subjects in the photographs. Apart from Harrison and Kim Major, whom I already knew. I didn't tell him why.

'When Pam gets back we'll have a look,' he said. 'You never know. But of course we don't promise to be infallible.'

'I've heard you're hot stuff,' I said.

He grinned when I spoke. 'We do all right,' he said.

'What got you into this line of business?' asked Dawn.

Tony shrugged. 'Who knows? Just a series of accidents really. Pam and I have always been fascinated by...' he hesitated, 'I'd say popular culture but that makes me sound like someone on *The Late Show*,' he said. 'You know, things that are happening. Music, dance, clothes. We started to collect sixties and seventies stuff seriously when we were living together before we got married. I was a mod when we met, and so was Pam. We bumped into each other first at the Lyceum. We

were very young. It was a long time ago. Twenty-five years. Longer.'
He smiled at the memory, and his smile warmed the room. 'We got a
load of stuff out of junk shops and jumble sales,' he went on. 'Things
people didn't want then, but are worth a packet now. A few other
people, at the BBC and places like that, heard about us and what we
were doing, and asked us to research for them. We not only did the
research, but we hired out the props too. Simple.'

'Nice work,' I said, as Pam came back with a tray, put it on the
table next to Tony, and poured out four glasses of wine.

I asked if I could smoke, and Tony nodded and I lit a cigarette.

'So can we look at the photos?' he said.

Dawn got the envelope out of her bag and passed it over to him. As
she did so, the cat snorted, opened its eyes, then closed them again.

Pam Taffler pulled up a chair next to her husband's, and switched
on the Anglepoise lamp that stood on the corner of the table, and
pulled it close to the photographs. I saw the light catch the dull
surface of the top one, and it flared in my eyes, and I looked away.
Dawn continued to stroke the sleeping cat's head, and I sipped at
my wine, and looked past her out of the window over the view of
Shepherd's Bush and beyond. A plane with its navigation lights
twinkling was making its descent into Heathrow and I could just
hear through the double-glazed windows the sound of its engines as
they were throttled back to slow the aircraft down.

You could tell straight away that the Tafflers had been together a long
time. The way they spoke, finishing each other's sentences, searching
through their minds for shared memories. Almost telepathically. I
envied them. Whatever they'd been through in the last twenty-five-
odd years, they'd been through together. I *did* envy them. I'd never
had that, and I looked at Dawn again, and wondered how long we'd
have together, and whether or not we'd ever learn enough about each
other to be able to finish sentences like they could.

Pam got up again, and fetched a large magnifying glass from a
drawer in a bureau that was covered with yellowing copies of *Melody
Maker*.

'Jesus,' said Tony. 'Look at this one, Pam. Isn't that the... ? You
know the place. Down by where Biba's used to be. That restaurant.'

'No,' said Pam. 'It's Gino's in the King's Road. I recognize those
lights.'

'Are you sure? I could have sworn...'

'I know it is. We went there to a wedding reception. That bloke who used to be in that band. You remember. He married my friend Gillian.'

'The Glitter Band?'

'No. Before that. Andy Fairweather-Low's band.'

'Amen Corner.'

'That's right.'

'Yes I remember. Course it is. And who's that with Jay Harrison?'

'Who, him?' Pam stabbed her finger on to the photo.

'No, her. With the headband.'

'She looks familiar,' said Pam. 'Wasn't she a groupie?'

'Probably,' said Tony. 'It'll come back to me.'

And it did. Plus lots of other names from the past. Some vaguely familiar, and others that meant nothing to me, but obviously quite a lot to the Tafflers. For over an hour they were lost in reminiscences as Dawn and I sat and drank our wine, and I smoked, and Dawn stroked the cat.

Tony Taffler made notes on a pad as they went. It seemed most of the faces had vanished. Died, either by their own hands or through various accidents or diseases. The mortality rate for the group of people photographed was high. Individuals who had lived fast, died young, and left corpses in various degrees of attractiveness.

When they got to the last photo in the pile, Tony said, 'Christ!'

I looked up sharply at the tone in his voice, and Pam gave him a bemused stare through her specs. 'What?' she said.

Tony pointed at the photo. 'Look who's there.'

'Where?' said Pam.

'There. In the front with Harrison. All over him like a dirty shirt.'

I stood up and looked over their shoulders. The photo had been taken in someone's flat. It looked like a party was going on. Jay Harrison and Kim Major were at the front of the photograph. Harrison looked awful. Fat and dissipated with long greasy hair curling over his face. Kim looked better, but not much. Draped over Harrison's shoulder was a tall, well-built geezer with long, flowing hair, a flower-patterned shirt and jeans. Next to Kim stood a much shorter man. Fat, with a sort of Nehru jacket buttoned tightly across his chest. A whole coterie of grinning idiots holding glasses or joints or both were behind the star and his girlfriend and their two chums. Each face brightly lit by the flash that had been used.

'Him?' I said, pointing at the long-haired bloke.

'That's right,' replied Tony. 'Remember him, Pam?'

I looked down at her face, and she shook her head.

'You should,' said Tony with a grin. 'He came round enough times when we were living in Notting Hill. He grew a beard.'

She shook her head again.

'Julius Rose,' Tony said triumphantly. 'He used to do a bit of dope dealing. Do you remember now?'

'Is that Julius Rose?' asked Pam, with astonishment in her voice.

'Course it is.'

'Crikey, he put on some weight.'

'He did. And next to Kim is...' Tony Taffler screwed up his face in concentration. 'That geezer that Julius was webbed up with all the time. A slimy little git. Always trying it on for a few bob. Bill... Billy... Billy Sanger... No. Sayer. That's it. Billy Sayer.'

'I remember,' said Pam. 'I loathed him.'

'Who didn't?' said Tony. 'I never knew what Julius saw in him.'

'Julius Rose. Who would believe it?' said Pam.

'What kind of drugs?' I asked.

Tony pulled a face. 'Nothing serious. A little hash. Grass. Acid. Small time.'

'They all look pretty matey there,' I said.

'Don't they just,' agreed Tony. 'Maybe Julius just gave Jay a suppository.' And he smiled.

'God, but it was a long time ago,' said Pam. 'I wonder whatever happened to him?'

'I know exactly what happened to him,' said Tony. 'I saw him last week. Didn't I tell you?'

'No. You saw him? Where?' said Pam.

'I'm sure I told you,' said Tony, then shook his head. 'It was when I went round to Jenny and Peter's place. They've got satellite TV. Julius Rose was on.'

'On what?'

Tony grinned. 'You'll never guess. I was sure I told you. How could I have forgotten? He's an evangelist with his own show. Brother Julius. I nearly pissed myself.'

'What was the name of the show?' I asked. If 'show' is how you describe a religious programme. But from what little I'd seen of television evangelism in the past, that's exactly how I'd describe one.

Come on down. Or come on up and meet thy maker.

Tony screwed up his face as he thought. '*Redemption Cometh*,' he said. 'I think that was what it was called.'

Perfect, I thought. Cometh on down. 'Catchy,' I said. 'And the name of the church? Do you remember?'

He screwed up his face again, then shook his head. 'No. But it was quite a mouthful.'

'Why didn't you tell me?' said Pam.

'Sorry, I forgot,' replied Tony.

'How could you forget something like that?'

'Sorry,' he said again. 'No one's perfect.'

'What channel is it on?' I asked.

'One of the Astra channels,' said Tony. 'It's on every night at seven apparently.'

'I'll check it out,' I said.

'They gave an address for the place at the end. For sending donations and stuff, you know. I think they're very big on donations. They'd have to be if Julius Rose was involved. He was always very big on donations even in the old days. It was in one of those squares at the back of Notting Hill Gate...' He hesitated as he thought.

'Powis Square?' said Pam helpfully.

'No. The other side of Westbourne Grove. You know.'

'Leinster Square.'

'No.'

'Pembridge.'

'That's the one.'

'Well done,' I said.

'There you go, Nick. I know where at least one of this lot is,' and he tapped the photos. 'And here are some other names. But I've no idea where to locate the ones that are still alive.' He passed over the pad that he'd been making notes on.

'Thanks,' I said. 'You've been a big help.'

'If I track any of the others down, I'll be in touch,' he said.

'Thanks again,' I said.

'All part of the Taffler service.'

'And send the bill to Kennedy-Sloane,' I told him.

'It'll be a pleasure,' said Tony Taffler.

We sat around for another hour or so, finishing off the wine we'd brought, and another bottle Pam found in the fridge, until about ten, when Dawn and I left and she drove the pair of us home.

'Any good?' she asked on the way.

I shrugged from the passenger side of the seat. 'Who knows?' I replied, 'but it's a start. All we need now is someone with a satellite dish so that we can catch the show. Then we'll pay Brother Julius a visit.'

'Think he'll know anything?'

'We'll never know unless we ask.'

'That's true.'

'So do you know anyone?'

'Anyone, who?'

'With a satellite dish,' I said patiently.

'Tracey's all cabled up where she lives.'

'I bet she is.'

Dawn looked over and put out her tongue. 'No, I mean she gets all the satellite channels.'

'Great,' I said to Dawn. 'Give her a ring when we get back and we can pop round tomorrow evening for a glass of wine and a little redemption on the box.'

16

But like many of the best-laid plans of mice and men, it didn't work out quite like that.

At around ten the next morning, as I was finishing a slice of toast spread with apricot conserve and a cup of freshly brewed coffee, and listening to Albert King on the CD player, the phone went. It was one of Dawn's records. And say what you like about my wife, she has unimpeachable taste in music. If you can't get that sort of thing right, then the relationship is probably doomed from the beginning. Albert was doing his 'Born Under a Bad Sign', when the dog and bone went. Maybe I should have taken it as an omen. I turned down the sound with the remote and fielded the call.

'Nick Sharman,' I said.

'Nick. Good. Just the man.' It was Chris Kennedy-Sloane. I recognized his voice straight off.

'Well, as you were calling me, that's hardly surprising, Chris. What's up?' I said.

'I need you to do a job for me.'

'I *am* doing a job for you, sort of. Remember?'

Dawn looked at me from where she was standing by the sink, rinsing off a plate, and raised one eyebrow quizzically. I shrugged back like I didn't know what was going on, and I didn't.

'No. Another job,' said Kennedy-Sloane.

'Blimey,' I said. 'Such riches of opportunity. What is it?'

'Are you busy tonight?'

'Yes, as a matter of fact I am. I was going to take Dawn to watch some TV round at a friend's, then catch a Chinese nosh on the way home.'

'Am I paying you a grand a day to watch TV?'

'*You're* not paying me a grand a day to do anything. It's a long story, Chris, trust me.'

'Christ on a bicycle, Nick, I never know half of what you're talking about.'

'That's the secret of my success.'

'Can't you watch TV another night? I need you this evening.'

'I didn't know you cared.'

'No jokes, Nick. This is serious.'

I lit a Silk Cut.

'You remember Angela?' he asked. 'I brought her to your wedding reception.'

'Who could forget?' I asked back.

'And you know that The Virgin Mary is in town?'

'Have you told the Pope?' I said.

'I said no jokes, Nick. You know who I'm talking about, don't you?'

Course I did. The Virgin Mary. The hottest recording act right about then. Hornier than Madonna. Sexier than Cher. Younger than either of them. Her managers and producers had taken the Memphis horns and layered them on top of a Tamla Motown rhythm section, segued in a sample of a John Bonham drum solo, sweetened the mix with strings from the Love Unlimited Orchestra under the direction of Barry White, and multi-tracked the Virgin's voice over the whole thing. And what did they get? A load of hit records, and videos, and films, and books, and T-shirts, and every other kind of merchandise you could decently shake a stick at, and some you couldn't. That's what they got, and I know that my daughter and her friends loved her.

'I know who you're talking about,' I said.

'She's doing a special concert tonight for charity at the Astoria in Charing Cross Road. She's brought over her whole show. The complete Rhythm Review. Just about everyone in the world is going to be there...'

'It'll be a bit of a tight squeeze, won't it?' I interrupted.

He ignored me and went on. 'And Angela's got a pair of invitations, and I can't take her. I've got to go out of town. Some last-minute family business has come up, and I can't get out of it.'

He was probably strangling his granny for her BT shares, I thought, but kept shtoom.

'So?' I said.

'Will you escort her?'

I looked at Dawn, who was busy putting clean crockery in the cupboard. 'Do what?' I said.

'You heard. You've got a tuxedo, haven't you? I want you looking smart.'

'As a matter of fact, no. We don't get a lot of call for them round Tulse Hill way.'

'So you've got plenty of time to get up to Young's or Moss Bros and hire one. I'll pay.'

'Listen,' I said. 'I'm grateful that you thought of me for the job. But...'

'But what?'

'But. You know. I've only been married for just over a week...'

All of a sudden, Dawn was taking much more of an interest in the conversation that I was having than she had previously.

'I'm asking you to take Angela to a reception. Not run away to Gretna Green with her,' said Kennedy-Sloane.

'Sure, but...'

'You're full of "buts" this morning, Nick. This is not like you. If I didn't know you better, I'd say you were acting like a henpecked husband. I never thought I'd see you under the cosh –'

That did it. 'How much?' I interrupted.

'How much, what?'

'How much are you going to pay for my services tonight?'

'Well, I thought a favour, maybe.'

'Bollocks, Chris. The going rate for me now is a grand a day. Remember? You just told me.'

I heard him swallow.

'Take it or leave it,' I said.

'But I only want you for the evening.'

I thought about it. 'A monkey then.'

'Five hundred quid.'

'Your grasp of the vernacular is impeccable,' I told him. 'Plus expenses of course.'

'OK. You got it. A limo will pick you up at six-thirty. I've booked a table at the Savoy Grill for dinner at a quarter to eight. The gig starts at eleven. The limo driver will have Angela's address. She's got the invitations. Hire a soup and fish. And take care of her. This is a big night. Loads of publicity. Make sure she gets her photo taken. I'm trusting you, Nick.'

'No problem, Chris,' I said. 'Thanks for thinking of me,' and I put down the phone.

Dawn was back by the sink, tapping the heel of one shoe. Now the fun could really begin.

'Dawn...' I said.

'What?'

'You remember Angela? The model that Chris brought to the wedding reception.'

'What? That long skinny tart with the big eyes for every man in the room?'

I couldn't have put it better myself. 'That's the one,' I said.

'What about her?'

I explained, and saw Dawn's eyes get slittier with every word.

'You want to go out with *her*?' she said when I'd finished.

'No. It's a job. Worth five hundred quid.'

'But you still have to spend the night with her?'

'I wouldn't put it like that exactly...'

'Then how would you put it?'

'I escort her to dinner, to the do. Make sure she gets maximum publicity. Then take her home. End of story.'

'It's a stitch-up. I saw the way she looked at you.'

'She looked at every geezer like that.'

'So?'

I shrugged. 'So it's a job. Puts food on the table and petrol in the motors.'

'So you're going to do it?'

'Not if you're totally against it.'

'I am.'

'I've said I'll do it now.'

'And you can't let your old mate down, now can you?'

'He got me the Harrison job. I owe him one.'

'All right,' she said, and every word dripped with icicles. 'Take the slag out. But if I think for a minute that you've laid one finger on her,

I'll kill the pair of you. And you know I mean it.'

The scary thing was that I did.

I got up and went over and held her tight. I knew what the trouble was. I knew that she remembered her first husband leaving the house with their daughter for the short drive down to where his parents were going to babysit while Dawn went to work. I knew that she remembered the copper coming to tell her that she'd never see either of them again after the van that her husband was driving was crushed in a pile-up. Not even to identify the bodies, the injuries were so bad. And I knew that she remembered the bad years after. Years of booze and drugs and loveless sex. Living without trust in a world of pain, and being knocked back and used at every turn. About crying so much from loss that she thought her eyes would turn white. I could feel her trembling as I held her, and without speaking I tried to let her know that I knew as much about pain and hurt as she did. And that I'd die before I inflicted any more of it on her.

She clung to me tightly, and I could feel her sobbing. Then she stopped and looked up at me, and smiled through the tears. 'Sorry,' she said. 'Bad moment. Of course you must do it.'

'You know that I won't do a thing except what I'm being paid for.'

'That's what worries me,' she said. 'Now go and get yourself some evening clothes. And, Nick.'

'What?'

'No frills on the shirt.'

'Come with me,' I said. 'Help me choose.'

'What? Get you all tarted up for that... *Tart.*'

'It's not for her. It's for us. Another honeymoon. Hastings. Remember?'

She smiled again, then said, 'What about that thing on the TV? One of us should keep working on the Harrison case.'

'Sod it. It's twenty years old. What does one more day matter, more or less? Come on. Come out with me now. It'll be fun.'

'You want me to?'

'Course I do. You're my baby, aren't you?'

'Am I?'

'Course you are. I'll buy you lunch in Covent Garden, and we can moan how it ain't like it used to be.'

'All right,' she said. 'But I'll go round to Tracey's tonight and catch the show. I'll video it and you can see it tomorrow.'

'You're superb, babe,' I said.

'Am I?'

'Twenty-four carat. Now are we going out or what?'

She nodded, dried her eyes, put on some fresh make-up and off we went. And we had the best day I can remember for years.

17

The limo was dead on time. It was a black stretch Ford LTD with a whole load of aerials sticking out of the boot. It must have been twenty-five feet long and it made the Chevy look small. It probably wouldn't start tomorrow after that. Some cars have souls, you know.

I'd chosen black silk for my suit. The most expensive that Young's had for hire. It was double-breasted with plain-bottomed trousers. I'd teamed it with a red cummerbund, a gleaming white shirt with French cuffs, a real bow tie that Dawn had to tie for me, and shiny black patent leather shoes. Dawn checked the tie for me one last time, when the limo driver sounded his horn outside.

'You look so handsome tonight,' she said. 'You're making me dead jealous. That bitch better leave you alone.'

'She will, believe me,' I replied.

'Will you be late?' she asked.

'Don't know. The damn thing doesn't start 'til after eleven. So I suppose I shall.'

Dawn brushed off my shoulders with the palms of her hands, then came up and kissed me on the side of the mouth. 'Be as late as you've got to be,' she said. 'Just don't let me down.'

'Never,' I said. And 'never' I meant.

She smiled at me and I smiled back.

'Enjoy the show on TV,' I said.

'Oh, I will,' she replied. 'I always enjoy watching religious programmes while my husband's out partying with lovely young models.'

I was going to say, 'Then you're in for a treat tonight', but I thought better of it.

I went down to the car, and the driver, dressed in something that closely resembled what I was wearing except that he was sporting a black peaked cap as an accessory and no cummerbund, jumped out of his seat and opened the back door of the car for me.

The limo was like a perfumed leather and wood coffin inside. The windows were tinted as dark as an autumn evening, and I could stretch my legs right out without touching the bulkhead. As soon as I was seated the driver pulled away, did a tight three-point turn and headed north.

Angela lived in Clapham, so we were there within twenty minutes. Her address was a row of villas at the east side of the common. I rang her doorbell. She answered via an intercom mounted at the side of the door, and when I told her who it was, she buzzed me up. She was waiting in her flat doorway when I reached the top of the stairs. She was as tall and slim as I remembered, and that night she was almost wearing a dress of red silk that was so small I bet I could have crushed it into the palm of one hand. Her make-up was flawless, and when I got close she sort of kissed the air about six inches to the right and left of my face. In the heels she was wearing she was exactly the same height as me, which seemed strange as I normally have to look down on people. Especially women.

'Come in,' she said. 'We've got plenty of time. You're very punctual.'

'The chauffeur was right on the button,' I said. 'And besides, that's what I'm being paid for.' Trying to get the relationship on the right footing from the off.

'Don't talk like that. You're my escort tonight. Chris and his damned family business. Do you want a drink?'

'Sure,' I replied.

'What do you want?'

'What've you got?'

'Anything.'

'What are you having?'

'A glass of wine.'

'Make it two.'

She vanished through a door into what I assumed to be the kitchen, and I took the opportunity to look round the place. Her flat was big. The whole top storey of the house. It was minimally furnished and the floors were polished wood. I went over to the huge uncurtained window which had a view of the common beneath.

She came back carrying two large goblets of white wine, and gave me one. 'Do you like the view?' she asked.

I didn't know if she meant her, or what was outside the window. I assumed it to be the latter. 'Yes. Have you lived here long?'

'About a year.'

'And before?'

'With my parents.'

We were drinking standing up, as I couldn't actually see anywhere to sit in the room, and I didn't want to ask.

'You're looking very handsome,' said Angela. 'I like your suit.'

'You're the second person to say that to me tonight,' I replied.

'Who else?' she asked.

'My wife.'

'Oh *her*.'

'Yes *her*,' I said. 'Mind if I smoke?'

'Of course not.'

I took out my Silk Cut and offered her one. She took it and I lit it for her and she blew out a long stream of grey smoke.

'Do you like my outfit?' she asked, and gave me a twirl, making sure not to spill her wine.

It was so short and low-cut, front and back, that I felt like saying, 'It'll be all right when it's finished', but didn't.

'Very attractive,' I said instead.

'Do you really think so? Good. Versace.'

Which meant it had a price tag in the low thousands.

'I hope you don't spill any gravy on it.'

'It doesn't matter if I do. I did some work for them last winter, and they've loaned it to me for tonight.'

'Nice work,' I said.

She shrugged, drained her glass, and said, 'Shall we go?'

'Whenever you're ready.'

She collected an evening coat that matched her dress from another room, and locked up securely behind us. We went down to the limo, which was sitting at the kerb with its exhaust pipe burbling to keep the air-conditioning going. I helped Angela into the back, averting my eyes from the flash of underwear she gave me, and sat next to her. She picked up the phone that went through to the driver's compartment and said, 'Any champagne?'

He said something in reply and she put down the receiver and said, 'Open the fridge.'

'Where?' I asked, looking round.

'There.' She pointed to a chrome handle and when I pulled it, a small door opened, and inside was a mini-bar stocked to the gills with booze, including a couple of bottles of vintage bubbly. As the car drew away from the kerb, I took out a couple of cold champagne flutes from their mounts inside the door, gave them to Angela, rescued a bottle of champagne, undid the foil, took off the latticework, and popped the cork without spilling a drop. She held up the glasses and I filled them both to the brim.

We spent the drive up to the Savoy finishing the bottle and looking out through the tinted windows at the poor unfortunates who had to take buses. It doesn't take much of this kind of treatment to turn anyone into a lousy snob.

The driver swung into the little street in front of the hotel, and the commissionaire leapt into action, and opened the door of the car for us. After I'd told the driver to collect us again at ten-thirty, we were ushered into the foyer, a fiver was transferred from my hand to the commissionaire's pocket, and we headed for the grill room where we were met by the maître d' who showed us to a table by the window with a view of the Embankment and the river beyond.

We ordered a pair of vodka martini cocktails and were left with the menus and the breadsticks, and Angela hauled out a packet of Marlboros and gave one to me.

'You're very good,' she said. 'Everything's going like clockwork.'

'It's easy when you've got a flashy car and driver, a pocket full of small-denomination notes and your absent host has an account at the place. If I tried getting in here as a regular punter, it might be a different story.'

'I'm sure it wouldn't,' she said. And who was I to argue?

The martinis arrived, and Angela ordered lobster and I chose rack of lamb. The wine waiter boogied on over and Angela wanted white wine, and I couldn't have cared less, and said I'd have white too, and the waiter recommended something that cost an arm, a dick and a leg, and I just shrugged and told him to bring it along.

We skipped dessert and ordered coffees and brandy and chatted away like we'd known each other for years, and before I knew it, it was time to go, and I signed for the meal, helped Angela on with her coat and went back out front to the motor which was parked in a no-waiting zone with its engine running again.

The driver headed down the Strand to Trafalgar Square and up Charing Cross Road to the Astoria which was under siege from about a thousand fans of The Virgin Mary. They were twenty deep at the front door, spilling out into the road, and holding up the traffic, and a score of dark-suited bouncers aided by about a dozen coppers were doing their best to keep a pathway open through the crowd to let the guests inside.

We joined the queue of expensive cars outside the theatre and the fans peered through the dark glass to try to see who was inside. Now I knew what a goldfish felt like.

Angela had a handful of invitations in her bag. Three in all. A silver one to get us into the building, a gold one to get us into the VIP enclosure, and a platinum one to get us into the *real* party, backstage after the show, she explained. When our car was at the front of the queue, one of the bouncers fought his way over to it, and she stuck the silver one against the glass, and he wrestled the door open and three of his mates, and a couple of uniformed policemen, formed a flying wedge to get us to the door, and inside to the foyer. As we made our way up the steps flashbulbs went off all around us like an artillery barrage. Well at least parts one and two of my job had been fulfilled. I'd got Angela to the gig, and she was getting her photo taken.

Once inside the place, Angela told me she had to go to the loo to freshen up, and I waited in the foyer and took a look round. Even though it was still early, the place was crawling with people. And what a feature they were. It looked like every mini-celeb and star-fucking roach in town had crawled out from under the gas stove, put on their best, caring nineties grunge gear and come looking for a good time in the name of charity. So what or who the hell were we saving tonight, I wondered. I looked around for inspiration and caught the eye of someone who looked as if he'd be at home in a re-make of *Night of the Living Dead*. The geezer was about fifty, very tall, stick thin, shaved bald except for a hank of purple, green and black hair over one eye, with a dead-white face, save for a thick coating of black eye-liner and matching lipstick. He sported three nose studs and his ears were pierced so many times, and held so many rings, that the lobes almost brushed the shoulders of his black lamé boilersuit, worn with wedge-heeled suede slingbacks.

He grinned, exposing a ruby mounted in one canine tooth, and lurched towards me in his ridiculous shoes.

'Hi,' he gushed as he got close. His voice was breathy and high pitched. 'Have we met?'

I shook my head, and he reached out one long, black, nail-polished, skeletal hand thick with rings. 'I'm Caspian,' he said.

I took the proffered mitten, which was cold and dry, in my right hand and shook it briefly. 'I'm Nick,' I replied.

'Delighted you could make it. Are you alone?'

'No,' I said. 'I'm with a friend. She's in the ladies' room.'

'Nice,' he said. 'What do you get up to with her?'

'Her usual escort couldn't make it tonight. I stepped into the breach,' I said. Cheeky bugger.

As I spoke I saw Angela heading our way.

'Here she is now,' I said.

Caspian turned and his face lit up. 'Angela darling,' he cried. 'Where have you been?'

He knew exactly where she'd been, but we were into freakspeak by then, and Angela replied, 'Working, Caspian. I see you've met Nick.'

'Such a nice boy,' he said. Boy. Well it's been a while.

They embraced without seeming to touch, and kissed each other's cheeks the same way.

'Shall we go in?' said Caspian. 'Are you staying for the party?'

Angela waved her invitations, and Caspian rolled his shoulders and shimmied his hips with pleasure. 'Wonderful,' he gushed. 'We can keep each other company.'

'Where's Sterling tonight?' asked Angela.

'Oh, he's off on location,' said Caspian. 'It's so tiresome. He's doing something for Peter Greenaway in Peru or Chile, or somewhere else equally unspeakable on the South American continent. I spoke to him on the phone on Sunday. It's all mosquitoes, tequila and guacamole from what I can gather, and some seriously unspeakable rough trade down by the docks.'

'I do hope he's being careful,' said Angela.

'It's a full-body condom job I believe,' said Caspian, lifting his plucked eyebrows at me. 'But boys will be boys.'

If he expected some comment from me on the subject he was going to be disappointed. Instead I just smiled and allowed myself to be led into the auditorium of the place, and through a barrier of red-velvet rope into the VIP area, courtesy of Angela and Caspian's gold invitations.

A waiter led us to a table in one corner. He was tall, bronzed, heavily muscled and lightly oiled, wearing just a suede loin-cloth and sandals. When we were seated he took our order for drinks. Angela asked for a spritzer, Caspian went for a Bloody Mary, and I asked for a whiskey sour. When Caspian finished admiring the waiter's bare behind as he went to the bar, he jumped up and said, 'I've just seen someone I simply must speak to. I'll be back directly, darlings. Don't do anything I wouldn't.'

Which was giving us a long rope from what I could gather so far, but I just smiled again, as he vanished into the crowd towards another table.

'Who the fuck is he?' I asked.

'A designer. He's very good. A sweetie in fact.'

'You've convinced me,' I said. 'And Sterling?'

'His lover. An actor. Sterling Rush. He had a part in *EastEnders* about a year ago. He had a market stall. Sold flowers I think. Had an affair with, what's her name?, in the pub. The fat one. You must have seen him.'

'The name doesn't ring a bell, but I'm sure I'd recognize the face,' I said. 'By the way, what is this all about tonight? I feel I should know in case I get into light conversation with anyone.'

'Save the Swordfish,' she said.

'*What?*'

'Save the Swordfish,' she repeated slowly, as if I was hard of hearing, or partly brain dead.

'I didn't know the swordfish needed saving.'

'Everything needs saving these days,' she said seriously.

'And all this is for some poor bloody fish that doesn't even know it's endangered.'

'Of course. Do you know that if we go the way we're going, by the year twenty thirty there'll be no swordfishes in the world? Not one.'

'Really. Well you learn something new every day.'

She nodded in agreement.

'And all these beautiful people really care about the fate of the swordfish?' I asked.

'Of course they do.'

'And nothing about the fact that their faces will be all over the papers tomorrow.'

'Don't be cynical.'

'As if,' I replied. 'I can just see this crew getting sleepless nights over their pals, the gentle little swordfishes.'

'Someone's got to,' said Angela.

I sighed, and spotted our waiter returning through the gathering throng. When he arrived I did my whiskey sour in one, and ordered another three refills. I could tell it was going to be a very long night.

And I wasn't far wrong.

The show itself was taking place in the auditorium next to where we were sitting, and people kept wandering in and out waiting for the action to begin. The men wore anything from full evening dress to full rodeo gear, and the women for the most part were minimally dressed and maximally obvious. Angela and I stayed at the table where we were sitting for the next half hour or so, and she greeted a stream of her friends and acquaintances to whom I was introduced but whom I immediately forgot, as I'm sure they did me. Our waiter kept bringing the whiskey sours and I was as happy as a pig in shit. Caspian rejoined us and kept up a constant snidy monologue on the other guests, their state of fashion victimness and their sexual and drug predilections. I saw two Rolling Stones, one ex-Beatle, one half of Bros and the geezer who used to mess around with the synthesizers in Roxy Music. I was also informed that Suede and Blur were in the building, plus Charles and Eddie and LA Fishbone, but I was none the wiser. Old age creeps up on all of us. There was also a bunch of soap opera stars, who all seemed to know Caspian, plus some very dodgy trannies who looked like bags of old bones wrapped up in taffeta and lace. So much for the glitterati, I thought, and had another whiskey sour.

Then I noticed a bloke clocking us from two tables down. He was tanned, with dark hair, about thirty-five, wearing a denim jacket with spangles above one pocket, and leather jeans. At this point I was nicely mellow and imagined he was a friend of Angela's or Caspian's or both. But every time I caught his eye he looked away and started to talk to his companion, a heavy-looking individual dressed in roadie gear of a western shirt and jeans. It didn't bother me at first, but every time I looked over, spangled jacket was screwing me, and he didn't look particularly friendly.

Angela was rabbiting to some clothes horse, and as soon as she'd split, I touched my charge on the shoulder.

'Yes, Nick,' she said. 'Sorry, am I neglecting you?'

'No. Do you know that geezer?'

'Who?'

I didn't look, but said, 'Two tables down. Denim jacket, leather strides.'

Angela peered past me and said, 'Who?'

Then I looked. But the ice cream and his mate had vanished, to be replaced by a blonde-haired dream in buckskins and her boyfriend dressed from top to toe in a red sparkly suit.

'Don't worry,' I said, 'I've had too many of these,' and tapped my glass. 'Must be getting paranoid.'

She smiled.

'Anyhow, I'm off to the gents,' I said.

'Take this with you. It'll cure your paranoia. Or make it worse,' and she pressed a white paper wrap into my hand.

'Thanks, Ange,' I said, and left my seat and went back into the foyer to find the gents.

Walking into the gents was like walking into Drugs 'R' Us. Everyone seemed to be cutting something out on every available flat surface. I pushed my way to the urinal and took a leak. A spare-looking individual in Oxfam chic with two-tone brown and white shoes stood next to me and said, 'Got a blade, mate?'

'Sorry,' I replied.

'Shit. Got a credit card?'

I shook my head. 'I bust my limit,' I said. 'And they cut it up.'

'That's the breaks,' he said, zipped up and left.

I did the same, then the door to one of the stalls opened and two Japanese came out, bowed to me and vanished through the door to the foyer. I went into the vacant stall, rescued Angela's wrap from my pocket and opened it. There was about a gram and a half of white powder inside, nicely crushed with just a few rocks for contrast. I touched the pad of my little finger to the powder and licked off the residue. I got a good freeze straight away. I'd thought it was coke, but you never know. It's some people's idea of a joke to give you a line of skag just to see how you cope. I'd been lying when I said I had no credit card, and pulled my trusty Access out of my pocket, dug up a pile of cocaine with the edge and snorted it up. Instant rush. I took the other half for badness, closed the wrap, licked the credit card clean, and returned them both to my top pocket. I went outside and checked my nostrils in the mirror for traces. I was clean, but when I looked at my reflection I didn't particularly like what I saw, and could hardly raise a smile.

I went back to our table, and by the roar from inside the auditorium it sounded like The Virgin Mary had made an appearance. 'Want to go in?' I asked.

'Not particularly,' said Angela.

'Well I am,' said Caspian. 'I want to see what horror the old bag's wearing.'

Not one of your designs, obviously, I thought. You bitch you.

'Go on then, Cas,' said Angela. 'Nick and I will stay out here and get drunk.'

Get, I thought? I've already got.

Caspian got up and sashayed into the gig, and I gave Angela back her wrap of coke.

'OK?' she asked.

'Primo.'

'I'm going to the little girls' room myself,' she said. 'Will you get me another drink?'

'With pleasure,' I said. And she got up and wiggled her skinny butt out of the room.

I caught the waiter's eye and he nodded without coming over, and called out our order for drinks to the barman. I sniffed the residue of coke up into my sinus, lit a Silk Cut, and wondered what Dawn was doing. I looked at my watch. It was well past midnight and inside the auditorium the joint was really jumping. I got up and went to the door and peered through. The stage was quite close, and The Virgin was making a sandwich with two almost naked black men, rubbing herself up and down them from neck to thigh while a vicious techno beat swirled out of the banks of speakers on either side of her.

I wonder what the swordfish would make of that, I thought.

By that time the waiter had delivered a fresh round of drinks, and I went back to the table again and sat down. As I did so, the door to the auditorium opened to allow a wave of noise and a huge geezer, dressed in the height of rock and roll chic, to enter. He was another roadie if ever I'd seen one. A brick-shithouse job wearing a dark blue cowboy shirt with embroidered pockets, pearl snaps for buttons, and two little metal arrows on the points of the long collars. With the shirt he wore tight blue jeans cinched in by a thick black leather belt with a silver longhorn head as a buckle. On his feet he wore very shiny, very tight looking, black high-heeled boots, and in his right hand he held a bottle of Old Gran'dad bourbon. He had a thick moustache, and long hair that hung below the brim of a straw cowboy hat. All in all, a sight for sore eyes.

Unfortunately, as he entered from the gig, Angela came back from the foyer, and our hero fastened his piggy eyes on her as she crossed the room in my direction.

'Hey, honey,' he called. 'Hold on there.' Yank. Predictable.

Shit, I thought. Just my luck.

The roadie weaved his way through the tables so that he could cut Angela off at the pass, and before she could get to me, he grabbed her upper arm with the hand not holding the bottle and said, 'What's the hurry, darlin'? Didn't you hear your ol' Babaloo callin' ya?'

Babaloo. Terrific, I thought, got up from my seat and moseyed on over to see good ol' Babaloo.

The hand that had hold of Angela's arm was the size of a small York ham, and when I got close it was obvious that Babaloo was viciously drunk. Dangerously drunk. Even drunker than I was, and that was my only advantage. Otherwise it was all downhill. I stopped in front of Babaloo and looked up at him, about seven feet tall in his heels and that ridiculous cowboy hat. 'Whoa, hoss,' I said. 'Unhand that maiden.'

I don't think Babaloo caught the intended irony of the remark as he peered down at me and said, 'Fuck off, dude. Cain't you see that the lady and me's about to get acquainted?'

'Nick…' pleaded Angela, and I knew I was getting into a bad situation.

'Babaloo,' I said quietly. 'If you don't let go of her arm, you and me's going to have to get acquainted ourselves, and that could end in a world of pain for one of us.'

And by the look of things I had an idea which of us it might be.

So did Babaloo. He looked down at me and laughed out loud, and his bourbon-laden breath almost singed my eyelashes off.

By then I was getting tired of the whole deal. Swordfishes, dress designers, models, roadies, groupies, The Virgin Mary and all.

'Your choice, boy,' I said, and stamped as hard as I could, putting all my weight on the top of my foot and on to one of his shiny, tight, black, pointy boots, just where all his toes must have been squashed together at the front. Babaloo roared like a bear, dropped the bottle of bourbon on to the carpet where most of its contents gurgled into the thin pile, grabbed at his foot with both hands and began to hop around on his other leg. His eyes were full of tears of pain, and he bellowed that he was going to kill me.

I punched him then. Right above the longhorn belt buckle where his shirt was tight across his belly. I hoped that there was more fat than muscle there, but I hoped wrong. My fist bounced off his hard abdomen like a gnat off a windowpane, and once again I knew that I could be in serious trouble. Babaloo was still holding his injured foot, so I kicked him just below the knee of his good leg. A goal-scoring kick that dropped him to the floor. He hit the carpet like a mighty Redwood tree being felled, and I could have sworn I felt the building shake. Babaloo's hat came off exposing a thatch of dishwater blond hair, and I kicked him again. This time in the head just to keep him on the floor. Unfair? Maybe. Ungentlemanly? Certainly. But from where I was standing the Marquess of Queensberry would have understood.

Right then, the doors to the auditorium opened again and two more roadies came in. By the looks on their faces when they saw Babaloo spread all over the carpet, and me standing over him, they were mates of his. Shit, I thought. Just my bad luck. And then Angela came to the rescue. She popped open her evening bag, stuck in her hand and withdrew a switchblade knife. It was a very pretty knife too, with a banana-shaped, light wood handle with shiny brass rivets and action, which, when she touched it, released a six-inch length of sharp Sheffield steel with a vicious click. Angela knelt beside Babaloo's prone figure, grabbed one of his ears and touched the blade to the top of it. 'One more step and I'll cut it off,' she threatened.

The two roadies froze.

'Get back inside and stay there,' said Angela.

They did as they were told.

She stood up, dropped the knife back into her bag, grabbed my hand and said, 'We'd better get out of here before they come back with reinforcements.'

I couldn't have agreed more, and together we ran back into the foyer and out into the street.

The fans had disappeared by then, and as I looked up and down Charing Cross Road for our car, I saw a flash of headlights, and our limo pulled out from where it had been parked and glided up to us. I opened the rear passenger door, Angela dived into the back, I followed, and the car moved off towards Oxford Street.

'I didn't know you carried a knife,' I said.

'You never know who you're going to meet.'

'That's true. Like Babaloo f'rinstance?'

She nodded.

'I think he's going to lose a few toenails, that boy,' I remarked.

'Thanks for saving me,' she said.

'And thanks for saving me. I thought my goose was cooked when that other pair arrived.'

'A pleasure,' she said.

The limo ran down Oxford Street, then turned into Park Lane and headed for the river. We crossed Chelsea Bridge, and drove up Queenstown Road to Clapham Common and Angela's flat.

I walked her to the door. What a gent.

'Want to come in?' she asked. 'I'll make some coffee, and we can have a last brandy.'

'I don't think so.' Although I was tempted.

'Scared of the wife?'

'Not really. Scared of myself more like.'

'What you might do?'

I nodded.

'No one would ever know.'

'I would.'

'A man of honour?'

'Not really,' I said again.

'We could have fun. The night is still young.'

'I'm sure we could.'

Angela studied my face in the light from a streetlamp. 'She's a lucky woman,' she said.

'There's a lot who'd disagree.'

'Not me, Nick.'

'Thanks.'

'So it's goodnight?'

'Looks like it.'

'Have you got my number?'

I shook my head.

'Do you want it?'

'A few months ago I would have died for it.'

'But not now?'

'No.'

'At least you're honest.'

'I try to be.'

'Well if you're ever in the area, you know where I am.'

'I do,' I said.

'Go on then, go home.'

I kissed her on the cheek, turned and went back to the limo. As I got in the back I looked at her front door, and she was still standing on the step, looking like a lost child. I waved, but she didn't wave back.

The chauffeur dropped me off at my place about one-thirty, and as I got out of the car I saw a thin line of dim light where the curtains in my flat hadn't been drawn properly.

'Looks like the missus is waiting up for you,' said the limo driver as I gave him a fifty for a tip. Not my money, remember.

'Looks like it,' I agreed.

'Well good luck, and thanks,' he said.

'Thank you,' I told him. 'I'm glad you weren't having a piss when we came out.'

'Why's that?'

'Long story.'

'I'll catch it next time.'

'If there is one, you will.'

'I see Angela all the time.'

'Aren't you the lucky one.'

'Could've done yourself a bit of good there tonight. If you don't mind me saying,' he added.

'Not in the least. But like you say, the missus is waiting. Night.'

'Night,' he said, and I walked to the front door fishing my keys out as I went.

The missus was indeed waiting for me. Sitting at the table wearing her black silk dressing gown.

And very attractive she looked too. 'How did it go?' she asked.

'It went.'

'How was Angela?' She pulled a face as she said her name.

'She was fine. She saved my bacon as a matter of fact.'

'How?'

And I told her. The whole story. Right until I dropped Angela off at her flat. Everything.

'Did you want to go inside with her?' Dawn asked.

'I'm here, aren't I?'

'But did you want to?' she pressed.

'It crossed my mind.'

'Why?'

I shrugged. 'She's a very attractive girl.'

'And she carries a knife.'

'There is that.'

'It turned you on that she was armed?'

'Yeah,' I said. 'It did as it happens. But I didn't go in with her. And I won't go in with anyone else. Ever.'

'Ever's a long time.'

'Not long enough for me to change my mind.'

'Why not?'

'Because of you.'

'And she said I was lucky?'

I nodded.

'She might be right.'

'I think I'm the lucky one,' I said. And I did.

'Perhaps you are,' said Dawn. 'And perhaps you're going to get luckier.'

'How come?'

She drew the skirt of her dressing gown back over her legs. She was wearing black stockings, and she drew something from the top of the right one. It was a flick knife. Black and evil-looking. She touched the button on the handle, and the long, thin blade leapt into view.

'Jesus,' I said.

'Women who can take care of themselves turn you on, do they?' she asked. 'How about this?'

'Where the fuck did you get that?'

'Tracey got it from a German punter years ago. I've had it since I started working with you.'

'And why were you carrying it in your stocking top tonight of all nights?'

'In case you came back smelling of sex or some strange soap that isn't in our bathroom, I'd've skinned the pair of you.'

And do you know I believed every word.

'Your trust in me is touching,' I said.

'I didn't come up river on a waterlily leaf last week, Nick. I know men.'

'Do you want to smell me now?'

'What would I smell?'

'Fear probably. Well, do you want to?'

'I want to do something with you, that's for sure.'

'What?'

'Come to bed and I'll show you.'

So I did.

18

I woke up with a king-sized hangover. Wine, champagne, cocaine and whiskey sours are not a good mixture. I felt as if a hundred little men in spiked running shoes were taking part in a marathon inside my cranium. Dawn saved the day. She was already up, and when she heard me moaning she thrust a cup of coffee and two aspirins under my nose.

'Feeling good, darling?' she said.

I shook my head and immediately regretted it. 'No,' I said.

'Serves you right for leaving me behind when you go out.'

'What difference would you have made?' I asked. Rather truculently as it goes.

'I could have got as drunk as you, and we could have stayed in bed together all day, nursing our heads.'

'Can't we... ?' I ventured. Hangovers always make me horny.

'Oh no. We've got work to do. I video'd that show last night.'

I'd forgotten all about it. 'How was it?' I asked.

'It wasn't *NYPD Blue*.'

'Was it *Mission Impossible*?'

'You can see for yourself when you get up. And wait 'til you catch the name of the church. You'll love it.'

'What is it?'

'Wait and see.'

'What time is it?'

'Nine.'

'I thought I might have a lie in...'

'Forget it, party animal. I want you out of that bed right now. I've got to change the sheets.'

'Give me a break,' I said.

'I am. Remember the knife.'

'Can I just finish my coffee?'

'Sure you can, sweetie pie. But don't dawdle.'

'Jesus, is this what our marriage is going to be like?'

She shrugged, and I knew that I wasn't going to win. But for some reason I didn't care. I just swallowed the aspirin and drank my coffee, got up and headed for the bathroom, showered and shaved and came back feeling much better. I dressed in a Levi's checked shirt and jeans, and Dawn, God bless her, put a plate of bacon and eggs, sausage, beans, tomatoes and toast on the table for me.

'You're a star,' I said.

She winked, and I dived into the food.

With my second cup of coffee and my first Silk Cut of the day I watched *Redemption Cometh*. Dawn sat on the sofa next to me and smoked half my cigarette.

The programme was a revelation. If not exactly *Revelation*. The name of the church was the Tabernacle of the Sepulchre of the Virgin Mary and Little Baby Jesus.

'Jesus,' I said as the pre-show credits rolled, echoing the name. 'Is this for real?'

'Seems so,' said Dawn. 'They take it very seriously anyway.'

'I bet they do,' I said.

The show opened with a squeaky-clean heavenly choir about two hundred strong, standing on a dark blue set decorated with stars that winked and blinked in the background, singing 'My Eyes Have Seen The Glory'. When they finished, the studio audience went potty, then pottier still when Brother Julius made his first appearance. I recognized Julius Rose from the photo, but might not have if Tony Taffler hadn't told me he'd grown a beard. The brother was still tall and well built, but his hair had thinned just a little. He was wearing a white three-piece suit with a darker shirt and tie.

'John Travolta,' said Dawn.

'Are the Bee Gees on later?' I asked.

'I don't think so. But if they're not, they're the only ones who aren't. Now shush, listen to this.'

Brother Julius was going into one. The first of several rants that punctuated the show. He stood at a dark wooden lectern with a huge Bible open in front of him. There was no messing with our Jules. Hellfire and damnation were his points of reference, and he never let anyone in the audience forget it. The first sermon was on the danger of drugs. Quite amusing I thought, if what Tony Taffler had told us about his previous occupation was true, and I had no reason to doubt it. Old Julius really got into it too. Foaming at the mouth, beating on the lectern and all.

'Does he heal the sick and raise the dead?' I asked Dawn. 'Make cripples walk and turn water into wine?'

'Wait and see.'

And of course he did. Not raise the dead or do the business with the water, but as soon as his talk about drugs had finished and the choir had sung 'Jerusalem', he came back in a freshly pressed suit and mingled with the masses.

He picked up a radio microphone and walked into the audience, who followed his every move with their eyes. The front row consisted of about twenty-five people of both sexes and all ages, in wheelchairs.

'Knew it,' I said, and lit another cigarette.

Brother Julius was calling on Jesus, and suddenly zeroed in on one particular wheelchair-bound punter. She was in her early twenties, dark haired, and pretty well twisted up from what I could see. Brother Julius knelt before her and asked her name.

'Tasmin,' she said.

'A very beautiful name,' said Brother Julius. 'How long have you been like this?'

'Forever.' The young woman's voice was barely a whisper.

'Then, my daughter, we shall have to change that. With the help of the blessed Mary and Jesus.' And he touched her lightly on the shoulder. The audience was silent as he did so. Nothing happened for ten long seconds, then the girl appeared to have a minor fit. I leaned forward to look as her twisted body began to straighten in front of my eyes. She put out her arms in front of her, and with Brother Julius's help she placed her feet on the floor in front of her chair, and with extreme care stood up. Julius stood back and she took two or three faltering steps before the congregation erupted in wild applause and the camera cut away.

'Christ,' I said. 'That was very good.'

'Fake?' asked Dawn.

'What do you think?'

She shrugged.

Then we went to the real business of the night. The first exhortation for money.

In a filmed clip, Brother Julius appeared to be in a Hollywood producer's idea of the Garden of Gethsemane. The grass was lush and green, the sky was blue, and the sun looked as if it had been polished. A stream tinkled pleasantly in the background, and little birdies twittered in the treetops. This time Jules was dressed in a long, flowing, white robe with gold detail, and an invisible choir hummed something melancholy behind the soundtrack.

'Brothers and sisters of the Tabernacle,' Brother Julius said in ringing tones. 'The work we do is necessary work to save the sinners of the world. Necessary, but expensive.' The choir hummed louder. 'And once again I must ask for your help. We need funds to go out into the wilderness to rescue the lambs of God that have gone astray.'

'He's good,' I said. 'I'll give him that.'

'I ask you, no, I *beg* you to dig deeply into your purses and pockets and send your donations to the Tabernacle of the Sepulchre of the Virgin Mary and Little Baby Jesus,' Brother Julius continued. 'Every penny that you give goes towards helping those who have turned away from the Saviour. And every penny is vital.'

On the screen appeared the address of the church. It was, as Tony Taffler had said, in Pembridge Square. I made a note of it.

'Jesus loves you, brothers and sisters,' said Brother Julius, as the choir burst into 'Rock Of Ages'. 'Show Jesus how much you love him in return. Send as much as you can. And God bless you.'

Fade to black.

I turned off the video then. I'd seen enough.

'There's more,' said Dawn.

'I'm sure there is.'

'He makes a deaf man hear again.'

'Course he does.'

'And he tells an old lady where her lost wedding ring is.'

'I'd expect nothing less.'

'You think he's a fraud?'

'Don't you?'

'He's got something,' she said.

'Sure.'

'So what do we do?'

'Pay him a visit, I think.'

Then the phone rang.

It was Chris Kennedy-Sloane.

'How did it go last night?'

'It went,' I said. I think I'd said that before.

'Angela got her picture in the *Mail* this morning.'

'Good.' I neglected to tell him that she almost got her name on an arrest sheet for threatening behaviour with a deadly weapon.

'I spoke to her just now. She says you acted like a perfect gentleman.'

'So I did. And hold that thought. I might need it as a reference one day.' And I winked at Dawn.

'Thanks, Nick. You did me a favour there.'

'A pleasure.'

'How's the other thing going?'

'Jay Harrison?'

'That's right.'

'Slow.'

'I've just had Lamar Quinn on the blower from LA. He wants a report.'

'There's nothing much *to* report.'

'Are you getting anywhere with it?'

'I'm doing my best.'

'Are you sure?' His tone had changed from one of gratitude to criticism.

'I'm on the case twenty-four hours a day. Except when I'm moonlighting for you. And that reminds me. You owe me a monkey plus exes for last night.' I told him how much I'd spent and got a strangled gasp as a reply. 'And Quinn's advance ran out yesterday,' I said, ramming my advantage home. 'I need more money from him too.'

'You amaze me.'

'Does he want me to carry on? I can always pack the case in and take a holiday you know.'

'Course he does. But he wants some results too. He's calling me back later.'

'Fine. Tell him I might have some news tomorrow. I'm following up some leads that your mates the Tafflers gave me. But remember this thing is twenty years old, for Chrissake. What does he want? A miracle?'

Saying that made me think of Brother Julius. Maybe with his help that's what I'd get.

'OK, Nick,' said Kennedy-Sloane. 'Don't throw a wobbler. I'll get you a cheque today.'

'Have it biked over,' I said. 'And don't forget my exes.' And I put down the phone.

'Problems?' asked Dawn.

'No. Chris just needs a firm hand now and again. Otherwise he gets out of line and tries to throw his weight around.'

19

We drove up to Kensington, and I parked the Chevy on a vacant meter in Pembridge Place. I took the photo of Julius Rose, Billy Sayer, Jay Harrison and Kim Major with me in a brown envelope.

Dawn and I walked in the summer warmth of the morning up to the square. The Tabernacle of the Sepulchre of the Virgin Mary and Little Baby Jesus's headquarters were in a terrace of half a dozen huge, three-storey, cream-painted houses on the west side.

'Impressive,' I said.

'Very nice,' Dawn agreed.

'Let's go and see if we can find Brother Julius,' I said.

The main entrance to the tabernacle was guarded by a heavy-looking number in a grey suit with a portable phone hooked on his belt.

'May I help you?' he asked in an American accent as we climbed the three steps to the front door.

'Brother Julius,' I said.

'Yes?'

'I'd like to see him.'

'Do you have an appointment?'

'Sadly no. We came on the off-chance.'

'Then it's impossible at this time,' said the heavy. 'His schedule prohibits it.'

He pronounced it 'skeddule'.

'I'm sure he could find us a moment in his busy day.'

'I'm sorry. If you care to leave your names…'

'Mr and Mrs Sharman. I wonder if you'd mind letting him know we're here.'

'Mr Sharman, I'm sorry, but Brother Julius has appointments the whole day.'

'You don't understand,' I said. 'This is urgent.' I'll always remember once being told that I had an inflated idea of my own importance. Which I freely admit I do. And of course the whole deal had already been around for twenty years or so. Which made it anything but urgent really. But the geezer got right up my nose, with his suit and his military haircut and his portable dog.

I reached over and tapped it. 'Now what I want you to do is get on that, or go yourself, and tell Brother Julius that Nick Sharman is here. And he wants to talk to him about Jay Harrison. Get that – J-A-Y-H-A-double R-I-S-O-N. Jay Harrison. If you don't, I'll be forced to get the police to talk to him, and I'm sure he wouldn't want a squad car parked outside his nice church all afternoon, would he?'

It was a bluff of course, but the heavy wasn't to know that.

The heavy looked me up and down and nodded, went into the doorway, drew the phone like a pistol, tapped out seven numbers and spoke to someone in a whisper so that Dawn and I couldn't hear. He paused, made an affirmative noise, said something else and came back looking like he'd lost a fiver and found a threepenny bit.

'He'll see you now,' he said grudgingly. 'I'm to take you in.'

'Lead on, Macduff,' I said.

He went through the big, glass front door into the air conditioned hush of a large foyer decorated in muted pastels, with huge vases of cut flowers everywhere and a painting in lurid reds, blues and gold of the Virgin Mary and little baby Jesus on the wall.

'It'll never get into the Royal Academy,' I said to Dawn, and she took my hand and squeezed it.

The heavy led us along a series of corridors until we came to a plain wooden door. He knocked and we entered. Inside was a wood-panelled office. Tastefully furnished, with a huge desk in front of the single window. Brother Julius sat behind the desk still dressed in his white suit, but this time with a pale blue button-down shirt and a dark tie. Next to the desk stood a huge geezer in a sweatsuit. He was young with long blond hair cut into a pudding basin, and looked something like Brian Jones. Before he died.

'Mr and Mrs Sharman,' said the heavy.

'Thank you, Brother Thomas,' said Brother Julius who rose to greet us. The heavy backed out of the room, closing the door gently behind him. Brother Julius shook Dawn's hand first, then mine. His grip was firm, smooth and dry, just like I'd imagined a TV evangelist's would be.

'Welcome, Mr and Mrs Sharman,' he said. 'My name is Brother Julius. This is my associate Brother Anthony.' Brother Anthony made no attempt to shake hands. 'I hope you don't mind him being present during our meeting.'

I shook my head.

'Please do sit down.' And Brother Julius indicated two comfortable-looking armchairs, one each side of the desk.

Dawn sat on one, smoothing her skirt down over her thighs. I took the other.

'You mentioned Jay Harrison,' said Brother Julius.

'I did.'

'Why would you think that that name would mean anything to me?'

'It obviously did.'

'Why?'

'Because it got us in here, and Brother Thomas was adamant that you had appointments all day.'

'He's been told to always say that. I get a lot of callers. My flock is extensive, and I just don't have time to see them all. But you haven't answered my question. Why did you think the name Jay Harrison would mean anything to me? Apart, of course, from the fact he was a singer who died. I take it that is the Jay Harrison that you refer to.'

'You take it right.'

'I remember him. But I still don't understand why you mentioned his name. What possible connection could there be between us?'

'You knew him,' I said.

'Did I?'

'Yes.'

'What makes you think that?'

'A little bird told me.'

Brother Julius looked puzzled. It was a perfect performance. Once again, exactly what I'd expect from a TV evangelist. 'I don't think so. And I'm sure I'd remember. Jay Harrison was very famous as I recall. I'm afraid your little bird was singing flat.'

I liked the way he said that. A real crim's way of putting it. Our Brother here was certainly not all he pretended to be. 'You recall perfectly,' I said. 'It's a shame you can't recall knowing him.'

'When was this?'

'Early seventy-two. Just before he died.'

'I met so many people in those days. Before I received the calling.'

He was beginning to get on my nerves. 'I'm sure you must have. Doing what you did would bring you into contact with vast amounts of people.'

'Doing what I did? And what exactly was that?'

'Don't you remember that either? Your memory is certainly far from perfect.'

'You tell me.' The smooth exterior was beginning to slip, just a little.

'Dealing drugs.'

The room was so quiet, I imagined I could hear my watch ticking.

'I beg your pardon,' said Brother Julius.

'You heard. Flogging opium to the masses. Almost exactly what you're doing now with all this.' I gestured round the room, taking in the office, the church, the whole nine yards.

'And who says I was dealing drugs?'

'Someone I met who knew you at the time.'

'The same little bird as before?'

I nodded.

'Name?'

'I don't think so. I protect my sources.'

'And I protect myself, Mr Sharman. I have taken the precaution of recording this interview, and I have Brother Anthony here as my witness. You have slandered me, and if you continue to do so you will hear from my legal representatives.'

I held up one hand. It was perfectly steady, which was a miracle considering the way I felt. 'Look at me shake,' I said.

'You obviously think you are a very amusing man, Mr Sharman,' said Brother Julius. 'An opinion I do not share.'

'I'm crushed,' I said. 'How's Billy?'

The room went very silent again. 'Who?' said Brother Julius.

'Billy Sayer. Your old chum.'

'Once again the name means nothing to me.'

'Jesus, Bro. You want to get one of those memory books. Except you'd probably forget where you put it. Jay Harrison, Billy Sayer. Old mates one and all, and you can't remember them. It's a shame.'

'I won't continue with this,' said Brother Julius.

'There's a rumour going round that Jay Harrison isn't dead,' I said. 'Any opinions on that one?'

He didn't answer, but instead said, 'Who *are* you?'

'I thought you'd never ask. I'm a private detective looking into Jay Harrison's *alleged* death.' I emphasized the word 'alleged'. 'I thought you might be able to help.'

'I've told you I know nothing of the man. This interview is terminated.'

'I wonder if the police would take that for an answer.'

'You're bluffing.'

Of course I was. Just like I had been when I'd mentioned them to Brother Thomas. But it was all extra seasoning for the pot.

I shrugged.

'I'd like you to leave now,' said Brother Julius.

'I'm not surprised that you're worried,' I said, ignoring his request. 'How much does this place take every week? How much do the faithful donate? It must add up. All the little bits of dough. How much? Go on, tell me. Fifty grand? A hundred? More? It's a nice little racket, Jules. I don't blame you wanting to protect it.'

Brother Julius stood up. He made quite an imposing figure I must admit. 'Mr and Mrs Sharman,' he said icily. 'I am a man of God, and I will not have God mocked in his own house. Brother Anthony here is a fifth dan, black belt in tae kwon do. He is not a violent man, but if I ask him he will put you out of the building. The choice is yours. Either go in peace or be removed.'

I looked at Brother Anthony, who hadn't moved in the whole time we'd been in the room. He looked capable of doing what Brother Julius said without mussing a perfectly placed hair on his head.

'Very well,' I said. 'We'll go. But we'll be back, don't worry about that.'

And we left. Brother Anthony showed us back to the main door. He didn't say a word as we went.

As we walked back to the car, Dawn said, 'Why didn't you show him the photograph?'

'Because you often learn more by letting people lie, than letting them tell the truth.'

'So what did you learn?'

'That he *was* lying about not knowing Harrison. That he's obviously bent. That the whole deal back there is crooked. That Brother Julius is no more a man of God than I am. *And* I've still got the photo to hit him with when we're good and ready.'

'What do we do now?'

'Now we get the car and park it up opposite the church and sit in it. Let's see what he does.'

I rescued the motor off the meter, drove up to Pembridge Square and stopped it on the yellow line opposite the front door where Brother Thomas was still standing. He gave us a long screw and I gave him a cheerful wave.

And that's where we stayed. There was a boozer on the corner which was handy for refreshment breaks, and to use their toilets. And at three I went and found a burger joint and bought lunch. When I left Dawn alone in the car I made her sit behind the wheel and lock all the doors. I didn't trust Brother Thomas as far as I could throw him. Brother Julius never showed his face, but as we were only watching the front it was conceivable that he toddled in and out of the back as and when he pleased.

At about five a police squad car showed up. The two cops inside got out, put on their hats and wandered over. I was in the driver's seat and rolled down the window.

'Good afternoon, sir,' said the older policeman. But even he only looked about nineteen, with a sad attempt at a moustache under his nose and the remains of his acne still on his cheeks.

'Good afternoon,' I said back.

'You know you shouldn't park on a yellow line.'

'I'm not exactly parked, officer,' I said. 'I'm just stationary.'

That didn't go down particularly well.

'According to our information you've been stationary here for about five hours.'

'But ready to move at a moment's notice if we're causing an obstruction, just like good citizens.' I gave him a big beamer when I said that, which wasn't reciprocated.

'We've had complaints,' said the younger copper, a real bruiser, with a broken nose, who looked like he should play for the Met's rugger first fifteen.

'What kind of complaints?'

'Complaints of harassment.'

'We're just sitting here.'

'Would you like to get out of the car, sir?' asked the older cop.

'Not particularly.'

'Just do it.'

So I did.

The Old Bill gave the motor the once over. They called the station with the index of the car for a PNC check, and once satisfied, checked the tax, the tyres, the exhaust and that the lights, indicators and horn worked. Then they gave me the once over too. I had my licence, the car's MOT, and insurance with me, and when they saw Dawn's name on the certificate, they asked for her licence too. The only thing they didn't do was breathalyse me. It would have been a waste of time. For once I'd only drunk mineral water in the pub.

'Very well,' said the younger copper when they'd finished. 'Now I'd like you to move the car out of the square.'

'Why?'

'Because I say so.'

'This might also be construed as harassment,' I said.

'There is a complaints procedure,' said the younger copper. 'You should know all about that.'

'Meaning?' I asked.

He grinned. 'Don't piss on my head and tell me it's raining, *Mister* Sharman. We know who you are. Now just get the fuck out of here and don't let us see you parked around the square again.'

I thought about arguing, but didn't bother. Dawn and I were just wasting time sitting outside the church anyway. So I shrugged, put the car's papers away, got in and drove off. The squad car followed us back to Notting Hill, then peeled off with its blue light flashing on some other mission.

'Cheeky bastards,' said Dawn. 'They had no right to do that.'

'They're the law,' I said. 'And it's handy to know that Brother Julius has friends in high places. He must buy a job lot of tickets for the policeman's ball.'

'What now?' asked Dawn.

'What do you reckon?'

'Let's go and see Miss Simmons again. Hyde Park Mansions isn't far. I want to see if her intercom's been fixed.'

20

I parked the Chevy in the residents'-only parking space in front of the block, and Dawn and I went to the front door. The concierge was at his station behind his desk, the door was locked and all was right with his world until we rang the bell and he looked up and saw Dawn. I swear he went white as he buzzed us in. Dawn walked straight up to him and said, 'Has Miss Simmons's intercom been fixed yet?'

'Yes, ma'am,' he replied politely.

'Very good. See how easy it was? We're going up. Is that all right?'

'Of course. She's in,' he replied.

'Keep an eye on our car,' Dawn said to him. 'It's the big American station wagon parked right outside. We wouldn't want it towed away or clamped, would we?' and she found a handful of change in her bag and gave it to him.

'It'll be fine, ma'am,' said the concierge, and Dawn and I went to the lift which was standing open.

We went up to Miss Simmons's floor and along to her flat. I used the knocker, and after a minute or two the door opened a crack.

'Miss Simmons,' said Dawn. 'Remember us?'

'The detectives,' said Miss Simmons. 'Nick and Dawn, isn't it? How nice of you to remember an old woman. Do come in.'

She led us through to the sitting room and insisted that we stay to tea.

'Can I help?' asked Dawn.

'You can warm the pot while I make some sandwiches. I've got a tin of salmon in the cupboard, and some cucumber.'

'That sounds fine,' said Dawn, and she followed Miss Simmons in the direction of the kitchen, and I sat on the sofa.

They'd been gone for about ten minutes before Dawn returned carrying the big silver tray containing a plate of neatly quartered sandwiches, some cake and biscuits, three cups and saucers and three side plates, which she put on the dining table. Miss Simmons followed with the teapot, which she put next to the tray. She took off the lid and gave the contents a stir with a teaspoon.

'Shall I be mother?' asked Dawn.

'If you don't mind, dear,' said Miss Simmons. 'I don't very often get waited on.'

'You should,' said Dawn. 'By the way, talking of that, did your door buzzer get mended?'

'Yes. Funny you should mention that. A very nice young man came only two days after you were here and fixed it.'

'I hope you asked for his credentials before you let him in,' said Dawn. 'There's some very funny people about these days.'

'Of course I did. In fact the porter came up and told me he was coming. I must say that it's rare to see him get off his backside.'

Dawn grinned to herself. 'And it's all right now?' she asked.

'Yes. The porter tested it for me himself.'

'Good.'

By then Dawn had filled the three cups with a strong, hot brew of tea and passed one to Miss Simmons and one to me. The old lady asked us if we wanted sandwiches. We both did and she gave us the side plates and passed the large plate of food round. I took half a dozen. I was suddenly hungry, and they were only small.

'I'm glad to see you've got a good appetite,' said Miss Simmons. 'I'll make you some more if you want.'

'He's just greedy,' said Dawn, giving me the kind of dirty look my mum used to give me if I hogged the grub at a birthday party when I was a kid.

'These are fine,' I choked round a mouthful of bread, butter, tinned salmon and cucumber. 'Just fine.'

Miss Simmons asked if we'd had any luck with the case. I told her we had. At least partly thanks to her. After all, if she hadn't kept Kim Major's belongings safe for all those years we would never have known about Julius Rose.

'It's so exciting,' she said when I'd finished.

'But still not conclusive,' I observed.

'And that cemetery,' she said. 'It sounds terribly spooky.'

'It was,' said Dawn.

After we'd finished the tea, sandwiches, biscuits and cake, Dawn and I made our farewells and left. I don't think Miss Simmons wanted us to go. Dawn sussed that out too. 'Can we come again?' she asked.

'Any time at all, dear,' said the old lady. 'I'd love to hear what happens in the end.'

'You will, I promise,' said Dawn, and kissed her on the cheek. I did the same and Miss Simmons saw us to the door and we went back downstairs.

'Your car's fine,' said the concierge when we exited from the lift.

'I didn't expect anything else,' said Dawn, as we walked across the foyer and out of the main doors.

21

We drove home, lay about the flat all evening, had a pizza delivered for dinner, and went to bed to eat it in front of the late film.

The next morning we stayed in the sack until eleven doing what ladies and gentlemen do together. I couldn't think of a finer way of earning a grand a day than being screwed by Dawn twice in quick succession, even if I had to make the breakfast after.

I'd just soaked up the last of my egg yolk and tinned tomato juice with the remains of a slice of toast when the telephone rang.

It was Chris Kennedy-Sloane again. 'Well?' he said.

'Not bad,' I replied, giving Dawn a wink as she chewed on her last mouthful of grilled bacon. 'How's yourself?'

'That's not what I meant, and you know it,' said Kennedy-Sloane tetchily. He'd probably been up since seven dealing with matters in the financial world, and I guessed his ulcers were biting.

'Kaolin and morphine,' I said. 'Does them the world of good.'

'I don't know what you're talking about, as usual. What I want to know is, have you got any news for me?'

I could have made some even more facetious remark in reply, but I could tell his patience was wearing thin. 'What about?' I asked sweetly.

'The case of course. Jay Harrison. You do remember, don't you?'

'Of course I do.'

'I've had Lamar Quinn on the phone again. He's getting impatient. He wants some results.'

'I'm not a bloody magician. I can't conjure results out of thin air.'

'You said you might have something today.'

'I might.'

'Like what?'

'I don't like giving out information in bits and pieces. I'd rather wait until I'm sure of all my facts.'

'He's threatening not to pay you any more.'

'I've got your cheque.'

'Have you paid it in yet?'

I hesitated. The damn thing was still on the top of the TV set. 'Might've,' I said.

I could almost see him shaking his head. 'I can still stop it even if you have, which I know you haven't. And I will unless you tell me how far you've progressed.'

I knew he wouldn't. We went too far back for that, especially as part of the cheque was what he owed me personally, but if he was making even empty threats, then he was obviously getting heavy stick from his principal in the matter, and it was time to stop kidding around. 'OK, Chris,' I said, 'I give in.' And I told him.

I told him how helpful the Tafflers had been. I gave him the full SP on the photographs I'd found in the case that Miss Simmons had kept in her attic. And finally I told him about the Tabernacle of the Sepulchre of the Virgin Mary and Little Baby Jesus, and Brother Julius aka Julius Rose, ex-dope dealer to the stars.

'Doesn't sound like much,' he said sniffily when I'd finished. 'Not for a thousand quid a day.'

'It was your fucking idea to charge that much. What do you want? Commission?' I said.

There was silence at the other end of the line. 'OK, Chris,' I said, 'don't answer that.'

'So what are you going to do now?' he asked.

I didn't have a clue really. Pour myself another cup of coffee and chill out with the daily paper seemed favourite, but somehow I didn't think that was the answer he was looking for. 'I'm getting right on the case,' I said. 'Trust me.'

He sighed. 'Looks like I've got no choice,' he said, and hung up in my ear with rather more force than was really necessary.

'Everything all right?' asked Dawn.

'Just perfect,' I said. 'That fucking septic Quinn wants to stop our wedge.'

'Cheeky sod,' she said. 'It would serve him right if we went straight back to bed and had another fuck.'

Afterwards we showered and got dressed. I put on Levi's, a checked cowboy-style shirt and dark blue leather bumper boots, and pulled on my battered old Schott. Dawn wore a leather biker's jacket, with enough zips and studs to give a metal detector terminal indigestion, over a plain white T-shirt, faded Lee Riders and pink Converse All Star, Chuck Taylor, high-top canvas baseball boots. I think the rock and roll was going to our heads.

Around four we went down to my office to check the mail and any messages on the answer machine. Now don't get me wrong. If there'd been something worthwhile to do we would have done it. But there wasn't as far as I could see. We had our noses up a cold trail, and there was nothing to do but wait and see if anyone came to us.

Which is exactly what they did.

I went across to the pub and got four bottles of cold lager, and Dawn and I sat, me behind my desk, she in one of the client's chairs, and drank them.

Happy families.

It was a warm afternoon, and I left the front door open so that we could check out the ragga that the cabbies next door were listening to on their radios.

The sun was over the pub roof and shining straight through the window in front of us, and I was checking out my wife's thighs the way that newly married men are supposed to do, when a shadow fell across the floor, and my desk, and me. I squinted up, and saw a massive figure, made even bigger by the angle of the sun and my sitting down, standing in the doorway. I looked at Dawn again and she looked at me. That time I ignored her thighs.

'Brother Anthony?' I said. And it was. Last seen at the Tabernacle of the Sepulchre of the Virgin Mary and Little Baby Jesus. They were really going to have to do something about that name. He stepped through the door and stood on the carpet in front of my desk. He was still huge, but not so big as he'd seemed to be standing in the doorway. Not manageable mind, but not as daunting as he had been.

'What can I do for you?' I said.

'Brother Julius sent me, sir. He doesn't want you to bother him any more.' It was the first time I'd heard him speak, and he had a Texas drawl. Very big on Americans was our Brother Julius.

'It's my job, Brother Anthony. Bothering people. That's how I find out what's true and what's not.' That was the idea at least. Of course, like many ideas of mine, it didn't always work out.

'Brother Julius doesn't care about your job, sir. He cares about the church, and he cares about the people who worship at the church.'

'The people who donate their money to the church, you mean,' I said.

Brother Anthony didn't bother justifying that one with an answer.

'Doesn't Brother Julius care about the truth?' I asked.

Brother Anthony shrugged this time.

'I can't stop. Sorry,' I said.

'Then I'll have to stop you, sir.'

He was bloody polite, I'll give him that.

'How?' I asked.

He shrugged. He knew that I knew how he'd stop me.

Interesting. As Brother Julius had insisted on telling me, Brother Anthony was a fifth dan, black belt in tae kwon do, which I knew was some kind of Korean karate. Now in stories and films, if our dauntless hero comes across some martial arts expert, one of two things happens. Either, our hero is even better at martial arts than the person he meets, or, if he's not, he just hauls some huge gun from where he's got it hidden and blows the martial artist away. Always good for a few yuks down at the local Odeon, that.

Unfortunately the time I tried to learn jujitsu I felt such a fool wandering around in my jammies and bowing to anything that moved that I only went once.

And that particular afternoon I wasn't carrying.

This could turn out to be extremely embarrassing. And painful, I thought.

I stood up and moved to the side of the desk. The side closest to Dawn. I was thinking that maybe if I hid behind her skirts everything would be copacetic. From the look in Brother Anthony's eyes as he followed me with them, I was wrong.

'Brother Anthony,' I said. 'I know that you're a bit handy. I understand that, and I admire you.'

Flattery now.

He nodded his agreement.

'So listen. I'm not a rucker. Not any more. If I took you on I'd be fighting well out of my weight. How old are you anyway?'

'Twenty-five, sir.'

'See. I'm nearly fifteen years older than you, and you outweigh and outreach me. Besides, I've not been too well. And, you know... Well you don't know, so I'll tell you. I've been shot, stabbed and beaten up several times in my life. It wouldn't be right. You'd hate yourself if you hurt me. I mean, the whole point of the discipline that you practise... the art, is that you don't pick on the defenceless. Am I right?'

'That's correct, sir.'

'So if I won't fight back, it kind of negates the whole point of it. The almost religious intensity of the experience. And I know that you're a religious boy. The honour. The chivalry. Get what I mean?' I was on a roll by then and I could see that Dawn for one was well impressed. I wondered how Brother Anthony was reacting. 'And besides,' I said. 'I've only been married for a little while to this fine woman here.' I gestured at Dawn. 'Just think how she'd feel to see me humiliated in front of her. It could ruin our relationship.'

With that I thought I'd covered every base.

'But, sir,' he said. 'Brother Julius sent me to stop you asking any more questions.'

'And, Anthony,' – I dropped the 'Brother' bit, I just couldn't carry on with it – 'as far as I'm concerned, you've done it without one blow being struck.'

He looked puzzled. 'But Brother Julius said that I should insist.'

'Surely only if I didn't listen.'

'Yes, but...'

'You've done it,' I said again. 'You've convinced me. I've learnt my lesson.'

He looked puzzled again. 'So I can go back and tell Brother Julius that you won't bother us again?'

'Of course you can.'

'But what happens if you're lying?'

Shame on you, I thought. 'Then, Anthony, my old son,' I said, 'you come and find me and beat the shit out of me.'

He reddened. 'I'd rather you didn't use that kind of language, sir.'

'I apologise, Anthony,' I said. 'From the bottom of my heart.'

He thought about what I'd said and came to a conclusion. 'That's good,' he said.

'I knew you'd see it my way.'

'So I'll say goodbye, sir, ma'am,' he said, and shook hands, first with Dawn, and then I moved round the desk and shook his hand too.

'Give my regards to Brother Julius,' I said.

'I will, sir.'

And he turned to leave, and I picked up one of the empty lager bottles that was sitting on the edge of the desk and slammed it down on his head. He heard the sound of the air being displaced as I aimed the blow, and he half turned, and the bottle caught him just above the ear. Another second or two and he would have managed to do some karate move and taken me out there and then. I was lucky.

Brother Anthony hit the carpet in front of my desk like a log and a small cloud of dust rose from the pile. I'd have to get the vacuum cleaner out soon.

Dawn looked up at me. '*Haven't been well?*' she said.

I shrugged.

'*Chivalry?*' she said.

I shrugged again.

'*Honour?*'

'I never said I was Sir Lancelot.'

I knelt down beside Brother Anthony's prone form. The skin above his ear was broken, but not badly, and there was some blood in his yellow barnet. I felt for his pulse. It was strong and regular. 'He'll be OK,' I said.

'You were lucky,' she said, echoing my previous thought. 'Another half a second and he'd've had you.'

'Whole second,' I said. 'Maybe longer. Do try to be a little more exact.'

'What are you going to do with him?' she asked.

'No probs,' I said, and went to the door. Donny, one of the cabbies with whom I was quite pally, was lounging on the bonnet of his Ford Sierra in front of the cab office.

'Donny,' I said. 'Want a fare?'

'Sure,' he said and came off the bonnet and walked up to my door. 'Who?'

'Him,' I said, gesturing to Brother Anthony's body.

'Jesus,' said Donny. 'What's up with him?'

'Too many of those,' I said, pointing at the lager bottles on the desk.

'Where to?'

'Notting Hill. Pembridge Square. A church. He's a God-fearing boy. Just likes the sauce a little too much for his own good.'

'He won't throw up in the car will he?'

'No.'

Donny noticed the blood in Brother Anthony's hair. 'He looks like he needs a hospital more than a church.'

'He'll be fine.'

'I'm glad to hear it. *Doctor*.'

'Twenty quid,' I said.

That clinched it. 'Give me a hand with him, then,' said Donny.

We lifted Brother Anthony up and half carried, half dragged him to Donny's motor and wedged him into the back. I gave Donny a pony in fivers, the address of the church, and Brother Julius as the man to deliver him to. Donny got in behind the steering wheel and drove off in the direction of town, and I went back to the office where Dawn was waiting. 'What now?' she said.

'Now we go off and have something to eat at that Caribbean restaurant near the George Canning, and you drive us back to Pembridge Square where we can have another chat with Brother Julius.'

'Why?'

'Because I got to him yesterday. If I hadn't he would never have sent that stupid lump round to try to shut me up. He over-reacted. There *is* something going on in that bent little church of his. Something to do with Jay Harrison. I was only guessing before, but now I know for certain.'

'But why would Harrison pretend to be dead for all this time, and now suddenly ask for money?'

'The only way to find out is to go back and see Brother Julius.'

'And Brother Anthony,' she said.

'Could be.'

'He won't let you get away with the trick with the lager bottle twice.'

I shrugged.

'He won't,' she said again.

'But this time I'll be packing iron,' I said. Packing iron. What a glorious term. Just like Gary Cooper in *High Noon*.

'Sometimes I don't know why I married you,' Dawn said in exasperation.

'For my brilliant personality,' I said. 'And the raw excitement of my animal magnetism. Not to mention the sex and drugs and rock and roll. And there's plenty of all those in this case. So are we off?'

She sighed, but came along anyway.

She drove me home and I went up into the crawl space in my roof where I had amassed quite an armoury over the last few years. Early that evening, for comfort and convenience I chose a nifty Glock 9mm automatic with a fifteen-shot clip and weighing in at about two pounds fully loaded.

I checked the clip and wrapped the gun in a Sainsbury's plastic bag and put it in a lockable compartment in the back of the wagon. I don't know if Mr Chevrolet planned it that way, but the Glock fitted perfectly, and didn't rattle a bit as we drove over Tulse Hill.

'Park right in front, love,' I said as we went. 'And I hope we get the window table. I want to keep an eye on the car. I don't want it stolen. The thought of some idiot, probably stoned half out of his head, driving around in this motor with that pistol in his possession is not a pleasant one.'

'You later, you mean,' said Dawn tartly.

I didn't bother to answer. The woman already knew me too well.

We did get a parking space right outside the restaurant and the table by the window. I ordered a Yellow Bird from the waitress as soon as we sat down. It's a cocktail made from five kinds of rum, banana liqueur, coconut liqueur and fruit juice. I believe the islanders use it to get well stoned when the marijuana crop gets blown away by a hurricane. And by Christ it works. After a couple of those fuckers it's hard to tell which way is up.

For dinner we had shark soup, chicken gumbo, ackee, rice, peas and sweet potatoes. Delicious. After all that and three Yellow Birds, by the time we left, I felt no pain.

Dawn drove us up to Notting Hill and parked the Chevy round the corner from Brother Julius's money machine. We arrived at about eight. The street was pretty much deserted and I got the gun from its hiding place, discarded the plastic bag and stuck the pistol in the waistband of my jeans at the back, under the lightweight silk Hugo

Boss double-breasted jacket I was wearing. I always like to be smart when I'm going to church.

I let off the safety catch but didn't rack a bullet into the chamber. Doing that is a sure way to shoot yourself in the arse if you carry a gun like that.

We walked round to the front arm in arm. Just a couple of the faithful going to worship. We went straight to the front door. It was locked and Brother Thomas was nowhere to be seen. I rang the bell, and after a minute or so it was answered by an acolyte I hadn't seen before dressed in a long white robe.

'I want to see Brother Julius,' I said.

'We're in the midst of recording next week's services,' said the robed figure. 'He's in private meditation now.'

Probably counting his cash, I thought. 'Tell him that Nick Sharman wants to see him.'

'I'm sorry,' said the man. 'It's impossible at this time. The strain is enormous. We have to record two more hours tonight. He cannot be disturbed.'

'It's very important,' I said. 'A matter of life or death.'

'What is it concerning?'

'The future of the Tabernacle,' I said sincerely.

The acolyte hesitated, then said, 'Very well. Come inside.' And he allowed us to stand in the foyer while he went through the door that Brother Thomas had taken us through the previous day.

Ten minutes passed and I was starting to get impatient. I wondered what would happen if I got the Glock out and let off a few rounds into the ceiling. I was just curious. That was all.

Before my curiosity could get the better of my common sense, the door opened again and Brother Julius stood in the doorway. He was alone. He was dressed in his usual white three-piece suit, a white shirt, white tie and white shoes. I would have bet my life that his shorts, socks and T-shirt were white too. My life and Dawn's. Perhaps I was about to. 'Two choc-ices and a vanilla cornet,' I said.

He wasn't amused at my levity. After all, making money is a very serious business. 'I have a service to conduct,' he said. 'What do you want?'

'A little chat.'

'About?'

'You know very well.'

'I have nothing further to say on that subject. I've told you all this before. You are getting rather tiresome, Mr Sharman.'

'You can talk to me or the police. Take your choice.'

'The police wouldn't be interested. Unless of course you are referring to the unwarranted assault on Brother Anthony that you perpetrated earlier this afternoon. I think they might be very interested in that.'

'You sent him round to threaten me. I dealt with the threat as I saw fit. Reasonable force and all that. *And* you owe me twenty quid for the cab.'

'You tricked him,' said Brother Julius through gritted teeth.

'Then he was easily tricked. You should have sent someone with a little more experience.'

'Next time I will.'

I took a step towards him. That was the sort of old bollocks I was used to, but I'd had it done by experts in the past. Brother Julius was just an amateur as far as I was concerned. A joker. A punter who was beginning to get right up my nose with his piousness. 'Don't try and frighten me, son,' I said. 'You're way out of your league. And even if the Old Bill don't want to know, and I'm not a hundred per cent convinced of that, perhaps Her Majesty's Inland Revenue would. All the money you collect from donations in a year. And a large part of it in cash. A slimebag like you is bound to cream some off the top. You wouldn't be able to resist. How are the books? The people I'm working for have got plenty of money too. And money talks. If I make enough noise, someone is bound to take notice. I don't care. I've got nothing better to do. And I'm being well paid to do it.'

He thought about what I'd said and asked, 'Who exactly *are* you working for?'

I told him. It was no secret.

He hesitated. He obviously knew exactly who Lifetime Records were. 'Very well,' he said. 'Come with me.'

He led us back through the corridors to his office. We met no one as we went. He opened the door, and stood back to let us in. I entered first, Dawn followed. Standing against the wall opposite us was Brother Anthony.

22

He stood looking at the three of us. I noticed that there was a large strip of Elastoplast above his ear, half hidden by the fall of his blond locks. 'Hiya, Tone,' I said. 'How's the head?'

Brother Julius ducked out of the room and closed the door behind him. I heard a lock click. 'Stepped out for some air?' I said. 'It is kind of close in here.'

Brother Anthony didn't bother to answer, he just went into some karate stance. One leg in front of the other, knees bent, his left arm extended from the shoulder, then bent at the elbow across his body, palm flat at chest height, his right arm straight down his side to the elbow, then up to form a T under his left palm. If that wasn't terrifying enough, he began to move his arms around, clenching and unclenching his fists just like Bruce Lee in *Enter The Dragon*. And you remember what happened to Bruce Lee. He exhaled with a hiss and I took the Glock out from under my jacket and stuck it in his face. He looked sort of sad at that, as though I'd disappointed him somehow.

'On the floor, stupid,' I said. 'Face down.'

He did as he was told. I was quite pleased at that. Remember there was no bullet in the chamber, and I had a good idea that he could have offed me before I worked the action.

There was a roll of sticky tape on Brother Julius's desk. 'Dawn,' I said. 'Get that tape. Tie him up.' I knelt down beside Brother Anthony and cocked the pistol. 'No tricks, son,' I said. 'Otherwise

I'll blow a hole in your head that'll make what happened to you this afternoon look like nothing.'

Dawn got the tape and pulled off about two feet of it and wrapped it around his wrists, then another and another until his hands were tightly bound. Then she did his ankles and finally wrapped a triple length around his head covering his mouth. I checked that his breathing was clear and tried the door. It *was* locked. 'Key,' I said.

Of course he couldn't speak which didn't help. I should have waited until we knew we could get out before gagging him, but no one's perfect, as I've mentioned before. I went through his pockets and found three keys on a ring. The second one worked the lock on the office door.

I eased the door open and peered into the corridor. It was empty. Brother Julius had obviously thought that I was no match for Anthony. Just shows how much he knew.

I beckoned for Dawn to follow and we went out. I shut the door behind me, locked it, and using the butt of the pistol as a hammer, broke the key off in the lock. Nifty, or what?

Dawn hadn't said a word the whole time. I looked at her and she was grey and sweaty, and I held her tightly for a second, not speaking, just sending get-well messages to her with the embrace.

'I thought he was going to kill you,' she gasped. 'Or that you were going to kill him.'

'No,' I replied. 'He's just a big idiot. He hasn't got a clue what's going on. There's other fish to fry here. Are you going to be OK?'

She nodded.

'Let's go and find the shark then,' I said.

We walked down the corridors of the church, which were completely deserted, up some stairs and along more empty halls, until I heard something. I stopped, and Dawn bumped into my back. 'What?' she said.

'Hear that?' I asked.

She cocked her head. 'Someone singing,' she said.

'The song,' I said. 'Don't you recognize it?'

She shook her head.

'It's "Just Do It",' I said. 'Dog Soldier, number one, 1968. I bought it. I loved it. And it's him singing. Jay Harrison. I swear.'

She looked at me as if I was mad. 'It's a record,' she said. 'Someone's got the radio on.'

'No. There's no music. It's Harrison. It must be.'

She looked at me as if I was mad again, but I ignored the look.

'Come on,' I said. 'Let's go see.'

We followed the sound along the corridor, and the closer we got to the source, and the louder it became, the more I was convinced that it was Jay Harrison singing. I'd recognize that distinctive voice anywhere. It had been one of the soundtracks of my adolescence, and it brought it all flooding back. The colourful clothes, the first taste of illegal drugs, the fumbling with skinny girls in mini-dresses at all-night parties where Dog Soldier records were compulsory. The whole bit.

Dawn and I turned a corner and the voice was coming from behind a closed door in front of us.

I touched the forefinger of the hand not holding the Glock to my lips and tried the handle. It turned, and I pushed the door open and looked inside.

The room was small and light. The walls were white and the only furniture was a single camp bed covered with a thin blanket. Facing the window opposite the door, back towards us, was a massive figure. He was easily as big as Brother Anthony, dressed in something resembling army fatigues. His hair was long, halfway down his back, but the crown of his head was totally bald, like a monk would wear it. He was singing the chorus to 'Just Do It' and was totally oblivious to our entrance.

I tapped the barrel of the gun on the door and the figure stopped singing and turned to face me.

His face was like the rest of him. Gross. His cheeks and neck which bulged out over the collar of his shirt were smoothly shaven, and his forehead was covered with the bangs of his grey-brown hair. But somewhere behind the fat was the echo of the skinny young man I'd worshipped, like millions of others, when I was just a skinny boy myself.

'Jay?' I said. 'Jay Harrison?'

He looked at me, and his blue eyes were the ones that had looked out at me from a dozen album covers, a hundred posters and a thousand photographs.

'It is you, isn't it?' I asked.

'My name is Brother Simon.' His voice was soft, with the faint trace of an American accent in it.

I shook my head. 'No,' I said. 'You're Jay Harrison. I'd know you anywhere.'

He looked down at the pistol I was holding.

'Why do you bring a gun into the house of the Lord?' he asked.

'Because the house of the Lord is like any other house. Sometimes it needs cleaning.'

He made to make a step towards us and I shook my head. 'Don't do it, Jay,' I said. 'We mean you no harm.'

'What are you doing here?'

'Looking for you. I'm a detective. My name is Nick Sharman. This is my wife, Dawn. She works with me. Lifetime Records hired us after they got your letter.'

He nodded, and the fat on his face quivered. 'That was a mistake,' he said. 'I thought I was helping.'

'Helping who?'

'The Lord. Brother Julius. The church.'

'How?'

'By bringing in much-needed funds for the Brother.'

'Doesn't he get enough?' I asked.

'There is never enough for our work.'

I snorted.

'You mock us?' said Jay Harrison.

'Not you. But this place. I smell a rat here, and I believe his name is Julius Rose.'

'How did you find me?'

'It's a long story. I'll tell you about it sometime. But tell me something first. Why did you pretend to be dead?'

He pulled a face. 'That too is a long story,' he said. 'I was taking the devil's path. Then something happened, and I found a way of escape.'

'What was it?' I asked.

'Don't answer that,' said a voice from behind us. I turned and Brother Julius was standing in the doorway.

'Hello, doll,' I said. 'You're just in time.'

23

All four of us stood and looked at each other like characters in a play. I was still holding the Glock so I reckoned that I was the juvenile lead.

'Come on in, Jules,' I said. 'Are you alone?'

He gave me the snake eye, said nothing, but did as he was told.

'Shut the door, doll,' I said, and once again he obeyed. 'Sit on the bed. We've got a lot to talk about.'

He did that too.

'You as well,' I said to Jay Harrison. 'Nothing personal, but you're a big boy and this gun is getting heavy.'

Jay Harrison joined Julius on the bed, and I relaxed and took out my cigarettes and leaned against the door jamb. 'Don't mind, do you?' I asked.

Neither of them objected, but then they were hardly going to. I was heavily armed and the chance of a little passively acquired lung cancer was the least of their worries.

'Jay,' I said. 'Tell me what happened.'

'When?'

'April seventh, 1972. The morning you died. Or didn't, as it turned out.'

He looked at Julius, then back at me, put his head in his hands and started to cry.

He looked like a big, fat baby sitting there rocking back and forth and sobbing fit to bust. Dawn walked over to the bed and sat on the far side of Jay and put her arms as far round his huge body as they'd go. 'Don't cry,' she said. 'You'll be all right. No one's going to hurt you.'

It was obviously just what the big man wanted, and he leaned into Dawn's body until I was afraid he was going to crush her against the wall.

After a minute or two he pulled himself together and sat up straight, but Dawn stayed with him and held one of his big hands in both of hers.

He looked up into my eyes again and began his story.

'I was a very bad man in those days,' he said. 'I can't remember a lot of it, but I think I was trying to kill myself long before I joined the band. And when we started making huge amounts of money it got even easier. Perhaps I wanted to die so badly that what happened was inevitable. I died by proxy. But it was what I wanted to happen in reality.

'It all started around the spring of sixty-six. I was doing a film course at Berkeley. But what I wanted to be was a poet. Rimbaud was my hero. I wanted to be just like him, and I tried my best. That was when I met Joey Loder. He was on the same course as me. He played piano in bar bands to earn money to pay for his classes. My family had money. They were rich. I had no problems with anything like that. All I had to do was to attend a few lectures during the day and hang out at nights. I was writing a lot of poetry, like I said. I showed some of it to Joey and he said he'd set it to music. He was a good songwriter. Some of the stuff I was writing was pretty far out. All about death and destruction. But Joey made me write some simple lyrics, just so that publishers would listen. We sold some stuff too. Then Joey met Jake who played guitar, and who had a friend who was a drummer. I was renting a cottage on the beach and we jammed there for a couple of months, and it sounded good. We made a tape, came up with the name Dog Soldier and Columbia gave us some studio time. I was drinking a lot and taking acid, and I wanted to record all the weird stuff. Columbia hated it, but we got a gig at a club called The London Fog. They wanted us to play covers of Beatles and Stones hits. We did it too, but we always dropped in a few of our songs. One night a guy from Lifetime came in and heard us. He liked what we did, and with a bit of a fight got us on to the label. We made the first album. They cut down "Just Do It" from seven minutes to two and a half, and released it as a single. The next thing we knew, we'd knocked The Byrds off the top of the hot one hundred.' Jay Harrison smiled at the memory. 'Boy, but they were mad. And Columbia too. The Byrds recorded for them, and they'd thrown us out of the studio for partying too hard.' Suddenly he remembered where he was and sobered up. 'And I don't blame them. We didn't care what we did. Then the bandwagon started rolling, and things went from bad to worse. You know about Dog Soldier?' he asked me.

I nodded, and lit another cigarette. 'I had all your records,' I said.

'You must have been pretty young.'

'I was.'

'Anyway, we sold a lot of records, went on TV, toured for nearly five years non-stop. It was like living in the eye of a hurricane. Crazy. We were always in trouble. Getting busted for trashing hotels and wrecking hire cars, and eventually it all had to end one way or another. The albums were getting worse. No one cared about the songs any more. All we cared about was money, drugs, sex and booze. We had such a bad reputation in the States that I decided to get out for a while. I was on bail... You know about that too?'

I nodded.

'So I decided to come over here for a visit. I brought Kim with me. You guys in England really loved the band. More than in the States by then, I guess. But then you Brits were well known for being pretty bad people yourselves. I was taking a lot of heroin. Drinking. Taking pills. Everything. And Kim was in an even worse state than me, if anything.'

'And all the goodies supplied by little buddy here.' I pointed the business end of the Glock in Brother Julius's direction.

Harrison nodded. 'That was the way it was then,' he said simply. 'They were strange days.'

I silently agreed with him. But then most of my life had consisted of strange days, and today was no exception.

'So what happened that night?' I asked.

'Don't tell him,' said Brother Julius.

I laughed out loud. 'You're in no position to tell anyone what to do,' I said. 'You're all alone, Jules. Brother Anthony is out of the game, no one else is around and Jay here wants to confess. It's good for the soul, so they tell me.'

'You always mock, don't you?' said Brother Julius.

'No,' I replied. 'I know the truth of that. Jay. Tell me. You'll feel better, I promise.'

Jay Harrison licked his lips. 'That night I called up Julius to score. Kim and I were strung out on smack, and we didn't have as much as a nickel bag in the apartment. Julius came round with Billy Sayer about midnight. He brought enough for Kim and me, and himself too. More than enough as it turned out.'

'You were using too, huh, Jules?' I said.

He didn't reply, and Jay Harrison continued. 'Billy was a virgin,' he said. 'He told us he was always scared of H. We didn't care. All the more for us. But Kim kept on at him. She was high and there was plenty. She wanted him to join us. Junkies are like that. She wouldn't leave him alone, and eventually he agreed to let her shoot him up. She made up a syringe and prepped him. She was jealous of all his fat veins. Most of hers had collapsed by then.' He disengaged his hand from Dawn's and rolled up one sleeve. His arms were a battleground of old needle scars. Even after all those years it was easy to see what a mess Jay Harrison had made of his own body in his youth.

He rolled his sleeve down again, took Dawn's hands in his, and went on with his tale. 'She was stupid. She'd made up a load enough for one of *us*. We were used to the stuff. Had a high tolerance level. Billy'd never used before. He turned blue. He went straight into a coma and never came out of it again.'

'You called an ambulance,' I said.

'Sure. There was no phone in the apartment. We were spending all our money on drugs, and the bills were huge. Kim used to talk to the States for hours at a time. We got cut off. One night when I was high I threw the thing out of the window and was never reconnected. If we needed to make international calls we'd go to someone's office. For local calls there was a pay phone just outside the door of the apartment block. I liked not being on the phone. No one could bother us. It drove Kim crazy. I'm sure she'd been born with a phone in her hand. But I was the boss, and what I said went.'

'So you called from a box?' I said.

Harrison nodded.

'One fourteen in the morning,' I said.

'How do you know that?'

'We looked into it.'

'I waited for a minute, then went back to the flat. I guessed I'd hear the siren and go back and meet them, or send Julius down. I was freaked out. When I got back to the flat Kim was freaked out even more than me. Billy was dead by then. His heart just gave out. She gave him the hit, she was convinced she'd be arrested for murder.'

'Manslaughter more like,' I said.

'Whatever. Anyway, she'd cleaned her fingerprints off the syringe and broken it up. All three of us were half crazy. When we heard the ambulance outside she wouldn't let me go downstairs again.'

'And they went away.'

He nodded.

'Then Kim came up with a plan. We'd talked about what would happen if I died. Jim Morrison, Janis Joplin and Hendrix were all dead by then. They were all as messed up as me, and we used to joke that they were better off dead than alive. She said that I could pretend to be dead. Take a rest. Get the cops back home, and all the people we owed money to, off our backs. And there was some insurance. About a hundred and fifty grand, American, with Kim as the benefactor. Julius told me that he had a place down in the country that I could stay at. An old house he'd bought, miles from anywhere.

'I told them they were crazy. But Kim said that we had a body that needed disposing of, and a pet doctor who let us have paper for drugs when we needed them. He should have been around that day, but he'd been called away to some patient or other out of town. If he'd been there when we needed him, Julius and Billy would never have come around that night. Kim went down to the phone and called him up. He was in bed, but got up and came straight over. In exchange for the promise of ten thousand pounds when the insurance came through, he made out a death certificate in my name. He insisted that we call an ambulance. It was risky, but we had to have official confirmation. Kim made the call.'

'At three oh five,' I said.

He shrugged. 'The doc said he'd just arrived. That Kim had called him too. He confirmed my death, and sent the ambulance crew away. He knew the local undertakers, and called them in. He promised them five thousand pounds if they were discreet. They accepted. Who wouldn't? They screwed down the lid on the box and took it away.'

'It was a crazy scheme,' I said.

But what did I expect? Logic and sense from a pop star junkie at the end of his tether, his crazy girlfriend and some dope-dealing future Jesus freak.

'Do you think I don't know that now?' said Harrison.

'And you hid out in the country?'

'That's right. At the house that became the first headquarters for the Tabernacle.'

'From little acorns…' I said.

The room fell silent. The air was thick and warm, and the rays of the setting sun coming through the smeary window panes caught motes of dust and held them floating in its embrace like tiny sea creatures in a bright ocean.

'One thing I want to know,' I said. 'After all that, after you've got a dead body that you need to dispose of permanently, why didn't you have him cremated?'

'My father wouldn't let Kim do it. He was a religious man himself. He had virtually disowned me, but he insisted that I was buried. Cremation was against his beliefs. He was my next of kin, so what he said went. He didn't want my body back in the family vault at home. He considered my life and the way I was supposed to have died to be a sin. But I was still his son. Kim and I used to go to Highgate to visit Karl Marx's tomb. My father agreed to buy a plot there and pay for the tomb and its upkeep in perpetuity. He didn't come to the funeral. None of my family did. And he never visited my grave as far as I know. Nor did my mother. They've both been dead for a long time now…' I saw the sadness in his face and he hesitated. 'It suited us at the time. We didn't want anyone from back home asking questions about what happened that night.'

'So Billy Sayer is still buried there,' I said. Not a question. Just a confirmation.

Jay Harrison nodded. 'To my eternal shame, he is.'

'But you visit the grave, don't you, Jay?' I asked.

He hesitated again. 'You know a lot about me.'

'That's my job.'

'Yes,' he went on. 'I go there sometimes at night. I find it peaceful. It takes me back to before all this happened. But how did you know?'

'I met someone who saw you, and described you. He goes there at night too, and almost every day as far as I can gather. There's a few of them hang out round your tomb. One in particular finds the place peaceful, just like you do. He lives rough in the cemetery. He treats your grave like a shrine. Or rather Billy Sayer's grave. I wonder how he'll feel when he finds out he's been wasting his time.'

Harrison didn't answer.

'So why decide to write to Lifetime Records now?' I asked. 'After all this time.'

'Like I said. The Tabernacle needs the money.'

'Is that the only reason?'

Harrison thought for a moment. 'I wanted to come back to life. I've been dead for twenty years. I wanted to be Jay Harrison again.'

'And what did you have to say about all this?' I asked Brother Julius.

'I thought it was unwise. But if Jay insisted I wouldn't stand in his way.'

'But you denied he was here. Denied even knowing him.'

'I didn't take to your attitude, Mr Sharman. I still don't. I see a dark side of you that I do not like.'

Talk about the pot calling the kettle dark.

'Why did you think it was unwise?' I asked. 'Because you were implicated in Sayer's death?'

'I had nothing to do with it.'

'You supplied the dope.'

'I didn't prepare the needle.'

'But you were there.'

'Kim Major killed him if anyone did.'

I saw Jay Harrison flinch at the words.

'But you were still there,' I went on. 'There's still a case to be made against you.'

'I doubt it. It was a long time ago.'

'And then you conspired with several others to pervert the course of justice. Not a nice thing for a future man of God to do. What about that?'

'The people involved are mostly dead now. The doctor, the undertaker, Kim. I can afford the best lawyers for both Jay and myself.'

'I think you might still do a little time. Both of you. And it wouldn't do much for the church you run.'

He pulled a face. He seemed to be getting more confident now that the story was out.

'So tell me, Jules, how did you progress from dealing dope to running this place?'

He pulled another face. 'I was called.'

'A road to Damascus job,' I said.

'If you wish to put it like that.'

'A revelation.'

He nodded.

I changed the subject. 'Did you see much of Kim Major after the funeral?' I asked.

He looked at me. 'I saw something of her, of course. She wanted news of Jay. It was impossible for them to meet, or even speak on the telephone. We all agreed on that.'

'Did she get the insurance?'

'Yes.'

'When?'

'I don't remember.'

'Come now, Jules. You must. There was the doctor to be paid, and the undertaker. And a hundred and fifty thousand dollars was a hell of a lot of money in those days. Did the cash come through quickly, or was it delayed for legal reasons? I mean, let's face it. The whole deal was iffy to say the least.'

'I don't think there was much delay.'

'Give me a clue. A month? Three? Six? Longer?'

'A month or two.'

'And she collected all that money, and only had to pay out fifteen grand sterling in bribes?'

'That's right.'

'Then tell me, brother, how come just three months after Jay Harrison allegedly died, she had to leave the flat in Hyde Park Mansions because she couldn't afford to pay the rent?'

24

The words dropped into the conversation like stones into a stagnant pool and sent out ripples that would have repercussions I couldn't possibly anticipate right then. If I'd've known what was to come I wonder if I would still have said them, or kept my big mouth shut. You work it out for yourself. I'm sick of trying.

Jay Harrison's great head turned towards Julius, then back to me, and I saw his hand grip Dawn's harder until her skin went white. 'That's impossible,' he said.

'No,' I replied. 'It's the truth. We've been to see the old lady who took over the tenancy of the apartment three months after you were supposed to have died. That's how we found out where you were. Kim left some photographs of you, her, Bubbah Jules here, and Billy Sayer, all getting cosy at some party or other, at the flat. The old lady kept them all these years in case she came back. She didn't know Kim was dead. I found some people who were around at the time and they identified Julius and Sayer. By coincidence, one of them had seen your boy here on the Tabernacle's TV show. Otherwise I never would have found you. Man, it's a fact. Ask my wife.'

Dawn nodded, withdrew her hands from Jay Harrison's grip and began to massage some life back into them.

Harrison turned and looked at Brother Julius again. 'That can't be right,' he said. 'You always told me that she was OK for money.'

Julius Rose looked uncomfortable, licked his lips and said, 'I didn't know.'

'Bullshit,' I interjected. 'You had to know. You were too closely involved.'

And then I got the first real inkling of what had happened all those years ago, and vocalized it. 'How about this then, Jules,' I said. 'You've got Jay stashed away down in the country. You've got Kim Major up here in London, scared as shit that she's going to get busted for giving Billy Sayer an overdose. You've got a coffin buried in Highgate Cemetery with Sayer's body in situ, and good old Kim gets a cheque for a hundred and fifty thousand dollars free and clear. I bet that was more than you'd make in ten years peddling dope round Notting Hill Gate. She's a spaced-out smackhead and you're her supplier. One night, as if in a dream, God comes to you and says, "Julie baby, I want you to start a church for me. But we need some dough to get it started." Maybe things were getting too hot for you on the drug scene. Maybe you really did see yourself as the second coming. Who knows? But I reckon that you put some pressure on Kim. What did you tell her? "I'll take care of the cash, babe. Pay the bribes to the good doctor and the undertaker that'll keep you out of Holloway jail, and maybe invest a little in a tabernacle I fancy opening. God said it'll be all right." Was that it? Did you rip her off? She couldn't speak to Jay because you had him safely under lock and key in some location out of town. And I bet you had someone keep him high as a kite, didn't you, son?'

By the look on Julius Rose's face I knew I was close.

'That was it, wasn't it? I bet it was a nice mixture of heroin and psychedelics. With maybe a few downers in there somewhere just to sweeten the mixture. A little cocktail to keep Jay docile, so's you could get on with the business in hand. On something like that he wouldn't know if it was Wednesday or Christmas, would he?'

I looked at the wreck that Harrison had become and I felt desperately sorry for the man.

'How long did that go on for? A long time I bet,' I said. 'Years? How many years, Jules? Up until quite recently I imagine. So meanwhile you bled the dough out of the poor bitch, and she had to move out of her flat. Where did she move to? Somewhere you could keep an eye on her and feed her the drugs she needed? Was that the deal? You're a regular little chemist, aren't you? And all along you're telling Jay that everything was hunky-dory. That she was doing fine.'

Brother Julius was shaking his head in reply, but he was starting to sweat. I was on another roll by then, and I pushed it as far as it would go.

'And maybe, just maybe,' I went on, 'a few months later you give her an overdose of her own. Was that it? Did you consider her a danger to your grandiose plans? Was she opening her mouth too wide about what had happened? Was the guilt getting to her? Was it simpler to kill her, than to let her blow the whistle on herself, and you, and Jay? Did you do to her what she'd done to your mate Billy?'

Julius was shaking his head faster, and drops of perspiration were flying off like rain. 'For pity's sake,' he said.

But I didn't feel any pity for him. 'Nobody would suspect, would they, Jules?' I pressed. 'She was just an accident waiting to happen. Everyone knew that. A terminal loser who'd just buried her old man, and was pushing the envelope of her existence every miserable day that she lived. Just another poor fucking messed-up drugs casualty at the arse end of the alternative society.'

I paused, then, with as much disgust as I could muster in my voice, I said, 'Was it your idea? Or did God tell you to do that too? Send her to heaven a few years before her time so that she couldn't blurt out what had happened one dark and moonless night to someone who might actually pay attention to what the poor, pathetic junkie had to say? Did you kill her, Jules? Did you?'

I don't know if all that I'd surmised was true, or even only part of it. But as I finished speaking, I saw that the blood had drained out of Julius Rose's face, leaving it grey and damp, and I knew that I wasn't far off the mark. He licked his lips again and said, 'That's ridiculous.' But his words carried no conviction.

'Is it?' I asked. 'I don't know so much.'

'*No.*'

'And when you had to give the sad news to Jay after she died, I bet you were real solicitous. I bet you told him that God's will had been done, didn't you?'

'Is it true, Julius?' said Jay Harrison. 'Tell me the truth.'

'And shame the devil,' I said. 'Isn't that how it goes?'

Julius leapt to his feet and, ignoring the gun I was still holding, lunged at me. I whacked him on the jaw with the barrel and he fell back on to the bed, clutching at his head.

'Stupid,' I said. 'I keep telling you.'

The room was silent, except for Julius Rose's whimpering as he cradled his damaged face in his hands.

'What are we going to do now?' asked Dawn after what seemed like an eternity.

'Get Jay out of here. I'll give Kennedy-Sloane a call. Tell him what's happened. He can get on to Lifetime in LA and tell them. Then I think an interview with a copper friend of mine is in order. Jay here should make a statement to the authorities as soon as possible. What do you reckon, Jay?'

'Whatever you think I should do.'

'That's it then. And we'll take Brother Julius with us. I reckon the Old Bill would love a little chat with him too. Whaddya say, Jules?'

Brother Julius said not a word in reply. And as far as I was concerned, his silence was as much a confession as if he'd admitted everything.

25

'Come on then, people,' I said. 'We've got to get out of here without running into any of the Brother's strong-arm boys.'

I went to open the door and took my eyes off Jay Harrison and Brother Julius for just a split second.

Bad mistake. I was caught wrong-footed as Harrison turned, picked up Brother Julius in his big arms and slammed his head against the wall so hard that his cranium put a dent in the plaster.

'Jay,' I shouted, and grabbed at his shoulder. It was like a gnat trying to get a full nelson on an elephant. He was nothing like the skinny young man in the poster I used to have. Under the fat that covered his body was hard muscle, and plenty of it.

He bashed Julius Rose against the wall again, and the sound of his head connecting with the plaster for the second time was like that of a melon being dropped from hand height on to a stone floor. I still had the gun in my hand, but I was hardly going to use it. Not even to whack Jay Harrison on *his* head. I wanted him conscious. There was no way that Dawn and I could drag his bulk through the corridors of the church and out to the car.

At that moment she decided to get into the act. 'Stop it,' she cried, and slid between Harrison and Julius. 'Stop it now.'

Surprisingly, the big man did as he was told and dropped Julius to lie awkwardly on the narrow bed. Dawn put her arms round Harrison and held him tightly. He embraced her back.

'Nice work,' I said as I examined Brother Julius's body. The side of his head that had hit the wall was unnaturally flat and when I touched it it felt like papier-mâché, and I could feel the blood seeping through his hair. I rubbed my fingers on my jeans and felt for a pulse at his wrist. There was none.

'You've killed him,' I said to Jay Harrison.

Harrison looked at me over Dawn's shoulder. 'He deserved it,' he said back, which might have been true, but didn't help a lot. 'I loved Kim,' he went on. 'She wasn't much, but she was mine. He lied to me all these years about what happened to her.' He looked down at Julius Rose's still form. 'All this time he used me. I was worth more to him dead than alive. And he pretended to be a man of God. How could he have done that?'

'Yes, Jay,' I said. 'But can we save the philosophical questions 'til later? Right now I think we'd better get out of here before someone comes looking for the preacher man. This is a right fucking mess.'

I checked the corridor outside. It was empty, and deathly quiet. I didn't know where everyone was. I was just glad they weren't in this part of the building. I returned the Glock to the waistband of my jeans under my jacket at the back. I figured that the sight of a loaded gun might alert even members of Julius's tabernacle that something was up.

We walked through the halls and down the stairs and didn't see a soul until we came close to Brother Julius's office where four geezers were standing together where the corridor dog-legged towards the foyer and the main entrance. Three of them were long-haired and shaggy, dressed for the best part in faded denim, the other was tall, dark-haired, about thirty-five, wearing a tailored leather jacket and black canvas jeans, giving the rest what looked like a serious pep talk.

They didn't look much like religious acolytes to me. More like a rock band's road crew, and the one who was giving them the bunny looked familiar, although for a moment I couldn't think from where.

And then I remembered. He was the ice cream in the spangled jacket who'd clocked me a few days earlier at The Virgin Mary's charity concert for distressed swordfish. Now, what the fuck was he doing here?

Then I found out. He saw me coming, said something to the other three, and before I could as much as reach for the gun under my jacket I was looking down the barrels of four extremely large and lethal-looking automatic pistols.

Shit, I thought. What now?

26

There was a door half open, opposite where we were all standing, and the dark-haired geezer gestured to it with the barrel of his automatic. Dawn, Jay Harrison and I went in. The four guys with guns followed. Inside was a general office with several desks, chairs and a row of dark green filing cabinets down one side. It could have been the office of any small-time commercial company but for the religious prints, framed on the walls. The dark-haired geezer shut the door behind himself. There was a silver key poking out of the lock. He didn't turn it.

Mistake.

He hitched one buttock up on the corner of the nearest desk and said, 'You're Nick Sharman.' He had an American accent, and his voice was slightly familiar.

I nodded.

'Mrs Sharman, I presume.' To Dawn.

Her turn to nod.

Then he looked at Jay Harrison. 'And who have we here?' he said.

Harrison said not a word in reply.

'So you found him?' said the Yank.

'Who?' I asked.

'Don't be clever. I'm Lamar Quinn.'

That threw me a bit. 'I thought you were in Los Angeles,' I said. 'Talking to Kennedy-Sloane on a daily basis.'

'I use a portable,' said Quinn. 'I can be anywhere in the world.'

'Satellites,' I said. 'What will they come up with next?'

Quinn ignored me. 'Jay Harrison,' he said instead, looking at Harrison hard. 'My, but you've changed some. But you're still in there, aren't you? Well done, Nick. I may call you Nick, mayn't I?'

'Call me what you like,' I said. But don't call me late for breakfast, I thought. The stupid things you think when you're being covered by four high-powered automatic weapons.

'So that's why you were so keen to get a progress report on what we'd found,' I said. 'You were just round the corner, waiting. You cunning old fox, you. I knew I shouldn't have told Kennedy-Sloane what I knew until I was sure.'

'But you were right.'

'Didn't do me much good though, did it?'

'The guys and I were impatient,' said Quinn, with a shit-eating smirk. 'Sorry.' He didn't look it.

I looked at the three blokes with him. Rednecks one and all. I didn't recognize any of them. The biggest had a tattoo of a tarantula on his massive right forearm. Scary. I wondered if he had a tattoo of a little old lady on the other. The little old lady who swallowed a spider, that wiggled and wriggled and tickled inside her. Just one more idle thought while I wondered what the hell to do next.

'Search them,' Quinn said to Tarantula. He stuffed his automatic into the waistband of his Levi's, under his heavy stomach, and carefully walked round the back of Dawn and Jay Harrison and me, being careful not to get into the other three's line of fire. He started by searching me, and turned up the Glock within ten seconds, which he tossed to Quinn who caught it easily in his left hand and stuck it into *his* waistband. Shame. I always liked that gun. Tarantula frisked me further, and found nothing more, then moved over to Dawn whom he gave a particularly close search, concentrating on her breasts and finishing by sticking his right hand under her crotch for a lot longer than was necessary, until I saw her grit her teeth hard from the pain, but she didn't make a sound.

'Leave her,' ordered Quinn. 'We're not here for that.'

I looked at Tarantula who looked back at me with a sneer. One day, I thought.

Tarantula finished by giving Jay Harrison the once over. 'They're clean, boss,' he said when he had finished. He was American too, but I didn't need to hear his voice to know that.

'Well,' said Quinn, when the man with the spider tattoo had rejoined him. 'This is perfect.'

'What now?' I asked.

'Now, I'm afraid, Jay Harrison has to become what the rest of the world has thought he was for all these years.'

'Dead, you mean,' I said.

'Precisely.'

'And why's that?'

'Come on, Nick,' said Lamar Quinn. 'You can do better. Why do you think?'

'Money, I suppose,' I said. 'The well-known root of all evil.'

Quinn nodded.

'Which is why you're here?'

Another nod.

'You've been doing a little injudicious dipping into Jay's royalties. Is that it?'

'Very good,' said Quinn. 'Very good indeed.'

'And not hard to work out. But you'll never get away with it.'

'That sounds like a line from *Hawaii Five-O*.'

Which it probably was, and none the worse for that. Some of my best lines come from trash TV of the seventies. I've made a study of it.

'You'll have to kill all three of us,' I said.

Quinn shrugged.

'And when certain people start asking awkward questions, won't it be strange when they find out that you were in the country when it all happened?'

'We're not,' said Quinn. 'Not officially. We came in with The Virgin Mary party. She's on Lifetime Records too. It wasn't difficult to arrange for the four of us to hitch a ride. Two 747 loads of band, crew, hangers on, costumes and equipment. Lots of room to get lost in. The planes taxied straight up to the limos and buses that brought us to London. No passport checks. No customs. With a star of her magnitude it's easier for the authorities to let us straight in. No hassle. If we bring a few illegal substances with us, so what...'

'Or a few illegal people,' I finished for him.

'Precisely,' he said. 'Your government doesn't want to cause an international incident by letting any over-zealous official in a uniform upset her creative flow. The Virgin's bigger than God at the moment.'

'Be careful what you say here,' I said. 'You never know who might be listening. This is where God hangs out, or hadn't you heard?'

He ignored me.

'*Someone* must know you're here,' I said.

'Sure. But most of them depend on me for their jobs. They're not going to tell.'

'So that was why you were at the concert the other night?'

I saw Dawn turn to look at me.

'He was clocking me,' I explained. 'I thought he fancied Angela.'

'As you would.' Dawn spoke for the first time since she'd entered the room.

A thought occurred to me. 'You didn't set this up with Kennedy-Sloane, did you?' I asked Quinn.

He shook his head. 'He doesn't know I'm in the country. Didn't I make that clear? He just happened to mention that you were escorting his girlfriend to the affair. He knows that I'm involved with the band at home. I asked around. Someone knew her, and you were sitting with her. Simple.'

Caspian had been sitting with her too, but then I doubt if anyone would have taken him for a private detective cum bodyguard. Mind you, the way things were going, I could say the same thing about myself. 'Good,' I said. 'I would have hated to have read him so wrong for all these years.'

'I guess you didn't,' said Quinn.

'Who are your friends?' I asked, looking at Tarantula and his two mates. 'Three of the seven dwarfs on steroids? Sneezy? Grumpy? Dopey?'

Quinn ignored my levity. He was getting plenty of practice at that. 'Old buddies of mine,' he said. 'We used to work together. I was a tour co-ordinator for some very big names during the first half of the eighties. These were my main men.'

The road crew from hell, I thought, but left it unsaid. Instead I remarked, 'And then you got into embezzlement. Good career move.'

He gave me a sour look, as if he didn't like what I was saying. Which was fine by me. He wasn't supposed to.

'But you didn't come all this way on a whim,' I said. 'And you were in England long before I told Kennedy-Sloane about this place. Why did you go to all this trouble on the strength of one lousy letter? You told me you get them all the time. What made this one different?'

'What made this one different was that it wasn't just one,' said Quinn. 'There were a whole bunch. And the later ones couldn't've been written by anyone else but the real Jay Harrison. I knew he was alive, I just didn't know where. I asked around and your name came up as the man most likely to find out. And you did.'

You fucker, I thought.

'You took me for a bit of a mug then, didn't you?' I said.

'If that means I took you for a ride, sure,' Quinn grinned as he said it. 'So where's the other guy? This Brother Julius character I've heard so much about, who's been keeping our friend out of the public eye for so long?'

'We had a little truth or consequence session,' I replied. 'The consequence is that he's deceased.'

'Really?'

'Really. Go look upstairs if you don't believe me. He's in one of the bedrooms at the back of the place, one floor up. He's the one with the head made of mush.'

'Who killed him?' asked Quinn.

'I did,' said Jay Harrison.

'Did you now,' said Quinn. 'Naughty, naughty.' He turned back to me. 'As a matter of interest,' he said. 'Who's buried in Harrison's grave? Did you ever find out?'

'Someone named Billy Sayer,' I replied.

'What happened?'

'It wasn't his lucky day.'

Quinn grinned again.

'Why did you steal my money?' Harrison said to Quinn suddenly. 'Why?'

'It was there,' said Quinn. 'A great lump of dead cash, just appreciating all the time and never being used.'

'But you had use for it?' I said.

'Sure,' said Quinn.

'How much?'

'Ten million. Twelve million. Maybe a little more.'

'Bad investments?' I asked.

'The market crashed. I couldn't recoup.'

'You lost it all on stocks?'

'Most. But we partied a little, didn't we, guys?' He looked at the other three for confirmation. Their smiles were all I needed.

'Up your nose?' I said.

'Some. But that's all water under the bridge now,' said Quinn.

Good metaphor, if you've done a lot of coke, I thought, but didn't say a word.

'I'm afraid the time has come to close the account,' Quinn said finally, as if it were pre-ordained.

'There'll still be people looking into where the money went,' I said. 'Even if you kill us all.'

'It'll take for ever. Maybe by then I can pay the money back.'

'And maybe you won't.'

'That's hardly your problem,' he said.

And wasn't that the truth?

The seven of us looked at each other in silence for a moment.

End of song, beginning of story, as Louis Armstrong said in *High Society*, I thought. Now what the hell got me into that?

'I think it's time for us all to leave quietly,' said Quinn. 'We've got a couple of cars outside. We don't want to attract any undue attention here, do we?'

Don't we? I thought. Just the opposite as far as I was concerned. But I had no say in the matter.

'Sam. You and Eddie ride herd on Nick and his lady. Joe and I'll take care of Harrison.'

The two roadies who hadn't spoken, and who I assumed to be Sam and Eddie, put away their guns and headed in Dawn's and my direction. Tarantula, who must have been Joe, did the same with his, and moved towards Jay Harrison.

Dawn said, 'I'm no one's fucking lady.'

Good for you kid, I thought, as she said it. That'll show 'em. Then she showed 'em properly.

From somewhere that Tarantula, or Joe, or whatever the hell his name was, had missed in his body search of her, she produced the flick knife that she'd had in her stocking top the night of The Virgin Mary concert. With a snap the blade appeared, and she straightened her arm and stuck it into Sam or Eddie's chest, alongside his right armpit. He looked down at the black handle of the knife as it protruded from his body and touched it almost in wonder.

We all stood perfectly still, until I grabbed Dawn's arm and yelled to Harrison, 'Jay. Let's go,' then kicked out at Lamar Quinn's gun hand and connected beautifully so that the automatic was torn from his grasp and landed on the far side of the desk where he was sitting with a thump. 'Move it, Jay,' I shouted, and he slammed Tarantula in the chest and sent him reeling against the roadie who hadn't been stabbed, and was clawing at the automatic in his belt, and I dragged Dawn out of the room, ripping the key from the lock as I went, closely followed by Jay Harrison. When all three of us were safely outside in the corridor, I slammed the door shut behind us, and locked it.

Not a shot had been fired.

'Come on,' I shouted, 'Let's get out of here.'

Harrison started in the direction of the foyer, but I caught his bicep and said, 'There might be more outside. Is there a back way?'

He nodded, and we went back in the direction we'd come, only this time he pushed through a set of swing doors into a tiled corridor, and Dawn and I followed. As the doors swung shut behind us, I heard the sound of the office door being smashed off its hinges, and shouting from behind us, but still no shots.

We dashed up a flight of stairs, and along yet another bare, starkly white-painted hall.

Harrison was starting to sweat, and his breathing was laboured.

'How far?' I said.

'Not far,' he gasped in reply. 'We can get through the church and out the other side.'

We moved off, but more slowly, and Harrison's breath was coming in stentorian gasps.

'Are you OK?' I asked, as we reached yet another door which led to one more bleak, concrete passageway.

Harrison leant one hand against the wall and put the other to his chest. From behind us I could hear the sound of boot heels clattering on the stairs. 'Just a minute,' he said.

'We've got to get going,' I urged him.

Dawn touched his face. It was as pale and sweaty as Brother Julius's had been when he'd been confronted in Jay's room. Not a healthy sight.

'He's ill,' said Dawn.

'He'll be a lot iller if that mob catch up with us.' I turned to him. 'Jay, we've got to get out of here, or find somewhere to hide.' The bare walls of the corridor seemed to mock me with their echo as I said it. You couldn't have hidden a cockroach where we were.

Harrison looked at me. 'I can't,' he said. 'I just can't. Thanks for trying to help, but I can't go on.'

'You must,' I said, but he just shook his head, smiled an angelic smile that made him look twenty-five years younger, and touched Dawn's hand with his own, as he leaned his back against the wall and slowly slid down into a sitting position.

I knelt down next to Harrison and felt for his pulse. There was none. I laid him flat and beat my fists down on to his chest, and the door we'd just come through burst open and Lamar Quinn, Tarantula and the roadie who hadn't been stabbed piled through, all carrying their guns, which I noticed were cocked, ready to fire. They slid to a halt when they saw us, and Quinn snapped, 'What happened?'

'Cardiac arrest,' I said. 'He's had a hell of a day.' I pinched Jay Harrison's nose closed and prepared to give him mouth-to-mouth resuscitation.

'Get him off, Joe,' said Quinn, and Tarantula grabbed me by the hair and dragged me away from Jay Harrison's still form. He threw me against the wall and gestured that I stay down.

'He's still got a chance,' I protested.

Quinn shook his head.

'You bastard,' said Dawn.

'Shut up, cunt,' said Tarantula. 'I haven't finished with you yet.'

'Leave them,' said Quinn. 'It's all over.'

'Is it?' I asked, from my undignified position on the floor.

'Sure. Harrison's dead. That's what we came here for. From natural causes too. Couldn't be better. Nobody'll ever be able to prove who he was now. There's nothing more that you can do. You've been paid handsomely, and I'll make sure you get a big bonus. I'll get the money to Chris Kennedy-Sloane as soon as we get back Stateside.'

'As easy as that,' I said.

'Sure. Why not? What do you care whether Jay Harrison is alive or dead?'

I thought about the poster I had on my wall again, and the records I used to listen to.

I cared.

'Not a lot,' I said. But I lied.

'So we part friends. And put all this down to experience,' said Quinn.

I nodded. 'Why not?' I said.

'Good,' said Quinn, and let the hammer of his gun down gently, put it away, then said to his companions, 'Guys, it's finished,' and reluctantly they too uncocked their pistols and returned them to the waistbands of their jeans.

'How about *my* gun?' I asked.

'I'll keep it as a souvenir,' said Quinn. 'I'll have it mounted on my office wall.' He grinned again. 'And now sadly we have to part. I won't say that it's been nice knowing you, but it's certainly been interesting. Come on, Eddie. Joe, let's get outta here. We gotta get Sam to a doctor.'

Joe Tarantula walked over to Dawn and swung his hand round and slapped her hard in the face. So hard that her cheek went white, then suffused with blood, leaving a strawberry-coloured mark mimicking the four fingers of his hand. I started to rise, but Quinn put his hand on the butt of his gun.

'That's for m'buddy ya stuck, bitch,' said Joe Tarantula. 'You're lucky I don't kill ya.'

'Joe,' said Quinn. 'C'm'on. We're finished here.' And the three of them went back through the door the way they'd come in.

27

So there the three of us stood and sat and lay. Well, two of us really. The third was just a shell. A dead husk that the spirit had left. I slid over and touched Jay Harrison's wrist again. There was still no pulse and his body was beginning to cool.

I got up and went over to Dawn and held her. The mark on her face was starting to bruise up, and I felt a hard tug of anger in my belly. 'How's your face?' I asked.

'I'll survive. I've had lots worse.'

That didn't make it any better.

'Is Jay dead?' asked Dawn.

I nodded.

'I liked him,' she said.

'Me too.'

'What do we do now?'

'Good question. Get the hell out of here I think is favourite. There's two dead bodies in the place and we'll have to answer a load of uncomfortable questions if we stick around.'

'So that's it?'

'What?'

'We take the money and run.'

'Did I say that?'

'You just said it to that American.'

'I thought it was preferable to getting shot.'

'So what *do* we do?'

'We go and find Lamar Quinn and his pals and wreak some serious havoc. I'm well pissed off. That geezer hit you. He didn't have to do that. No one hits my wife.'

'He hurt your pride you mean?'

'Christ, Dawn. Let's not get into all that now. He didn't need to hit you. Or hurt you when he searched you. And Quinn took the piss. And once upon a time I used to listen to Jay Harrison sing, and I thought that his songs might change the world. And Quinn thought that I wouldn't care what happened to him as long as enough cash changed hands. And yeah, they hurt my pride if you must know. You and my pride are pretty much all I've got in the world. Mess with them and take the consequences. Are those enough reasons for you? Or do you want more?'

Dawn pulled away and looked up into my face. 'You're OK, Nick,' she said. 'Sometimes I know exactly why I married you.'

I kissed her hard. 'Can we go now?' I asked.

'Where?'

'To see Mr Quinn.'

'We don't know where he is.'

'Don't we? You haven't been keeping up with the entertainment section of the daily paper. The Virgin Mary is starting a three-week stint at the old Hammy Odeon tonight. The Apollo they call it now. It's the hottest ticket in town. What's the betting old Lamar will be hanging out there?'

'But they've got guns.'

'So we get a gun.'

'Where?'

'Wanna bet Julius had one?'

'Where would it be?'

'Where all villains keep their guns. In the top right-hand drawer of his desk. Come on, babe, let's go see.'

We went downstairs back to Brother Julius's office. There were a few people around by then. Obviously all the action had attracted some attention. Dawn and I walked past them like we owned the place.

When we got to the door of the office I remembered I'd broken the key off in the lock. Smart move. It was still there.

Using my good foot I kicked at the door until it splintered and swung open. Brother Anthony was still lying, trussed and bound, where we'd left him. I'd almost forgotten he was there.

I knelt down beside him. He was still breathing, but not happy. I slapped him gently on the cheek and said, 'Not much longer, babe. Stick around.' Not that he had much choice in the matter.

I sat in the chair behind the desk and tried the drawers. They were all unlocked but one. As I'd surmised it was the top right-hand drawer. Brother Julius must have been as big a fan of old film noir as I was.

On the top of the desk was a hefty letter opener in the shape of a stiletto. I jammed it into the gap between the drawer and the desk, close to the lock, and applied some pressure. With a squeal the lock gave. Inside, along with some cheque books and letters, was a nickel-plated Colt .45 1911 A1 automatic, a spare, empty clip, and an almost full box of fifty .45 shells. Nice gun. Showed taste. A real man-stopper. Exactly what I needed. I grinned, took out the gun's clip and cleared the action. The chamber was empty, but the clip contained seven brass-jacketed rounds. I slapped it back home, chambered a round, took out the clip again and inserted a fresh bullet in the vacant space, cocked and locked the gun, put the spare clip in my pocket and gave the box of shells to Dawn.

'Hold these, doll, will you,' I said. Then I hefted the letter opener in my hand and gave that to her too. 'You did good, stabbing that wanker. You'd better have this. Might come in handy later. Where had you hidden the other knife by the way?'

'I always like to keep something up my sleeve,' she replied.

'Terrific,' I said. 'Let's go.'

We walked out together. There was a small knot of people outside the room, but no blue uniforms. I showed them the gun and they let us pass. We walked through to the foyer, out of the main doors and back to the car.

Then we went to Hammersmith.

On the way I got Dawn to load the spare clip with ammunition. It might turn out to be a busy night.

28

The wide pavement outside the Apollo was pretty much deserted when we rolled by. I looked at my watch. The show had to be well started. I drove the Chevy round looking for somewhere to park, past a couple of vanloads of Old Bill waiting for the riots to start. They might not have to wait long. I kept driving and looking. Fat chance. Every street and parking lot around the theatre was locked up tight with vehicles. I eventually found a space within walking distance, just about big enough for a Ford Escort, and slammed the Chevy in, front wheels and bonnet across the pavement, the big estate back end stuck out into traffic. If it got a bash, too bad. That's what we pay insurance for.

We bailed out, I locked the motor and off we went. Just before we got to the Apollo, I stopped Dawn and said, 'Are you sure about this?'

'What is there to be sure about?'

Diamond.

'It's going to get heavy.'

'That's what I signed on for.'

Twenty-four carat.

'I love you,' I said. And I meant it. I hope that when you say it to a woman and really mean it, it makes up for all the times you said it to a woman, and didn't.

'I love you too,' and she came close and kissed me. 'Is that a loaded pistol in your pocket, or are you just glad to see me?'

'Both,' I said.

'How are we going to get in?' asked Dawn, suddenly serious. 'Won't the place be sold out?'

'You just watch,' I said, and we crossed over the road to the theatre which had a big THE VIRGIN MARY RHYTHM REVUE PLUS SUPPORT sign plastered across the front where they used to advertise what movie was playing.

There were a few disappointed punters peering through the big glass doors of the place and, as we headed towards them, several shady-looking geezers detached themselves from the shadows and headed our way. The first one to get close was a ratty specimen wearing an orange and turquoise shellsuit and Nike high-tops.

Fashion god.

'Need tickets, folks?' he asked. 'The Virgin's due on any minute.'

'You read my mind,' I said. 'How much?'

'Front stalls, thirty-nicker tickets, to you, guv, and your lovely companion, a snip at a ton each.'

'Getaway,' I said.

'And I'm losing on the deal,' he said.

'Course you are,' I remarked.

'Come on, guv. You know it makes sense. Buy from Terry, your satisfaction guaranteed. Established nineteen eighty-five.'

'That gives me a lot of confidence.'

'So it should, guv. So it should.'

'They're not forgeries?'

'Would I?' he pleaded. 'Ask anyone. I'm here every night, regular as clockwork. I couldn't *afford* to knock out snides.'

'All right, Terry,' I said. 'You've talked me into it.'

His sense of relief was almost palpable. He must have over-bought for the evening, and time was getting on.

Quick as a flash two tickets appeared in his hand from nowhere.

'Over here,' I said, and we walked back into the gloom from where he'd appeared, and I pulled out a handful of cash.

'Got many left over?' I asked.

'A few. That's part of the game.'

'So's this,' I said, and kicked him just below the knee. He went down on to it on the pavement with a crack, and I said, 'Give us all you've got, son. This is a hold-up.'

'Christ,' he said, and I raised my fist as if to hit him. I was getting well sick of the rock and roll game. Everyone involved was at it. Give me an honest tea leaf any day.

'All right, guv,' he moaned. 'Hold on.' And he pulled out another handful of tickets which I took off him.

'Thanks, Tel,' I said. 'Ain't free enterprise grand? Now you just stay here quiet for a bit, and none of us will be making a claim on our medical insurance. Get my drift?'

He nodded, and I patted him on the shoulder, and Dawn and I went back round the corner and towards the main entrance.

'That was a bit naughty,' she said.

'I've never liked touts,' I said. 'He was lucky I didn't take his money too,' as I returned mine to my back pocket.

A few of the punters were still waiting by the doors. 'Want some tickets?' I said as we passed them.

Of course when you offer someone something for nish, no one ever believes you.

'How much?' said one spotty-faced midget in flared purple polyester strides, standing with half a dozen or so of his mates.

'Nothing,' I replied.

'What?'

'Take 'em or fucking don't,' I said, and stuffed them into his hand and passed through into the foyer.

Altruism, where is thy sting?

29

We walked into the foyer and across to the doors that led to the auditorium, past the concession stands selling The Virgin Mary CDs, tapes, T- and sweat-shirts, scarves, badges, books, posters and every other kind of shit the management and record company could screw the Billy Bunters for. I handed our tickets to the geezer in the monkey suit guarding the door, and he tore off the stubs and handed me our halves back. Inside I could hear the sound of the crowd like a wild animal about to be unleashed.

'She's on in one minute,' he said. 'You're just in time.'

I nodded, and we passed into the bowels of the theatre where a wave of hot air that smelled of perfume and sweat and adrenalin assailed us.

As the doors swung shut behind us, the lights went down and a recording of 'The Ride of the Valkyries' to which a thudding bass beat had been added boomed out of the speakers that ringed the theatre.

'I love the smell of napalm in the morning,' I whispered in Dawn's ear. 'It reminds me of victory.'

She looked at me as if I'd lost my mind.

As the music surged, the audience rose to their feet as one and the curtains on stage drew slowly back. The stage itself was black, and then, with a crack like thunder and a brilliant white light, began a pyrotechnic display that made Guy Fawkes' night look dull.

'Come on,' I shouted in Dawn's ear. 'Let's find the way backstage.'

We walked down the aisle on the right of the theatre where fans were already running down to the front for a better view of what was to come. Just by the side of the stage was a door with a dimly illuminated sign saying EXIT above it. We ducked inside as the band ran onstage and picked up their instruments to a roar from the crowd.

As the door hissed shut behind us, the music started with a hypnotic bass, electric organ and drum rhythm, and a howl of feedback from the lead guitar.

Dawn and I headed in the direction of the rear of the building, turned a dog leg in the passageway, and saw another geezer in evening dress, arms crossed, leaning against the wall, guarding an unmarked door. Bingo!

We walked up to him, and he pushed himself upright with a quizzical look on his face. On one lapel of his cheap dinner jacket was a badge that read Premier Security, with NORMAN typed neatly underneath in capitals. Premier Security, I'd had dealings with them before. Some of their operatives carried guns. On the other lapel was clipped a laminated *Access All Areas* backstage pass.

The sound of the music was muted back where we were and he had to raise his voice only slightly to be heard. 'Help you?' he said.

'Backstage?' I said in reply.

'Gotta pass?'

I nodded, reached under my jacket, pulled out the Colt .45, slipped the safety catch and stuck the gun in his lip. 'Access all areas,' I said.

30

The geezer's face fell. 'What the...' he said.

'Save it, son,' I said. 'You wouldn't even begin to understand. Dawn, take a squint inside. See if anyone else's about.'

She did as she was told, while I held the gun on the security man. She stuck her head round the door, then withdrew it. 'No one's there,' she said.

'Inside,' I said to Norman.

He did as he was told too, and we entered the backstage area of the theatre. Inside was a narrow corridor painted dark green and illuminated with dim bulbs mounted behind metal mesh, one every six feet or so at head height on the walls. The corridor was deserted and the sound of the band was louder. The Virgin Mary was screeching a song about the coming of Satan. Uplifting stuff.

'See if Norman's got a gun, babe,' I said to Dawn. 'Check his armpits, waist and ankles.' Dawn did as I asked her again, working from behind him. When she'd finished she shook her head. 'No gun,' she said.

Opposite the door we'd come through was another door made of slatted wood, with the words FIRE HOSE painted on it in faded red letters, and fastened with a small bolt that was old and pitted with rust spots. I slipped the bolt and opened the door, still keeping the gun on Norman. Inside was a small, dark cupboard with the requisite fire hose wrapped around a green iron skeleton shaped like a wheel that was bolted to the wall. On the floor were two battered water fire extinguishers.

'Get in there,' I said ripping the laminated *Access All Areas* pass off his lapel.

He started to protest and I pushed the barrel of the gun on to the end of his nose. 'It's loaded, Norm,' I said. 'And no one'll hear the shot. The music's too loud. Swallow it, son. I know it's a bastard, but you were just unlucky. You got the short straw tonight.'

He shrugged, sighed, turned, and went into the cupboard. I almost felt sorry for him, but not that sorry. I raised the Colt and whacked him on the side of his head, just below where his thick dark hair was parted. He stumbled and hit the floor. I shut the door and bolted it. I was getting good at hitting people from behind. Maybe I should start giving lessons.

Dawn didn't say anything, but I don't think she liked it.

'It's a dog-eat-dog world, babe,' I said.

She didn't reply, but I think she sighed too. Hell, it was her who wanted to be a detective. Get involved in the family business.

I pinned the laminated pass to her leather jacket. 'If this all goes pear-shaped,' I said, 'you can just melt into the background. Pretend you're a groupie or something.'

'Thanks,' she said.

'Don't knock it,' I said. 'Remember. No blow job, no backstage pass. Isn't that how it goes?'

At least that got a faint smile. 'I really don't know,' she replied.

'Come on,' I said. 'Let's go see what we can find.'

I stuck the gun back under my jacket and we went down the corridor in the direction that the noise of the band playing was coming from. Around the next corner, on top of a wheeled flight case, was a navy blue baseball cap with an elasticized strap at the back, and The Virgin Mary's corporate logo picked out on the front in yellow thread. I picked it up and tossed it to Dawn. 'Put that on,' I said. Her blonde mop was too distinctive and I wanted as few people as possible to remember her later.

She stuck it on her head at a jaunty angle.

'Rock chick,' I said. 'You really look the part now.'

'Cheers,' she replied, and I took her arm and we went off to see the wizard.

31

We walked around the next corner, and there was another, huge, silver, wheeled flight case shoved up against the wall. No hat on this one though. Instead a couple of serious babes were sprawled all over it. They were ignoring the music from onstage. I guess if you've seen one rhythm review you've seen them all. In fact, in my experience, the people who hang out with rock and roll bands never actually bother to watch them. Strange that. But true.

The babes were both blondes. In their late teens I guessed. They were both slim and pretty sensational-looking. In the street they would probably have stopped traffic. One was wearing sheer black tights with a black skirt that would have made a fairly decent pelmet when she was standing up. Half lying down, the way she was, it rode up her thighs and you could almost see what she'd had for breakfast. Almost, but not quite. But I did manage to work out that under the tights she was wearing white knickers. Hell, I'm a detective aren't I? With the skirt and tights she wore a white blouse sheer enough to let anyone, not just a detective, see the white lace of the camisole top she wore underneath. The other one was wearing a pair of ancient blue jeans, that looked like they'd been sprayed on, and a distressed Levi's jacket, open, over a tiny black bra that barely contained her full breasts, and pushed them up to show plenty of cleavage. Both wore high-heeled black boots with pointy toes. Handy for squashing bugs.

The pair of them also wore mirrored aviator shades. It must have been pretty weird looking at each other, because all they'd see was reflections of themselves. Come to think of it, that was probably the idea.

Naturally, they also both sported *Access All Areas* passes.

I felt Dawn stiffen when she saw them, even though we weren't touching. I just knew her by now, and the way she reacted to some other females, and I'd bet that if I'd looked at her, her eyes would have gone all slitty. I didn't look. I didn't need to. She didn't like them on sight, and that was the end of it.

In fact they pretty much looked like her, only ten years younger. But I thought this would be an inopportune time to mention it.

As we got up close, and I was doing my detective work on the one with the black skirt, she turned to her friend and said through a mouthful of pink bubble gum, 'We gonna check out the party, Pattie?' She was American. New York by her accent.

'Sure. Why not?' replied Pattie. American also. New York also. 'It'll probably be pretty much of a drag though.' She gave the impression that everything was probably pretty much of a drag to her. Sex. Drugs. Rock and roll. Life. Death. And everything in between. The whole kit and caboodle in fact. Jaded by twenty. Not bad.

I stopped, and Dawn almost cannoned into me. 'Where *is* the party?' I asked.

Two pairs of silver mirrors turned in my direction. I could see four of me. Hey, I looked OK.

'In the Green Room,' said the one that wasn't Pattie. She tugged her skirt down, but it was made of stretchy Lycra, and rode straight up again, thus accentuating the fact that her crotch was showing, rather than disguising the fact. I felt Dawn bristle beside me. I didn't mind at all.

'Where's that?' I asked.

'Upstairs. You can go right round the back, and take the elevator, or use the metal steps by the side of the stage.' She pointed a red-tipped finger in the general direction that we'd been heading.

'When does it start?'

'It already started.'

'Terrific.'

'You lost your pass, handsome? You won't get in without it,' the one who wasn't Pattie asked, and made the useless gesture of pulling down her skirt again. With a great effort of will, I didn't look up her skirt. It was tough, but I managed it. I could feel Dawn's eyes on mine, and I knew that if I merely flickered them in *that* direction, I was toast.

'He'll get in OK,' said Dawn. 'He's with *me*.'

Both the girls turned their bins in Dawn's direction. 'Oh really,' said Pattie. 'How divine.'

I felt Dawn bristle even more and, remembering that she had a knife stashed somewhere on her person, I said, 'The party beckons, honey. Let's go for it.'

'See you later,' I said to the two babes, and the one that wasn't Pattie wiggled her fingers in my direction.

Dawn glared at the pair of them, and I took her arm and gave it a gentle tug. She allowed me to lead her along the corridor. As we went I winked at Pattie and her friend whose name I'd probably never know. One or both of them might have winked back. Who can tell with mirrored shades?

But as we turned the next corner I heard the one that wasn't Pattie say, 'Cute.'

'*Cute*,' said Dawn, glancing back. 'I'll give her fuckin' *cute*.'

'Handsome too,' I remarked, and she punched me on the arm. Hard enough to hurt.

'What do you want to go to a party for?' asked Dawn.

'It's a start. We could look for Quinn and his mates all night down here. Let's swing with the in crowd. It can't hurt. And we can get a drink. I've been hitting people on the head all day. I think I deserve one. If there's no one we know up there, we'll come back down. OK?'

'If you say so,' said Dawn.

'And besides, the girls will be up there later.'

She hit me on the arm again. Harder this time, if anything.

We went deeper backstage, and the music got louder, and we passed a whole load more of the detritus of rock and roll as we went. Both animate and inanimate. Although sometimes it was pretty hard to tell the difference. But no one paid us any particular attention, and eventually, when we got right up by the stage, close enough to be able to see The Virgin Mary and her Rhythm Review cutting the mustard for the punters, we found a green-painted metal staircase that vanished upwards into the gloom of the cavernous roof of the building. We took the stairs up into darkness past the scaffolding for lights and a bunch of flats from some long-forgotten show that were festooned with weights on heavy ropes for counter-balance.

The music boomed from the walls as we climbed until eventually the stairs ended on a metal balcony with a heavy fire door at the far end.

'The Giant's kingdom,' I said above the sound of the music. 'Here there be dragons.'

'You're mixing your fairy tales,' said Dawn. 'And I hope you're not suggesting that I'm the cow that you're going to sell for a handful of beans.'

'As if,' I said back as I pushed open the door. When it closed behind us it cut out most of the sound, which was a relief. I was getting tired of The Virgin Mary's particular brand of heavy metal techno, or whatever it was, and I could have done with total silence. I must be getting old.

The words GREEN ROOM, with an arrow pointing further along the corridor we found ourselves in, were painted in fading green on the wall. A clue at last. We followed the arrow, then the sound of a lot of people having a good time, until we found the party.

There were a bunch of 'now' people standing in the corridor outside the room. There were a load more standing inside. They were all holding glasses. Some were holding two. Obviously booze was more appealing than The Virgin Mary. I could do no more than agree. There was a huge Premier Security guy in a Virgin Mary silk tour-jacket minding the door. His name plate read Big Mal. I almost fainted from fear. The bar on the far side of the room was crowded, and in one corner I saw, sitting on a window ledge, looking pale and unhappy, the geezer that Dawn had stuck with her flick knife. He was wearing a denim jacket. His uninjured left arm was in the sleeve, but the right sleeve hung empty and his right arm was in a sling. He was alone.

'He got fixed up quick,' said Dawn, when I pointed him out, as we stood by the open door.

'Probably got a doctor with the show,' I said. 'Or one on twenty-four-hour call. If he'd gone to hospital, he'd still be in casualty. And giving a description of the crazed individual who put a knife into him to some big, hairy copper. How does this go? Blonde, about thirty, slim, and sexy as hell.'

Dawn smiled. 'Goes pretty well,' she said.

'Hard one to swallow though,' I remarked. 'But not impossible. Some chicks are out of control these days. I blame women's lib.'

She punched me on the arm again, but not so hard this time. 'Doesn't look too well, does he?' she said.

'Nor would you if you'd been stabbed less than two hours ago. But he's no party pooper, I'll say that for him.'

'What are we going to do?'

'Ask him where the rest of the guys are hanging out.'

'Go on then.'

The security guy didn't seem to care that I didn't have a pass and let the pair of us into the room without a second glance. I snagged two glasses of wine from a passing waiter, gave one to Dawn and we circulated. We headed in the direction of the guy with the bad arm, but surreptitiously, listening to a lot of music biz bullshit being talked as we went. He didn't notice us. But then, he wasn't looking.

When we sauntered up to him, he was staring in the other direction, and I said, 'Sam?'

He turned and said, 'Yeah,' before he realised who we were.

'Hi, Sam,' I said. 'Remember us?'

He stiffened, and a wave of pain passed over his face.

'Where's the rest of the pumphouse gang, then? Left you all dressed up and nowhere to go?'

'What the fuck are you doing here?' he said. 'They said you were out of it.'

'We lied,' I said. 'I know we deserve a severe talking to, because of it, but there you go. So come on, Sam, tell me true, where are they?'

'Fuck off.'

I touched him on his right shoulder and he winced. 'Painkillers starting to wear off, are they?' I asked.

'I'll get the security guy,' said Sam. 'Get you tossed out on your ass.'

'And I bet I'll start to gibber in panic,' I said. I opened my jacket and let him see the checkered walnut butt of the Colt. 'And then I'll shoot him. And then I'll shoot you. And it seems a shame to spoil the party so early on in the proceedings.'

Sam breathed out. His face was white and greasy. He should have been in bed, not at a bun fight. 'They're downstairs,' he said. 'In the tuning-up room. At least that's where they were. They'll be up here later.'

'Cheers, pal,' I said, and punched him playfully on the right shoulder. Just like we were two old buddies sharing a rock and roll anecdote. His face went from white to a dirty grey, and he passed out and hit the floor with a thud. I knelt beside him, lifted up his head by his hair and slammed it down hard. The crowd parted into a circle around us and the security guy pushed through.

'He fainted,' I said. 'Too much strong liquor on an empty stomach I expect.'

The security guy got out his walkie-talkie, and Dawn and I pushed through the crowd back to the corridor.

32

We went back down the metal stairs to the stage level. Old Mary and the boys were still beating it out twelve to the bar. It didn't sound any better than before. I hadn't got a clue what my daughter and her friends saw in them. But that's what makes horse races, so they tell me.

A member of the road crew came off stage carrying a cherry-red Fender guitar with a couple of broken strings that cork-screwed back over the solid body of the instrument. Another clue. Follow the Fender and maybe find the tune-up room. Probably find a load of trouble too, but that's what we were here for.

I motioned with my head in the direction of the roadie to Dawn. She got it straight away. There's no flies on her. We followed the geezer as he went through a door and down another corridor that echoed with music. At the end was yet another door through which he passed. I stuck my head in after him. There were maybe ten geezers inside, including Lamar Quinn, Eddie and Tarantula. Babaloo was in there too, one foot in a cowboy boot, one in a soft slipper, plus the two roadies that Angela had threatened with her buck knife.

I pulled my head out quick before anyone noticed. 'Shit,' I said to Dawn. 'I think we might have bitten off more than we can chew here.'

'Why?'

'Remember, I told you about Babaloo? The night I was Angela's escort.'

'I remember,' she said, and her eyes went all slitty again. The love of a good woman was all very well, but sometimes it could get a trifle wearing.

'He's in there with Lamar and Eddie and the geezer with the tattoo who gave you a slap. And several other crew members who remember me with something less than affection.'

'We take them out then,' said Dawn. I could see she was beginning to enjoy herself.

'Odds of better than five to one,' I said.

'Tough on them.'

Maybe the love of a good woman was worth it after all. I squeezed her arm. 'Got your shiv?' I asked.

'Always. Never know when I might run into a private detective needs a good sorting.'

I nodded, smiled, kissed her quick before she could get the knife out, then drew the Colt, unlocked the safety, kicked the door to the tune-up room open and walked in.

33

There was another guy, one I'd never seen before, with long red hair tied back in a pony tail, playing one of those National guitars with the chrome finish and an electric pick-up through a little Pig Nose amplifier. The music was just about loud enough to drown out the sound of the band onstage, and the guy seemed to be enjoying himself. I pissed on his parade by shooting the shit out of the amp. It exploded in a hail of wood, metal and plastic, and a shower of sparks.

Bad manners it might have been, but it certainly got everyone's attention.

'I'm from the society of Hammersmith music lovers,' I said as the echo of the shot echoed round the walls, and the room filled with gunsmoke and the smell of used cordite. 'Have gun, will travel.'

Dawn came in behind and stood with her back to the wall, the letter opener in her hand. 'Meet my trusty assistant, Robin.'

The room was silent, except for the boom of the bass from onstage. 'Isn't anyone going to say "Hi"?' I asked.

Tarantula was standing right in front of me, and I broke his nose with the barrel of the Colt. I couldn't resist it, although I would have been better just keeping everyone in the room where they were until the police arrived. But he'd slapped Dawn, and I wasn't going to forget that in a hurry. So I whacked him in the face, and watched the blood and snot spurt out of his nostrils, like water from a pair of twin faucets. Good deal, I thought as he sank to his knees, clutching at his face. Served him right.

Then things started to happen fast. Babaloo was sitting by the light switches, and he reached up and knocked them off. The room was windowless, and darkness fell like a guillotine blade. I jumped to one side, felt the softness of Dawn's body and pulled her away from the door. Someone else drew a gun and fired. For a split second I wondered if it was my Glock he was using. The bullet smashed into the wall close to my head. So close that I felt the draught. Too fucking close. In the muzzle flash I saw bodies moving every which way. I fired once in the direction that the shot had come from, heard a high-pitched scream, and pushed Dawn out through the door into the corridor.

We ran back in the direction of the stage. I was running backwards, keeping an eye on the door to the tune-up room. It opened slowly and I blasted off two shots that splintered the wood of the door, which closed again quickly. We smashed through the first door that the roadie carrying the Fender had used, and the sound of the band crashed round our ears.

There was a crowd of people of both sexes standing by the side of the stage watching the show reach its climax. One woman turned at our entrance, saw the gun in my hand, turned back, did a double take, and nudged the bloke standing next to her.

He turned too, and I showed him the gun properly and yelled, 'It's not your business. Scram. Get this lot out of here.'

'What, man?' said the geezer. I almost had to read his lips.

'Fuck off,' I screamed. Was this bloke stupid, or what?

'But, man, I'm with the band,' he shouted.

A more ridiculous reason for getting into the crossfire from semi-automatic weapons I had yet to hear, so I stuck the gun into his face and repeated my instruction, 'Fuck off. Or I'll shoot,' I added for emphasis. By this time everyone was in on the act, and the little crowd broke and vanished towards the front of house. Probably looking for Norman the security man. Good luck.

The shit was that we couldn't hear anything but the music. No voices, no footsteps, and this close to the stage even gunshots would be muted down to nothing. The Virgin Mary's band was *loud*. And I mean really loud.

The door to the corridor going back to the tune-up room opened slightly, and I fired. How many bullets had I got left? Shit, I'd lost count. The door puckered where the bullet hit, and closed again. I checked the clip on the Colt. Two bullets were left, plus one in the pipe. I had the spare clip but I needed to conserve ammunition, or get hold of another gun.

I bent my head down to Dawn's ear and screamed, 'Upstairs is favourite.'

She must have heard because she squeezed my hand with hers, and we made for the metal steps.

Halfway to the top, the door below that I'd fired at opened and Quinn, Eddie, Babaloo and a couple of other roadies came into the backstage area. They spread out and peered around trying to see us, but didn't look up. People don't.

Three-quarters of the way up, the door to the landing where we were heading opened, and Big Mal from Premier Security sashayed into sight, a revolver in his hand. Sam must have come to, and told him what was happening. I should have bounced his head on the floor a few more times. I fired upwards and the bullet spun off the metal of the landing in a shower of sparks. Big Mal fired back twice, the bullets going wide, and ducked back behind the door. Below us, Quinn, Eddie and the roadies must have seen what was going on, and they started up the steps.

Dawn and I were fucked. We couldn't go up and we couldn't go down. I looked across at where the scaffolding which stood against the back wall of the theatre jutted out only a few feet from the metal banister of the staircase where we were standing.

'On there,' I yelled at Dawn. 'Get on the scaffolding and get across to the other side of the stage.'

Dawn did as I said, and hopped over on to the thin metal piping. I followed. I didn't hop. Heights have never been my forte. We clambered across to the centre of the scaffold. I looked down. Big mistake. Directly below me was the drum riser at the back of the stage where a sweating percussionist in a singlet and shorts was giving his twin bass drum kit a severe hammering, droplets of sweat flying off his body and catching the lights like diamonds. I looked back, and Quinn and Eddie were at the banister. They both raised their guns and fired. I pulled Dawn down, and the fusillade of bullets spanged off into the darkness at the other side of the theatre.

Eddie climbed on to the scaffolding behind us. I fired and missed.

One bullet left. Beside me was one of the bags of ballast that acted as a counterweight for the flats. I grabbed it and pushed it with all my strength in his direction. He ducked, and it flew over his shoulder, but he straightened up too soon to fire again. The weight caught him on the way back on the side of his head, and he dropped his gun, which fell, unnoticed by the performers, on to the stage below.

'Get down,' I screamed at Dawn, as Eddie swayed perilously only a few yards away from us. She started, and I followed, firing as I went. The last .45 round in the Colt tore a groove of denim and flesh out of Eddie's meaty thigh, and the breech of the gun blew back empty. I stuck the useless weapon in my jacket pocket and went after Dawn like a fly on a Lego tower.

Halfway down I stopped, and took the empty clip out of the Colt, replaced it with the full one, and racked a bullet into the chamber. Eddie was still above me hanging on to the scaffold for dear life. Blood was pouring from his wounded leg and dripping down on to the stage. I looked for his gun on the floor but couldn't see it.

Dawn hit terra firma behind the far bank of speakers. I was sick of going down slow, so I stuck my gun into my pants, reached out and grabbed a rope that hung down in front of me, tested it for strength, and, once satisfied, slid down it and landed at the back of the drum riser. There was a roadie there, poised like a runner in the shadows, ready to cater to the drummer's every whim. He looked at me in amazement as I dropped down beside him, and opened his mouth to shout something. On the assumption that everyone not with us was against us, I retrieved the gun from my pants and clubbed him on the side of the head, and went looking for Eddie's automatic. It was lying in the middle of a loop of cable. It was a Browning Hi-Power 9mm. I checked the clip. Nine bullets nestled there. Plus one in the chamber. Sweet, I thought.

But things weren't going so sweetly for Dawn. She'd been spotted by some beefy onstage security bloke, who must've thought she was a fan invading the stage to get closer to her idol. He'd grabbed her, and got her right arm up in a hammer lock. She was beating at him with the other, and he clouted her round the side of the head with his fist, and she went down at the side of the drum riser, hitting her head as she went. I shot him with the Browning. Every son of a bitch in the world was treating my wife like a punchbag. It had to stop.

The bullet tore a slice from his shoulder, and he went down like a felled tree. I started to make my way towards Dawn to see how she was, when the evening finally started to get really out of hand. Even with all the noise that the Rhythm Review were making, you couldn't have a full-scale gun battle backstage at a major London music venue without someone noticing what was going on.

Someone, somewhere suddenly pulled the onstage power and put up the house lights. Possibly not the best plan in front of three thousand fans hungry for The Virgin's music, but we all make mistakes. The band ground to an unamplified halt, even the sound of the drums falling to a manageable level, before the drummer dropped his sticks and stood up. In the body of the auditorium the fans ceased their clapping and yelling, looking at one another in puzzlement. The Virgin Mary herself, a diminutive, black leather-clad figure, with a mass of red, curly hair that fell almost to her waist, looked around in disbelief, then threw her dead microphone to the stage. 'What the fuck... ?' she said.

I stopped where I was as the audience began to bay in protest at their entertainment being cut short, and Lamar Quinn, now halfway down the scaffolding, with one of Babaloo's buddies close behind, fired at me. The bullet rang off a crash cymbal and ricocheted up towards the ceiling, and I strafed the scaffold with a spray of bullets from the Browning in retaliation. The Virgin screamed as the slugs whined round the back of the theatre, and dived beneath the bank of keyboards next to her. Someone in the audience screamed too, and as other voices took up the scream, in panic, three thousand people turned as one and headed for the exits.

34

One of my bullets must have hit the roadie who was slightly above Quinn on the scaffolding because with a cry he lost his footing and crashed down through the smoke-filled air in a thunder of broken wood and plastic and a domino effect of falling cymbals on to the drum kit, sending the drummer diving for cover. Quinn fired again and I jumped back and bumped into the lead guitarist. 'Better go, son,' I said. 'It's getting kinda dangerous round here.'

He didn't need to be told twice. He just unhooked his instrument from round his neck, dropped it on to the floor and ran. On the far side of the stage, the bass guitarist did the same and joined the keyboard player in a mad dash for safety. I looked round. Members of the audience were scrambling for the doors, and I heard shouts and screams as some were trampled underfoot in the panic. A bunch of uniformed police, probably from the vans I'd seen outside, was fighting to gain control of the mob and calm them down.

When I looked up into the scaffolding again, Quinn had vanished.

I spun round on my heels, a pistol in each hand, desperately trying to find out where he'd gone, but I couldn't see him. 'Shit, shit, shit,' I repeated, and Babaloo came limping through from stage left, a gun in his fist, firing as he came.

One of his bullets tugged at the leather of my jacket, and I shot him in his good leg, and he tumbled to the ground.

I walked over to where he was lying, moaning gently, kicked him in the head for the second time in our short acquaintanceship, picked up his gun and stuck it in my pocket, then remembering Dawn, went back to look for her.

Before I could reach her, a voice beside me said, 'Put the guns down,' and Quinn appeared by the bank of keyboards. He picked up the cowering Virgin by her long, thick, Titian curls, and dragged her in front of him to act as a shield. He hooked his left arm around her neck and put the huge, fully cocked automatic pistol he held in his right at her temple. 'Do it,' he ordered. 'Or I'll blow her head off.'

And he knocked me for sounding like *Hawaii Five-O*. I wondered what film he'd got that immortal line from.

But I did as I was told and gently laid the Colt and the Browning on the stage in front of me.

'And the other one,' he said.

I shrugged, took Babaloo's gun from out of my pocket and laid that on the stage too. Checkmate.

'And everyone keep very still, or she gets it,' he shouted.

More scenes from the movies. Everyone's in showbiz. Everyone's a star. But it seemed to work.

We all stood silently. Me, the few punters, crew, and hangers on that were still in the auditorium, and the cops who had come in through the doors. It was hot on the stage under the lights, and I could smell my own sweat and fear mixed in with the stink of the crowd, and the adrenalin and sweat of the band, who until recently had been centrestage.

Now, a more dramatic show was unfolding here.

I was the closest to Quinn, so I spoke. I tried to think of some B-movie dialogue of my own. 'Don't be stupid,' I said. 'Put the gun down, Lamar. It's all over.' It sounded like Broderick Crawford to me. I hope he had more luck with it than I did.

'Shut up, Sharman,' spat Quinn in reply. It was Sharman now. I wondered what had happened to 'Nick'.

My mouth was dry, and I tried to get some saliva going. I would have killed a puppy for a beer. A litter of puppies for a beer and a cigarette.

'How far do you think you're going to get?' I asked. 'Even with her.'

The Virgin Mary locked eyes with mine, and I tried to reassure her with a look. I don't think it worked.

'Far enough.'

'You've blown it, son,' I went on. 'Give me the gun. Let her go. She's got nothing to do with any of this.'

He laughed without a lot of feeling. 'This bitch is worth a billion dollars. I can get anywhere I want to go with her in tow.'

The Virgin looked at me again. She might have been worth a billion dollars, I didn't know. But right then she was just a frightened young woman who needed my help. 'Get me a plane to Cuba. Fuelled up and ready to go. Is that the deal?' I asked.

'Something like that.'

'Forget it, son. There'll be marksmen following you everywhere. Let her get a foot away from you, and one of them will blow your head off your shoulders.'

'No. She's too valuable. No one will be shooting anyone while she's around.'

'Get real, will you,' I said. 'You've got no chance.'

He took the gun away from The Virgin's head and levelled it at me. The bore hole looked to be about as big as a dinner plate and as black as an undertaker's hat. I felt myself wince as I looked down it. I didn't want to, but I did anyway.

'I've got nothing to lose,' said Quinn. 'Nothing at all. I'm getting out of here and she's coming with me. And you're going to take us.'

'Where?'

'The airport. It's not far, is it?'

I shook my head. 'A few miles down the motorway.'

He walked to the front of the stage, dragging The Virgin with him, but keeping the gun on me. 'You cops,' he shouted. 'Who's in charge?'

A uniformed inspector walked down one of the aisles. 'I am,' he said.

'What do they call you?'

'Inspector Field.'

'OK, inspector,' said Quinn. 'I want a fast car, gassed up and ready to roll, outside. And I want it there ten minutes ago. Get me?'

The inspector nodded.

'And no tricks. I'm not fooling. I want a phone in it. When we're moving I'll let you know what I want next. You know who this is?' He squeezed The Virgin's throat until she gagged.

'I am aware,' said Field. *I am aware.* Ain't our policemen wonderful?'

'Then be aware also that this guy,' Quinn gestured to me with the gun, 'is going to drive us where I want to go.'

'Which is?' Field again.

'Heathrow airport. And I don't want to get involved in any traffic snarl-ups. So get the roads cleared.'

'I'm afraid that's beyond my authority –'

'Fuck your authority. This is The Virgin Mary. If I get screwed, she dies. And this mook too.' He gestured with the gun at me again.

Mook. I ask you.

'So get the authority,' Quinn continued. 'Or get someone *with* the authority. Come on, man, get moving. I ain't got all day.'

'There are people here who are hurt,' protested the inspector. 'At least let me get them some help.'

'Fuck 'em. And you,' said Quinn. 'Now get moving or do you want this bitch dead?' And he squeezed The Virgin's face with his left hand until she squealed.

With all the dignity he could muster, Inspector Field turned and walked back up the aisle.

'And get those other cops outta here,' Quinn ordered. 'They're making me nervous.'

Field made a shooing gesture with both his arms and the uniforms melted away like snow on a sunny morning.

'And you fuckers,' screamed Quinn at the odd person standing around, 'get lost.'

They did. Until finally, apart from us onstage, a few still bodies by the doors were all that were left in the place.

'So now we wait,' I said.

'Cor-rect,' said Quinn, who seemed to be in a better mood after exercising a bit of authority.

'Why don't you cut her some slack,' I said, referring to The Virgin. 'You'll strangle her if you're not careful. She won't be much use to you then.'

Quinn relaxed his hold on the singer's throat and she leaned forward and coughed.

'Lamar,' she said in a choked-up voice. 'What the hell are you playing at?'

'Shut up, cunt,' he ordered. 'I don't have to listen to your crap any more.'

Old scores were being settled.

'That's no way to speak to a lady,' I said.

'She's no lady,' said Quinn. 'I remember when she was hanging around the offices, screwing anyone she thought could do her some good.'

'She must have screwed the right people,' I said. 'You pissed off because she gave you a blank?'

He pulled her back tightly and ground the barrel of the gun into her head. 'Shut up,' he said. It seemed to be his favourite expression.

Then, from the far side of the drum riser where she'd fallen, and behind Lamar Quinn's back, Dawn appeared, clutching the letter opener that I'd given her, what seemed like a lifetime ago, in Julius Rose's office. Her feet were quiet in her soft-soled Converse baseball boots. She had blood in her hair, a bruise on her forehead, another beneath her left cheekbone, and a wild look in her eyes. In fact I wouldn't have been surprised if she'd clamped the knife between her teeth, worn camouflage paint, and had a necklace of human ears around her neck.

Quinn kept his gun on me, and I tried to catch Dawn's eye without him realising she was there. I didn't want her to do anything that would make his trigger finger tighten by reflex and blow The Virgin's head off. It wasn't her fault she'd got involved.

'This isn't going to work,' I said.

'It'll work,' said Quinn confidently.

I shook my head, trying to get through to Dawn that I meant her. 'No,' I said. 'Not yet.'

'You don't know what you're talking about,' said Quinn.

'I know British coppers,' I replied. This time talking directly to him, to keep his attention on me. 'They don't like being talked to like that.'

'Fuck 'em.'

'If you say so.'

'I do. And I'm getting tired of listening to you.' He took the gun away from The Virgin's head and pointed it at me again. Which was just what I wanted him to do. I looked over the girl's head, and Quinn's shoulder, and Dawn was less than a yard away from his back, and I saw that her knuckles were white on the handle of the knife.

'Don't screw around,' I said. 'You won't shoot me.'

'Won't I?'

'No.'

'Why not?'

'Who'll drive you to Heathrow?'

'I'll find someone.'

'Dream on, son. I'm your only hope.'

'Don't you believe it.'

Now I was getting tired of listening to him. 'Do it, Dawn,' I said.

Quinn laughed again. 'Do you expect me to fall for that old one?'

'No. Not if it *was* that old one. But it's true.'

'You jerk. I think I might just finish you off anyway. I don't trust you.'

'But of course. I, on the other hand, have the greatest faith in you,' I said, and I saw his finger tighten on the trigger. So did Dawn, and with an unearthly shriek she covered the last few feet between her and the American and drove the point of the letter opener into the side of his neck. Blood jetted from the wound, and the force of her attack knocked his gun arm round and away from me. The gun went off and the bullet slammed into one of the huge speakers at the side of the stage.

Quinn dropped the gun, let go of The Virgin Mary, and put his hand up and tugged the knife out of his neck, which only allowed the gush of blood to increase. He stood for a moment looking down at the weapon that had wounded him, then he made one step and dropped to his knees, let the knife slip from between his fingers and fell on to his face, where he kicked two or three times before lying very still, the blood still pumping out from the puncture under his jawbone.

The Virgin Mary looked down horrified at Quinn's body, then at me, then at Dawn, until her face crumpled into tears and she reached for my wife who held her tightly.

Inspector Field appeared from the back of the auditorium and I went to the front of the stage and said, 'Cancel the car. He won't be needing it.' Then I sat on top of one of the monitor speakers and tried hard not to cry myself.

35

When the smoke finally cleared, the body count was pretty high, and someone had to be held responsible.

Guess who?

Dawn and I were both arrested and taken to Hammersmith police station in separate cars. We were searched, our personal belongings confiscated, and after Dawn had been seen by a surgeon who treated the wound to her head, we were allowed to make a telephone call each.

Dawn called Chas at home and told him what had happened. I'd said he'd be the first to know. He probably wasn't, but I did my best. I called Chris Kennedy-Sloane on his mobile and filled him in on the details. He was at the station within half an hour with his own personal brief in tow. Apparently, so too were the world's press, who laid siege to the place. The Virgin Mary was big news. So was the fact that Jay Harrison had been alive for the past twenty years.

Dawn and I were interviewed separately with the brief in attendance. He told us not to answer any questions.

We concurred.

Later we were charged with the following: Murder; Attempted murder; Possession of unlicensed firearms; Possession of a deadly weapon; A couple of offences under The Prevention Of Terrorism Act that I'd never heard of; Criminal conspiracy; ABH; GBH; Wounding; Assault; Breaking and entering; Trespass; Criminal damage; Robbery; Possession of controlled substances, because they found half a joint in Dawn's leather jacket, and they even did me for obstruction with the Caprice when they found out who'd been driving it.

After that they put us into separate cells, and as far as I could tell, wanted to throw away the keys.

Lifetime Records had more money than God. They also had more lawyers than God, if God had been into litigation They also had The Virgin Mary and Dog Soldier signed up to the label. When the powers that be learnt that Lamar Quinn, their vice-president in charge of Jay Harrison's royalties, had been systematically looting the account for years to the tune of over eleven million dollars, and had threatened The Virgin's life to boot, they also realised that they had a huge embarrassment on their hands.

Within three hours, their British lawyers started arriving on the scene. Within ten, their US lawyers, jet-lagged, weary, and red-eyed showed up, assistants, secretaries and all. Within twenty, a coterie of Japanese super-attorneys jetted in.

Within twenty-four, the murder charges had been commuted to manslaughter, and after a brief court appearance, Dawn and I were out on bail.

Lifetime stumped up the not inconsiderable amount of money it took to get us out. I think the coppers were glad to see the back of us, and of the newspaper and TV reporters who were blocking the road outside the police station. We were rushed in secret to a safe house that a film company subsidiary of the record company kept for starlets to recover from their abortions, and that top executives used for a bit of nookie on the QT.

When she heard about that, Dawn insisted on the sheets being changed.

That's my girl.

In fact the safe house was a vast penthouse, on top of a block of offices near Victoria Station.

Chris Kennedy-Sloane's retainer was increased, and he moved in with us. Lifetime hired a security company to give us 24-hour-a-day cover. I told Kennedy-Sloane to make sure it wasn't Premier. They might have a grudge to bear.

Dawn and I stayed there for the three months until the trial came up. It wasn't a bad life. We had a live-in maid and blue-ribbon chef.

There was a huge roof garden and a gym with jacuzzi and sauna. The place was wired for cable, and Lifetime opened an account for us at Harrods for books, videos and any records that Lifetime themselves couldn't supply.

And they continued to pay us our grand a day plus expenses. Mind you, the expenses by then were minimal, but the wages came in handy. We got a cheque every Friday, regular as clockwork, and Kennedy-Sloane paid it into our bank for us.

The Virgin Mary came to visit a couple of times. She was convinced that Dawn had saved her life. She was right. She was good fun. And she had a very fine coke dealer.

Lifetime's lawyers worked diligently, night and day, on our defence. Their publicity people worked diligently, night and day, on getting us good press.

Tracey looked after our flat and watered the pot plants.

I even took Dawn back to Highgate cemetery one day as I'd promised what seemed like an eternity ago. The tomb had been splashed with red paint the colour of blood. There was no sign of Chrissie, Bird, Malcolm or Dandy. Obviously they hadn't appreciated that their hero had just pretended to be dead. On the way out I asked the attendant if he knew anything about them. He just snorted and said, 'Good riddance.'

On the day that the trial started at the Bailey, the Crown Prosecution Service offered no evidence on any of the charges. The Virgin Mary was in the public gallery. She was dressed all in black, including the veil on the little hat that was tilted over her red fringe.

Dawn and I walked free out into the street to a blinding greeting of exploding flashbulbs.

I took Dawn on the promised second honeymoon in Hastings on the bonus that Lifetime paid us not to sell our story to the papers. I'd be embarrassed to tell you how much it was.

The moral of the story is that on the day of the incident at the Hammersmith Apollo, The Virgin Mary had one single and three albums on the *Music Week* charts. The single was at number four, going down. The albums stood respectively at numbers five, fourteen and thirty-eight. Dog Soldier were a no-show.

Ten days after Dawn saved The Virgin Mary's life, and Jay Harrison died for real, The Virgin Mary's single was number one, and her albums had climbed to numbers one, four and seven. Dog

Soldier's *Greatest Hits* had crashed in at number two on the album charts, and the band had another six entries on the top seventy-five. Lifetime Records reported increased interest and sales of both acts in every territory on the globe, including the old USSR.

That's what you get for dying, or almost dying, if you're in show business.

C'est la vie.

Falls the Shadow

by Mark Timlin

The Eighth Nick Sharman novel

Working in a bar has proved too dangerous for Nick Sharman, so he's back in the private investigation game.

His first job, looking for a lost Highland terrier called Prince, shouldn't be too demanding; a quick visit to the owner's ex-husband and a mention in the local newspaper ought to trace it. But Sharman has reckoned without a skinhead nutter by the name of Eddie Cochran.

Then there's the call from Sunset Radio. Late-night phone-in DJ Peter Day has managed to upset an unpleasant splinter group, not to mention a paranoid caller, John from Stockwell; and now his post contains more than the usual fanmail; nothing explosive however… so far. Sunset wants Sharman to mind Day – though he'd rather concentrate on Sophia, the secretary with the habit of wearing dresses that cling to every curve of her body. But even Sharman couldn't ignore the grisly contents of the next package delivered to the station – or let the threat of further bloody killings go unanswered…

Praised as 'the best private eye in London'
– *Liverpool Daily Post*

978-1-84344-481-7   £12.99

Ashes by Now

by Mark Timlin

The Ninth Nick Sharman novel

Nick Sharman stumbles home with two exotic dancers, Sandi and Mandi (aka Tracey and Dawn), which is fun for him until he gets a phone call from the past that ruins everything. Sailor Grant has just been released from prison, doing hard time for a crime he didn't commit.

A police officer's daughter had been found raped and murdered. Someone had to be found, so Sailor Grant, the local nonce, was sent down. Sharman always had his doubts, but that part of his life is over. Sailor keeps phoning and wants Sharman to help get justice, Nick tells him to leave him alone. The next day Sailor is dead and has left Sharman a note. The coppers Millar and Collier invite him to read the note, and then they beat him half to death. Lying in hospital, Nick realises that he must solve it before those close to him are killed. So with a little help from his friends Charlie, Chas and Monkey (a burglar, who can break into anything), Sharman must shed the truth about the events from his past.

'Timlin's blood-spattered tale of police-going-bad is a reminder that South London has badlands to rival any in the US'
— *Mail on Sunday*

'Vintage Timlin, full of lovely-jubbly London language'
— *Time Out*

'Mean streets, sleazy bars, brutal bent coppers… as British as a used condom in a fogbound London taxi, and graced with a pair of delightful floozies worth the fare to Wandsworth to meet'
— *Observer*

'Blistering, belligerent… Timlin's depiction of seedy South London streets is scary because it rings true… Tightly plotted, tautly written and thoroughly recommended' — *Tribune*

978-1-84344-624-8   £12.99

About Us

In addition to No Exit Press, Oldcastle Books has a number
of other imprints, including Kamera Books, Creative Essentials,
Pulp! The Classics, Pocket Essentials and High Stakes Publishing
> oldcastlebooks.co.uk

For more information about Crime Books go to > crimetime.co.uk

Check out the kamera film salon for independent, arthouse and
world cinema > kamera.co.uk

For more information, media enquiries and review copies please
contact Frances > frances@oldcastlebooks.com